Icelandic Folktales

Icelandic Folktales

Introduction by Rósa Þorsteinsdóttir

General Editor: Jake Jackson

FLAME TREE
PUBLISHING

This is a FLAME TREE Book

FLAME TREE PUBLISHING
6 Melbray Mews
Fulham, London SW6 3NS
United Kingdom
www.flametreepublishing.com

First published 2024

24 26 28 27 25
1 3 5 7 9 8 6 4 2

ISBN: 978-1-80417-816-4

Contributors, authors, editors and sources for this series include: *Icelandic Legends*, collected by Jón Árnason, translated by George E.J. Powell and Eiríkur Magnússon, 1864 and 1866; 'The Story of Frithi of the Bold' and 'The Story of Gunnlaug the Worm-Tongue and Raven the Skald', translated by Eirikr Magnusson and William Morris, 1875; *Seven Icelandic Short Stories*, edited by Ásgeir Pétursson and Steingrímur J. Þorsteinsson; *Icelandic Fairy Tales*, edited by Mrs. Angus W. Hall, 1897.

Designed and created in the UK | Printed and bound in China

Contents

Series Foreword **8**

Introduction to Icelandic Folktales **10**

Romantic Nationalism in Iceland 11

Jón Árnason, the Folktale Collector 11

Konrad Maurer, a Cultural Conduit 12

The Folktale Collection of Jón Árnason 14

The Translators 15

The Tales – Legends 17

Tales of the Divine and the Devil 18

The Tales – Sagas 19

Icelandic Folktales? 20

The Mighty & the Brave **23**

The Story of the Three Princes 24

The Story of Thorsteinn, the King's Son 34

Sigurdr, the King's Son 41

The Story of Hermódr and Hádvör 53

Carl's Son, Little, Trittle and the Birds 60

The Story of Frithiof the Bold 65

The Story of the Farmer's Three Daughters 96

History of Líneik and Laufey 101

Honour & Adventure **111**

Hildur, Queen of the Elves 112

Katla's Dream 118

Gold-brow 122

The Story of Jón Asmundsson 127

The Wizards in the Westmann Islands 137

The Story of Grímur, Who Killed Skeljúngur 142

The Story of Gunnlaug the Worm-Tongue
and Raven the Skald 155

The Elves, Giants & Beasts **193**
The Giantess and the Granite Boat 194
The Five Brothers 200
The Story of Audunn and the Bear 206
Helga 212
The Genesis of the Hid-folk 218
The Fisherman of Götur 219
The Grateful Elfwoman 221
Thórdur of Thrastastadir 221
The Magic Scythe 223
The Father of Eighteen Elves 227

The Divine & the Devil **229**
The Steward of Skálholt 230
Boat Language 232
The Wonderful Quern 234
The Devil's Marriage 239
Late Will the Souls of Priests Be Filled 241
Rosamunda 243
The Exorcism 247
The Priest and the Angel 247
The Soul of My Own John 252
The Sin Sacks 254

Series Foreword

STRETCHING BACK to the oral traditions of thousands of years ago, tales of heroes and disaster, creation and conquest have been told by many different civilizations in many different ways. Their impact sits deep within our culture even though the detail in the tales themselves are a loose mix of historical record, transformed narrative and the distortions of hundreds of storytellers.

Today the language of mythology lives with us: our mood is jovial, our countenance is saturnine, we are narcissistic and our modern life is hermetically sealed from others. The nuances of myths and legends form part of our daily routines and help us navigate the world around us, with its half truths and biased reported facts.

The nature of a myth is that its story is already known by most of those who hear it, or read it. Every generation brings a new emphasis, but the fundamentals remain the same: a desire to understand and describe the events and relationships of the world. Many of the great stories are archetypes that help us find our own place, equipping us with tools for self-understanding, both individually and as part of a broader culture.

For Western societies it is Greek mythology that speaks to us most clearly. It greatly influenced the mythological heritage of the ancient Roman civilization and is the lens through which we still see the Celts, the Norse and many of the other great peoples and religions. The Greeks themselves learned much from their neighbours, the Egyptians, an older culture that became weak with age and incestuous leadership.

It is important to understand that what we perceive now as mythology had its own origins in perceptions of the divine and the rituals of the sacred. The earliest civilizations, in the crucible of the Middle East, in the Sumer of the third millennium BC, are the source to which many of the mythic archetypes can be traced. As humankind collected together in cities for the first time, developed writing and industrial scale agriculture, started to irrigate the rivers and attempted to control rather than be at the mercy of its environment, humanity began to write down its tentative explanations of natural events, of floods and plagues, of disease.

Early stories tell of Gods (or god-like animals in the case of tribal societies such as African, Native American or Aboriginal cultures) who are crafty and use their wits to survive, and it is reasonable to suggest that these were the first rulers of the gathering peoples of the earth, later elevated to god-like status with the distance of time. Such tales became more political as cities vied with each other for supremacy, creating new Gods, new hierarchies for their pantheons. The older Gods took on primordial roles and became the preserve of creation and destruction, leaving the new gods to deal with more current, everyday affairs. Empires rose and fell, with Babylon assuming the mantle from Sumeria in the 1800s BC, then in turn to be swept away by the Assyrians of the 1200s BC; then the Assyrians and the Egyptians were subjugated by the Greeks, the Greeks by the Romans and so on, leading to the spread and assimilation of common themes, ideas and stories throughout the world.

The survival of history is dependent on the telling of good tales, but each one must have the 'feeling' of truth, otherwise it will be ignored. Around the firesides, or embedded in a book or a computer, the myths and legends of the past are still the living materials of retold myth, not restricted to an exploration of origins. Now we have devices and global communications that give us unparalleled access to a diversity of traditions. We can find out about Native American, Indian, Chinese and tribal African mythology in a way that was denied to our ancestors, we can find connections, match the archaeology, religion and the mythologies of the world to build a comprehensive image of the human experience that is endlessly fascinating.

The stories in this book provide an introduction to the themes and concerns of the myths and legends of their respective cultures, with a short introduction to provide a linguistic, geographic and political context. This is where the myths have arrived today, but undoubtedly over the next millennia, they will transform again whilst retaining their essential truths and signs.

Jake Jackson
General Editor

Introduction to Icelandic Folktales

THE LATTER HALF of the nineteenth century in Iceland was defined by political discussion and the question of independence from Denmark. The discussion for independence began as early as 1848 when King Frederick VII gave up his absolute monarchy.

The primary argument was that Iceland had never really been part of Denmark, but a singular state where the language was always Icelandic and where Icelanders had always had their own independent laws, as explored by Gunnar Karlsson ('The Emergence of Nationalism in Iceland' in *Ethnicity and Nation Building in the Nordic World*, 1995 and *Iceland's 1100 Years: The History of a Marginal Society*, 2000). Even though Icelanders could also refer to their medieval literature, which was written in the vernacular, it became necessary to create a modern national culture in this country striving for independence (Terry Gunnell, 'Daisies Rise to Become Oaks: The Politics of Early Folktale Collection in Northern Europe' in *Folklore* 121(1), 2010). This was, of course, in parallel to the romantic nationalistic movement in Europe. The influence that followed the folktale collection of the Brothers Grimm and their publication of *Kinder-und Hausmärchen* (Children's and Household Tales) in 1812 and *Deutsche Sagen* (German Legends) in 1816 were a part of a wider movement inspired by thinkers such as the German philosopher Johann Gottfried von Herder in the late eighteenth century; men who had argued that the 'unsullied' ancient *Volksgeist* of countries was to be found first and foremost in the poems, songs and folktales of the rural working classes. The resulting collection and publication of 'national' folk poetry, folk legends and fairy tales in countries such as Germany, Denmark, Norway, Scotland and Ireland was closely bound up with the creation of not only new forms of 'national' art, literature, music and theatre, but also with new works on history, new dictionaries of language and dialect, and the national images used in political struggles for national independence.

Romantic Nationalism in Iceland

The Icelandic process of folktale collection and its relationship to the development of new styles of 'national' theatre, art and music is not much different to those observed in these neighbouring countries. It piques interest how much connection those involved in Iceland had to those involved abroad. Konrad Maurer, for example, had close links to the Grimm brothers; George Stephens, who also knew the Grimms and the Icelandic intellectual elite in Copenhagen, was closely involved in the collection and publication of Swedish folktales; Eiríkur Magnússon, who together with George Powell translated Jón Árnason's collection into English, and Guðbrandur Vigfússon, who was involved in the publication of the Icelandic collection, both knew George Dasent, who translated Peter Asbjørnsen and Jørgen Moe's Norwegian collection into English and encouraged John Francis Campbell to embark on his key collection of Scottish folktales. The new 'folklorists' thus found themselves in influential positions within new national (and international) networks of writers, thinkers, politicians, academics and artists (most of those named here will feature below). The Icelander Jón Árnason (1819–88) was a typical example, closely associated with politicians, scholars and artists both at home and abroad as discussed by Terry Gunnell ('Jón Árnason and the Collection of Icelandic Folk Legends: Ripples, Flotsam, Nets and Reflections' in *Grimm Ripples: The Legacy of the Grimms' Deutsche Sagen in Northern Europe*, 2022).

Jón Árnason, the Folktale Collector

In his memoirs, Jón Árnason writes that his interest in listening to folktales awoke early and no one visiting his childhood home was free of regaling folktales, even though he was so frightened that he had to ask his mother to hold him in her arms as he went to sleep. That interest clearly developed as Árnason grew up, because in 1845 he and Magnús Grímsson (1825–60), who at the time studied at the Latin School, joined up to 'collect all the ancient lore of the people' they could find, as Árnason states in his foreword to the collection *Íslenzkar þjóðsögur og ævintýri* (1954). Grímsson was supposed to collect stories and Árnason's other material, such as poetry, riddles and descriptions of games. Truthfully, it can be said that this year marked the beginning of folkloric collection in Iceland because George Stephens (1813–95), an English scholar living in Sweden, also wrote a proposal to start collecting folklore in Iceland. This proposal was put before the Royal Society for Nordic Antiquaries in Copenhagen. It was agreed upon, and the following year a questionnaire was published in Iceland with little result. Árnason and Grímsson fared marginally better and their collection was published under the title *Íslenzk ævintýri* (*Icelandic Fairy Tales*) in 1852, the first printed collection of folklore to contain material from Icelandic oral tradition. Despite the title, there are no fairy tales to be found in the book. It contains a few poems and legends, some quite adventurous. Árnason (1954) said himself that the book 'at first met few friends in Iceland', but Icelanders in Copenhagen, and Germans, gave it a warmer welcome. The lack of interest in Iceland itself appears to have discouraged the two collectors, but in 1858 the German lawyer and professor of judicial history Konrad Maurer (1823–1902) travelled in Iceland and collected folktales, among other things.

Konrad Maurer, a Cultural Conduit

Maurer had great influence on the collection of Icelandic folktales, both by collecting himself and by encouraging Árnason and others to do the same. It was Jacob Grimm who had aroused Maurer's interests in linguistics, history and folklore during the latter's student years in Berlin. Later, Maurer spent some time in Copenhagen learning Icelandic and preparing for his trip to Iceland. The legends and tales he collected from Icelandic tradition were published in German in 1860. Some indications are that Maurer, the Icelandic-speaking foreigner, was more trusted as a listener by the Icelandic storytellers than the fellow countrymen who were higher up the social ladder (Rósa Þorsteinsdóttir, 'Konrad Maurer: Cultural Conduit and Collector' in *Grimm Ripples: The Legacy of the Grimms' Deutsche Sagen in Northern Europe*, 2022). He believed that because of the country's isolation and little-changed ways of life over the course of many centuries, the folktales preserved in Iceland were pure and unsullied. Maurer will certainly be long remembered in Iceland for his research on sagas and ancient law, and for supporting the country's struggle for independence. However, his greatest influence on Icelandic culture was in the collection and publishing of folktales. He encouraged Árnason and Grímsson to continue gathering folklore and promised to find a publisher for the tales in Germany. On 25 March 1859, Maurer wrote to Árnason from Germany and informed him that he had reached a verbal agreement with the Leipzig publisher Rost, with regard to publishing the latter's folktale collections in two or three volumes (the Royal Library in Copenhagen holds letters written to Árnason by non-Icelanders under the shelf mark NKS 3009 4to).

Grímsson died in 1860, so it fell to Árnason to finish the work. Maurer's letter initiated a long series of deliveries of material between Munich and Reykjavík, most of which stopped off in Copenhagen on the way. Indeed, soon after Árnason started sending material to Germany, Maurer suggested they should both send all their letters and packages via the Icelandic, Copenhagen-based scholar Guðbrandur Vigfússon (1827–89), allowing him to review the contents. This was partly to speed up the process because mailing to Iceland was both sporadic and difficult, but also because Maurer wanted Vigfússon to read over and correct the narratives, believing that his Icelandic was not fluent enough to meet the task. Vigfússon thus became a full participant in the editing of the folktale collection. Subsequently, the first volume of Árnason's *Íslenzkar þjóðsögur og æfintýri* (*Icelandic Legends and Folktales*) was published in Leipzig in 1862, 50 years after the Brothers Grimm had begun to publish folktales with the first volume of the

Kinder-und Hausmärchen. Árnason's second volume followed in 1864. Thus, Maurer played a key role in the publication of Árnason's collection of folktales – the first large collection of Icelandic folktales to be published. Finnur Sigmundsson, the editor of a selection of letters to and from Árnason, states in the Prologue to the volume in question that 'Jón Árnason can never be thanked enough for his work in collecting and publishing folktales. Nonetheless it is clear that he never would have managed this colossal task without the help of Maurer, and no one was more forthcoming about that fact than Jón himself, as can be seen in his letters' (*Úr fórum Jóns Árnasonar*, I 1950).

The Folktale Collection of Jón Árnason

Árnason did not collect all the folktales by interviewing informants; rather, he chose to write to friends and scholars all around Iceland, including an overview covering what he most wanted them to collect. Many individuals responded to his call and sent stories. This continued after 1864 when both volumes of the projected work had been published, so that nearly 100 years later, when a reprinted, complete edition of his collection was published in 1954–61, it filled six volumes. The enduring value of this collection for Iceland is evident, as it was recently voted the tenth most important work in the Icelandic literary canon.

The title of the work suggests that the material it contains was 'Icelandic' and the first edition of the folktale collection rapidly spread through the country. This was in no small part because the Icelandic Literary Society in Copenhagen immediately purchased 800 copies and distributed them to its members at no cost to them. This probably played its part in furthering the belief that Icelandic folktales were monotonous, without considering that many of the tales contained localized references. Even though the stories – and the fairy tales especially – belonged to an international folktale tradition, Árnason's collection was a great influence on nationalistic views. Many readers viewed it as a primary source of Icelandic folk belief and tales, believing the stories to be unique to Iceland and separated from other nations.

Of course, the collection contains Icelandic legends and wonder tales for the most part but there are also some tales that clearly came from foreign traditions but ended up circulating in the oral tradition of Iceland.

The Translators

Most of the stories in this publication come from the folktale collection of Jón Árnason and most were translated by the Welshman George E.J. Powell (1842–82) and Eiríkur Magnússon (1833–1913). Magnússon was born in eastern Iceland but met Árnason when he came to Reykjavík in 1848 to attend school. They both resided in Reykjavík until 1862 when Magnússon moved to London to oversee the printing of a new translation of the Bible in Icelandic. He moved between London, Germany and France until 1871 when he took a post as a librarian at the Cambridge University Library and held that post until 1909. During that time he also completed his Master of Arts degree and taught Old Icelandic. Magnússon and Powell were aquainted aboard a ship sailing from Iceland to England in 1862. Powell was a wealthy Icelandophile and supported Magnússon for a time after his arrival in England. In return, Magnússon tutored Powell in Icelandic and together they translated an Icelandic saga, which was never published, before they then translated a selection from the folktales of Árnason (Andrew Wawn, *The Vikings and the Victorians: Inventing the Old North in Nineteenth-Century Britain*, 2000).

One letter from Powell to Árnason has been preserved. Powell writes from Copenhagen and talks about the latter pointing out to Magnússon that they need approval to publish their translations from the German publisher. Powell says he has already written to Leipzig and awaits a reply. He then closes his letter with these words: 'I am sparing no pains to turn out the book perfectly, both as regards text and illustration, and I earnestly hope that it not prove unworthy of the talented collector.' A transcription of Powell's letter is available online at https://ismus.is/tjodfraedi/bref/26 (February 2024).

Magnússon wrote letters to Árnason only four times and they all concern his and Powell's translations and the publication thereof.

Letters to Árnason from Icelanders are preserved at the Árni Magnússon Institute for Icelandic Studies in Reykjavík under the shelf mark NKS 3010 4to. Many of them have been transcribed and made available online at https://ismus.is/tjodfraedi/bref/?samsafn=2 (February 2024).

The reason Árnason and Magnússon were not great correspondents could be that the former and the aforementioned Guðbrandur Vigfússon were good friends. Vigfússon moved to England from Copenhagen in 1864 and became a librarian at the Oxford University Library. He lived out the rest of his days in Oxford. Magnússon and Vigfússon were close when they first arrived in England, but grew to become sworn enemies (Wawn, 2000). From Magnússon's letters to Árnason, it can also be seen that the latter was, for some reason, not content with Magnússon and Powell's Preface, even though it is in some part a translation of Vigfússon's Preface to the Icelandic publication. Through Powell, Magnússon was introduced to the artist, poet and writer William Morris (1834–96), whom he taught Old Icelandic and joined in translating several Icelandic sagas (Gunnell, 2022; Wawn, 2000). Among those are two in this publication, 'The Story of Frithiof the Bold' and 'The Story of Gunnlaug the Worm-Tongue and Raven the Skald'. Morris was also very much an Icelandophile and travelled to the country on two occasions. In 1871, he travelled with Magnússon and then again in 1873. Even though it is likely he met Árnason in Iceland, there are no sources to confirm it (Gunnell, 2022).

The third Icelandic saga, 'The Story of Audunn and the Bear', as in this collection, was translated by Gabriel Turville-Petre (1908–78), an English philologist who specialized in Old Norse studies.

Three tales that also come from the folklore collection of Jón Árnason were translated and adapted by Mrs Angus W. Hall, of which not much is known. In the Preface to her publication *Icelandic Fairy Tales* (1897), Mrs Hall has this to say about the Icelandic stories: 'In their original form, many of the stories are somewhat crude and rough for juvenile reading. This it has been the Editor's endeavour to ameliorate by eliminating all objectionable matter, while at the same time preserving the originality and local colouring which most of them possess'.

The Tales – Legends

Perhaps another reason for Árnason's resentment of the translation by Magnússon and Powell was that they did not translate the stories with complete accuracy. This can be seen in their Preface, for example in the first volume (1864) where they state:

> *We have not translated closely; we have amplified, we have expunged, we have inverted. Where stories were told barely and nakedly, we have coloured and clothed them; where irrelevancies occurred, we have either got rid of them or harmonized them with the text; where incidents or descriptions have been given out of their proper places, we have changed their position.*

In the second volume (1866), they go on to say: 'But the prevailing features of our originals, their simplicity, their vigour, their tone, and the spirit in which they were written, we have religiously guarded.'

These partners translated stories from all categories of Icelandic folktales and claim to have translated about a third of the tales in Árnason's collection. It was Maurer who first categorized the tales in his publication from 1860, where he divided them into: 1) mythological stories (gods, elves, water and sea beings, trolls); 2) stories of ghosts; 3) stories of magic; 4) stories of natural phenomena; 5) stories of religious import (God and the devil, saints, heaven and hell, God's punishments); 6) historical legends; 7) fairy tales or wonder tales; 8) humorous tales. Árnason accepted this classification in his collection but added tales of outlaws as a separate class.

This publication includes selected stories from some of these categories. Here you will find legends of elves or the hidden people, trolls, ghosts and magic, and quite a few 'stories of religious import', wonder tales, and last, but not least, three sagas from the Middle Ages. Folktales have often been defined by how much the storyteller emphasizes the truthfulness of the tale. This definition originates to the Brothers Grimm, who said: 'The fairytale is more poetic, the legend is more historical' (*The German Legends of the Brothers Grimm*, 1981). The fairy tales speak of non-descript persons and happen 'once upon a time', whereas the legends are told as if they are true, as Elliott Oring has pointed out ('Legendry and the Rhetoric of Truth' in *Journal of American Folklore* 121, 2008). They tell of certain people at a certain time and are linked to specific places. This connection to places is very strong in Icelandic legends. Einar Ólafur Sveinsson (2008) claims that Icelandic

> *folk-legends comprise an enormous group of stories, and cover the usual stories of trolls and elves, ghosts and wizards, dreams, weird happenings, beasts, people of heroic past and outlaws. A mass of placenames is embedded in these stories, and some independent stories are solely concerned with the explanation of placenames. Almost all these stories are given Icelandic locations, and they often concern people known to history.*

Legends of hidden people and trolls, in particular, are connected to the surroundings and nature of Iceland. Stones and rock formations are claimed as petrified trolls and hidden people are a type of nature spirit who reside in cliffs and hillocks. Powell and Magnússon also point this out in their Introductory Essay in *Icelandic Legends: (Collected by Jón Árnason)*, 1866, wherein they explain, '...the country itself is the most natural father of that folk-lore to which the brains of the people gave birth'.

Tales of the Divine and the Devil

Of these tales, Powell and Magnússon state in their Introductory Essay:

> *In the fifth group of tales Árnason has classed Legends, in the narrower sense of the word, that is, stories which touch upon religious and ecclesiastical matters. Among these are many which illustrate the spite of the devil against God and God's best deeds and loveliest creations, a spite which invariably falls redoubled upon the evil one's own head.*

Many of these tales have a comical point of view where the Devil is mocked and comes to a just end in all cases. However, priests are also periodically mocked, and in some of the tales harsh criticism can be found of the clergy and their greed and injustice towards their subordinated parishioners.

The Tales – Sagas

At the same time as folktales were being collected in Iceland, a great interest arose among learned Britons of the medieval literature of Iceland. Among the most important were the sagas of the Norwegian kings and the family sagas, recounting the first generations of native Icelanders. It became fashionable among the learned to travel to Iceland and visit the places that had gained renown in family sagas – as did both George Powell and William Morris (Wawn, 2000).

'The Story of Gunnlaug the Worm-Tongue and Raven the Skald' is one of the family sagas, or the sagas of Icelanders as they are also called. It was composed at the end of the thirteenth century, but it is preserved complete in a slightly younger manuscript. The saga was translated by Magnússon and Morris and published in 1875 in *Three Northern Love Stories, and Other Tales*, with 'The Story of Frithiof the Bold', among others (Wawn, 2000).

Another kind of popular and important Icelandic saga were the so-called Kings' sagas, or sagas of Norwegian kings. Linked to them are the *þættir*, short stories about Icelanders and their dealings with the kings. 'The Story of Audunn and the Bear' is one of those, written early in the thirteenth century. The *þættir* often tell of young Icelandic skalds (poets) who spent time at the courts of the Norwegian kings reciting poems of praise dedicated to the monarch. In this story the occasion of the voyage is a less common one: the bringing of a polar bear as a gift to the Danish king . Legends that tell of a man who, after having been to the Norwegian king with a tame bear, decides to present it to the king of Denmark, can be found both in Scandinavia and Germany, but no earlier source for this motif is known other than in the story of Audunn. It is given an historical background insofar as it is set in the time of Harald the Hard-ruler, King of Norway (1046–66), and Sveinn Úlfsson, King of Denmark (1047–76), when the two countries were at war (*c.* 1062–64) (Steingrímur J. Þorsteinsson, Introduction, *Seven Icelandic Short Stories*, 1960).

'The Story of Frithiof the Bold' belongs to yet another saga genre, the so-called legendary sagas. It is preserved in an Icelandic manuscript from *c.* 1300 and supposedly took place in the eighth century. It was the first complete Icelandic saga ever published in English translation, in 1839, by George Stephens. During the nineteenth century, there were three separate English translations of the saga of Frithiof. Stephens claimed it was 'one of the most beautiful [sagas] in the whole cycle of Icelandic literature' and William Morris called it 'lovely … very complete and beautiful' (Wawn, 2000).

It just so happens that within Icelandic medieval literature this is the saga in which scholars have found the most Middle Eastern influence. This influence can also be found in younger tales that were collected from oral tradition in the nineteenth century when people thought they were collecting 'unsullied' Icelandic folklore.

Icelandic Folktales?

As mentioned above, Árnason relied on his friends and old schoolfellows to gather material when he resumed work on collecting folktales again in 1858. However, he did collect some tales himself from people he associated with in Reykjavík, mostly learned men and people in the upper echelons of society. Magnússon is, for example, credited as a source for one tale in the collection, a tale of dwarves that Powell and he discuss in their Introductory Essay in *Icelandic Legends*, 1866.

Most of the collaborating collectors were also educated men, and many were priests who were undoubtedly well read and familiar with a number of the foreign stories that had come to Iceland in printed books. It can thus be assumed that they would not have spent time copying such stories when there was enough 'genuine Icelandic' material among storytellers to record. Nonetheless, it is still possible to find some examples of stories that were brought from overseas, like the Middle Eastern collection *Arabian Nights*, in addition to other stories that clearly had roots in

European folktale traditions. So while their intentions were to focus on 'pure' Icelandic material, other material crept in. We have at least three examples of such stories here.

One individual who collected stories for Árnason was Jón Sigurðsson (1828–89), a wealthy farmer and Member of Parliament who lived in the north of Iceland. He clearly distinguished between foreign stories and Icelandic ones, as can be seen in a letter he wrote to Árnason dated 1 February 1860. He first writes of tales he believes to be genuinely Icelandic but goes on to add, 'then there is another story category that is common here, and rather like *One Thousand and One Nights*, I have jotted down one story from this category and send it to you, it is the story "Af þrem kóngssonum" [The Story of the Tree Princes].'

The story is 'Prince Ahmed and the Fairy Perî Bânû', and the Icelandic version is in substance very like that in the *Arabian Nights*, although it differs in many small details. These details appear to be part of an effort to make the events more familiar to an Icelandic audience. As Sigurðsson's words demonstrate, these stories were transmitted orally and people told them for entertainment.

The second tale that likely originates in *Arabian Nights*, 'The Story of the Farmer's Three Daughters', has been localized even more. It was so closely adapted to the Icelandic context and so unlike printed translations of the story that it is likely that neither the collector Sveinbjörn Guðmundsson (1818–85) nor Árnason were aware of its foreign origins. The characters in the story have Icelandic names and the topography suggests Icelandic society and landscape. Apparently, the story had long stopped being a 'foreign' story from a printed source and was now transmitted orally, so it had become an Icelandic oicotype (a story that travels across different nations and cultures).

The third tale that is obviously foreign is the tale 'Rósamunda', which Árnason transcribed himself from a woman storyteller. It had been translated into Icelandic from French early in the nineteenth century and continued into oral tradition.

Based on what has been outlined above, it is clear that it was not only 'Icelandic' stories that circulated orally in the time period under discussion and that material inspiration for some stories came from beyond Iceland.

It is exceptionally lucky for folklorists that some of those who collected stories for Árnason – and he, himself – did not filter out all the stories that came from foreign traditions. With that they opened a window into the extremely varied and international storytelling traditions of these times when national characteristics were otherwise being emphasized and the aim was to collect 'pure and unsullied' Icelandic folktales.

Rósa Þorsteinsdóttir is an associated research professor in folkloristics at the Árni Magnússon Institute for Icelandic Studies. She works both as an archivist and a researcher, while teaching courses on folkloristics at the University of Iceland. She has conducted research on the history of the collection of folklore in Iceland and has an interest in ethnomusicology.

The Mighty & the Brave

THOSE WHO ARE thoroughly acquainted with the literature of Iceland are agreed that, so far as the historical part of it is concerned, it holds a distinguished place among the literatures of the world, next indeed to the classics of ancient Greece and Rome.

And though its historians, the authors of its noble sagas, have been men of high learning and cultivated minds, its peasants, uncultivated and unlearned, have been those who have handed down to us the traditional lore of the country, the poetical and imaginative tales of elves, trolls, ghosts, goblins and monsters; some contenting themselves with telling them often by the winter fire; others adding stories from their own mental testimonies, and then committing them to paper.

The stories in this chapter focus on those who are superior, fearless, who fight for what – or who, as in the case of 'The Story of the Three Princes' – they want. Their courage may bring about unthought-of revelations, as in 'The Story of the Farmer's Three Daughters', or perhaps become its own reward.

The Story of the Three Princes

IT IS SAID THAT ONCE, in the days of old, there was a good and wealthy king, who ruled over a great and powerful realm; but neither his name, nor that of his kingdom, is given, nor the latter's whereabouts in the world. He had a queen, and by her three sons, who were all fine youths and hopeful, and the king loved them well. The king had taken too, a king's daughter from a neighbouring kingdom, to foster her: she was brought up with his sons. She was of the same age as they, and the most beautiful and accomplished lady that had ever been seen in those days, and the king loved her in no way less than his own sons.

When the princess was of age, all the king's sons fell in love with her, and things even went so far, that they all of them engaged her at once, each in his own name. Their father, being the princess's foster-father, had the right of bestowing her in marriage, as her own father was dead. But as he was fond of all his sons equally, the answer he gave them was, that he left it to the bride's own choice, to take for a husband whichever of the brothers she loved the most. On a certain day, he had the princess called up to him, and declared his will to her, telling her that she might choose for a husband, whichever she liked best of his sons. The princess answered: "Bound I am in duty to obey your words. But as to this choice of one of your sons to be my husband, I am in the greatest perplexity; for I must confess that all are equally dear to me, and I cannot choose one before the other."

When the king heard these answers of the princess, he found himself in a new embarrassment, and thought a long while what he could do that should be equally agreeable to all parties, and at last hit upon the following decision of the matter: that all his sons should, after a year's travel, return, each with a precious thing, and that he who had the finest thing should be the princess's husband. This decision the king's sons found to be a just and agreeable one, and they agreed to meet, after one year, at a certain castle in the country, whence they should go, all together, to the town, in order to lay their gifts before the princess. And now their departure from the country was arranged as well as could be.

First, the tale tells of the eldest, that he went from one land to another, and from one city to another, in search of a precious thing, but found nowhere anything that at all suited his ideas. At last the news came to his ears that there was a princess who had so fine a spy-glass, that nothing so marvellous had ever been seen or heard of before. In it one could see all over the world, every place, every city, every man, and every living being that moved on the face of the earth, and what every living thing in the world was doing. Now the prince thought that surely there could be no more precious thing at all likely to turn up for him than this telescope; he therefore went to the princess, in order to buy the spy-glass if possible. But by no means could he prevail upon the king's daughter to part with her spy-glass, till he had told her his whole story, and why he wanted it, and used all his powers of entreaty. As might be expected, he paid for it well. Having got it, he returned home glad at his luck, and hoping to wed the king's daughter.

The story next turns to the second son.

He had to struggle with the same difficulties as his elder brother. He travelled for a long while over the wide world, without finding anything at all suitable, and thus for a time he saw no chance of his wishes being fulfilled. Once he came into a very well-peopled city, and went about in search of precious things, among the merchants, but neither did he find nor even see what he wanted. He heard that there lived, a short way from the town, a dwarf, the cleverest maker of curious and cunning things. He therefore resolved to go to this dwarf, in order to try whether he could be persuaded to make him any costly thing. He got a guide to lead him to the dwarf, whom he found at home, and to whom he declared what he wanted. The dwarf said that he had ceased to make things of that sort now, and he must beg to be excused from making anything of the kind for the prince. But he said that he had a piece of cloth, made in his younger days, with which, however, he was very unwilling to part. The king's son asked the nature and use of the cloth. The dwarf answered: "On this cloth, one can go all over the world, as well through the air as on the water. Runes are on it, which must be understood by him who uses it."

Now the prince saw that a more precious thing than this could scarcely be found, and therefore asked the dwarf, by all means to let him have the cloth. And, although the dwarf would not, at first, part with his cloth at all, he, at last, hearing what would happen if the king's son did not get it, sold it to him at a mighty high price. The prince was truly glad to have got the cloth, for it was not only a cloth of great value, but also the greatest of gems in other respects, having gold seams and jewel-embroidery. After this, he returned home, hoping to get the best of his brothers in the contest for the damsel.

The youngest prince left home, last of the three brothers. First he travelled from one village to the other, in his own country, and went about, asking for precious things of every merchant he met on his way, as also on all sides, where there was the slightest hope of his getting what he wanted. But all his endeavours were in vain, and the greatest part of the year was spent in fruitless search, till at last he waxed sad in mind at his lot. At this time, he came into a well-peopled city, whereto people were gathered, from all parts of the world. He went from one merchant to another, till, at last, he came to one who sold apples. This merchant said he had an apple that was of so strange a nature, that if it was put into the arm-hole of a dying man, he would, at once, return to life. He declared that it was the property of his family, and had always been used in the family as a medicine. But, as soon as the king's son heard this, he would, by all means, have the apple, deeming that he would never be able to find a thing more acceptable to the king's daughter than this. He therefore asked the merchant to sell him the apple, and told him all the story of his search, and that his earthly welfare was based upon his being, in no way, inferior to his brothers in his choice of precious things for the princess. The merchant felt pity for the prince, when he had told him his story, so much so that he sold him the apple, and the prince returned home, glad and comforted at his happy luck.

Now nothing more is related of the three brothers, till they had met together at the place before appointed. When they were all together, each related the striking points in his travelling. All being here, the eldest brother thought that he would be the first to see the princess, and find out how she was; and therefore he took forth his spy-glass and turned it towards the city. But what saw he? The beloved princess lying in her bed, in the very jaws of death! The king, his father, and all the highest nobles of the court, were standing round the bed, in the blackness of sorrow, sad in their minds, and ready to receive the last sigh of the fair princess.

When the prince saw this lamentable sight, he was grieved beyond all measure. He told his brothers what he had seen, and they were no less struck with sorrow than himself. They began bewailing loudly, saying that they would give all they had, never to have undertaken this journey, for then, at least, they would have been able to perform the last offices for the fair princess. But, in the midst of these bewailings, the second brother bethought him of his cloth, and remembered that he could get to the town on it in a moment. He told this to the brothers, and they were glad at such good and unexpected news. Now the cloth was unfolded, and they all stepped on to it, and, in a moment, it was high in the air, and in the next, inside the town. When they were there, they made all haste to reach the room of the princess, where everybody wore an air of deep sadness. They were told that the princess's every breath was her last. Then the youngest brother remembered his wonderful apple, and thought that it would never be more wanted to shew its healing power than now. He therefore went straight into the bedroom of the princess, and placed the apple under her right arm. And, at the same moment, it was as if a new breath of life flushed through the whole body of the princess; her eyes opened, and, after a little while, she began to speak to the folk around her. This, and the return of the king's sons, caused great joy at the court of the king.

Now some time went by, until the princess was fully recovered. Then a large meeting was called together, at which the brothers were bidden to shew their treasures. First, the eldest made his appearance, and shewing his spy-glass, told what a wonderful thing it was, and also how it was due to this glass that the life of the fair princess had ever been saved, as he had seen through it how matters stood in the town. He, therefore, did not doubt for a moment that his gift was the one which would secure him the fair princess.

Next, stepped forward the second brother, with the cloth. Having described its powers, he said: "I am of opinion, that my brother's having seen the princess first, would have proved of little avail, had I not had the cloth, for thereupon we came so quickly to the place, to save the princess; and I must declare that, to my mind, the cloth is the chief cause of the king's daughter's recovery."

Next, stepped forward the youngest prince, and said, as he laid his apple before the people: "Little would the glass and the cloth have availed to save the princess's life, had I not had the apple. What could we brothers have profited, in being only witnesses of the beloved damsel's death ? What would this have done, but awaken our grief and regret? It is due alone to the apple, that the princess is yet alive; wherefore I find myself the most deserving of her."

Then a long discussion arose in the meeting, and the decision at last came out, – that all three things had worked equally towards the princess's recovery, as might be seen from the fact that, if one had been wanting, the others would have been worthless. It was therefore declared that, as all the gifts had equal claim to the prize, no one could decide to whom the princess should belong.

After this, the king planned another contrivance, in order to come to some end of the matter. He soon should try their skill in shooting, and he who proved to be the ablest shooter of them should have the princess. So a mark was raised, and the eldest brother stepped forward with his bow and quiver. He shot, and no little distance from the mark fell his arrow.

After that, stepped forward the second brother, and his arrow well-nigh reached the mark.

Last of all, stepped forward the third and youngest brother, and his arrow seemed to go farther than the others; but, in spite of continued search for many days, it could not be found. The king decided in this matter, that his second son should marry the princess. They were married therefore, and as the king, the father of the princess, was dead, his daughter now succeeded him, and her husband became king over his wife's inheritance. They are now out of this tale, as is also the eldest brother, who settled in life abroad.

The youngest brother stayed at home with his father, highly displeased at the decision the latter had given concerning the marriage of the princess. He was wont to wander about, every day, where he fancied his arrow had fallen, and, at last, he found it fixed in an oak in the forest, and saw that it had by far outsped the mark. He now called together witnesses to the place where the arrow was, with the intention of bringing about some justice in his case. But of this there was no chance, for the king said he could, by no means, alter his decision. At this, the king's son was so grieved, that he went well-nigh out of his wits. One day, he busked for a journey, with the full intention of never again setting foot in his country. He took with him all he possessed of fine and precious things, nobody knowing his rede, not even his father, the king.

He went into a great forest, and wandered about there many days, without knowing whither he was going, and, at last, yielding to hunger and weariness, he found himself no longer equal to travelling; he sat down under a large stone, thinking that his sad and sorrowful life would here come to a close. But after he had sat thus a while, he saw ten people, all in fine attire and bright armour, come riding towards the stone. On arriving there, they dismounted, and having greeted the king's son, begged him to go with them, and mount the spare horse they had with them, saddled and bridled in royal fashion. He accepted this offer, and mounted the horse, and after this, they rode on their way, till they came to a large city. The riders dismounted, and led the prince into the town, which was governed by a young and beautiful maiden-queen. The riders led the king's son at once to the virgin- queen, who received him with great kindness. She told him that she had heard of all the ill-luck that had befallen him, and also that he had fled from his father. "Then," quoth she, "a burning love for you was kindled in my breast, and a longing to heal your wounds. You must know that it was I who sent the ten riders, to find you out and bring you hither. I give you the chance of staying here; I offer you the rule of my whole kingdom, and I will try to sweeten your embittered life; – this is all that I am able to do."

And, although the prince was in a sad and gloomy state of mind, he saw nothing better than to accept this generous offer, and agree to the marriage with the maiden-queen. A grand feast was made ready, and they were married according to the ways of that country. And the young king took, at once, in hand the goverment, which he managed with much ability. And so time passed away.

Now, the story turns homewards, to the old king.

After the disappearance of his son, he became sad and weary of life, being as he was, sinking in age. His queen also had died, sometime since. One day, it happened that a way-faring woman came to the palace. She had much knowledge about many things, and knew how to tell many tales. The king was greatly delighted with her storytelling, and she got soon into his favour. Thus some time passed. But, in course of time, the king fell deeply in love with this woman, and, at last, married her and made her his queen, in spite of strong dissent from the court. Shortly, this new queen began meddling in the affairs of the government, and it soon turned out that she was found spoiling everything by her redes, whenever she had the chance.

Once, it happened that the queen spoke to the king, and said: "Strange indeed it seems to me, that you make no enquiry about your youngest son's running away, smaller faults being often chastised than that. You must have heard that he has become king in one of the neighbouring kingdoms, and that it is a common tale that he is going to invade your dominions with a great army, whenever he gets the wished-for opportunity, in order to avenge the injustice he thinks he has suffered in that bygone bridal question. Now I want you to be the first in throwing this danger off hand."

The king shewed little interest in the matter, and paid to his wife's chattering but slight attention; but she contrived, at length, so to speak to him, as to make him place faith in her words, and he asked her to give him good redes, that this matter might be arranged in such a way as to be least observed by other folk. The queen said: "You must send men with gifts to him, and pray him to come to you for an interview, in order to arrange certain political matters before your death, as also to strengthen your friendship with an interchange of marks of kindred. And then I will give you further advice, as to what to do."

The king was satisfied with this, and equipped his messengers royally.

Then the messengers came before the young king, saying they were sent by his father, who wished his son to come and see him without delay. To this the young king answered well, and lost no time in busking his men and himself. But when his queen knew this, she said he would assuredly rue this journey. The king went off, however, and nothing is said of his travels, till he came to the town where his father lived. His father received him rather coolly, much to the wonder and amazement of his son.

And when he had been there a short while, his father gave him a good chiding for having run away.

"Thereby," said the old king, "you have shewn full contempt of myself, and caused me such sorrow as well-nigh brought me to the grave. Therefore, according to the law, you have deserved to die; but as you have delivered yourself up into my power, and are, on the other hand, my son, I have no mind to have you killed; but I have three tasks for you, which you must have performed within a year, on pain of death. The first is, that you shall bring me a tent which will hold one hundred men, but which can yet be hidden in the closed palm; the second, that you shall bring me water that cures all ailments; and the third, that you shall bring me hither a man, who has not his like in the whole world."

"Shew me whither," said the young king, " I shall go to obtain these things."

"That you must find out for yourself," replied the other.

Then the old king turned his back upon his son and went off. Away went also the young king, no farewells being said, and nothing is told of his travels, till he came home to his realm. He was then very sad and heavy-minded, and his queen seeing this, asked him earnestly what had befallen him, and what caused the gloom on his mind. He declared that this did not regard her. The queen answered: "I know that tasks must have been set you, which it will not prove easy to perform. But what will it avail you to sit sullen and sad, on account of such things? Behave as a man, and try if these tasks may not indeed be accomplished."

Now the king thought best to tell all that had happened to the queen, and how matters stood.

"All this," said the queen, "is the rede of your step-mother, and it would be well indeed if she could do you no more harm by it, than she has already tried to do. She has chosen such difficulties as she thought you would not easily get over, but I can do something here. The tent is in my possession, – so there is that difficulty got over. The water you have to get is a short way hence, but very hard of approach. It is in a well, and the well is in a cave hellishly dark. The well is watched by seven lions and three serpents, and from these monsters, nobody has ever returned alive; and the nature of this water is, that it has no healing power whatever, unless it be drawn when all these monsters are awake. Now I will risk the undertaking of drawing the water."

So the queen made herself ready to go to the cave, taking with her seven oxen, and three pigs. When she came before the cave, she ordered the oxen to be killed and thrown before the lions, and the pigs before the serpents. But while these monsters tore and devoured the carcasses, the queen stepped down into the well, and drew as much water as she wanted. And she left the cave just in time, as the beasts finished devouring their bait. After this, the queen went home to the palace, having thus got over the second trial. Then she came to her husband and said: "Now two of the tasks are done, but the third, and indeed the hardest of them, is left. Moreover, this one you must perform yourself; but I can give you some hints as to whither to go for it. I have got a half-brother who rules over an island, not far hence. He is three feet high, and has one eye in the middle of his forehead. He has a beard thirty ells long, stiff and hard as hogs' bristles. He has a dog's snout and cat's ears, and I should scarcely fancy he had his like in the whole world. When he travels, he flings himself forward on a staff of fifty ells length, with a pace as swift as a bird's flight. Once, when my father was out hunting, he was charmed by an ogress, who lived in a cave under a waterfall, and with her he begat this bugbear. The island is one-third of my father's realm, but his son finds it too small for him. My father had a ring, the greatest gem, which each of us would have, sister and brother, but I got it, wherefore he has been my enemy ever since. Now I will write him a letter and send him the ring, in the hopes that that will soften him, and turn him in our favour. You shall make ready to go to him, with a splendid suite, and when you come to his palace-door, you shall take off your crown, and creep bareheaded over the floor, up to his throne. Then you shall kiss his right foot, and give him the letter and the ring. And if he orders you to stand up, you have succeeded in your task; if not, you have failed."

So he did in everything as he was bidden by his queen, and when he appeared before the one-eyed king, he was stupified at his tremendous ugliness, and his bugbear appearance; but he plucked up courage as best he could, and gave him the letter and the ring. When the king saw the letter and the ring, his face brightened up, and he said: "Surely my sister finds herself in straits now, as she sends me this ring." And when he had read the letter, he bade the king, his brother-in-law, stand up, and declared that he was ready to comply with his sister's wish, and to go off at once without delay. He seized his staff, and started away. He stopped, now and then, for his brother-in-law and his suite, to whom he gave a good chiding for their slowness. They continued thus their march, until they came to the palace of the queen, the ugly king's sister; but when they arrived there, the one-eyed king, cried with a roaring voice to the sister, and asked her what she wished, as she had troubled him to come so far from home. She then told him all the matter as it really was, and begged him to help her husband out of the trial put before him. He said he was ready to do so, but would brook no delay.

Now both kings went off, and nought is told of their journey, till they came to the old king. The young king announced to this father his coming, and that he brought with him what he had ordered last year. He wished his father to call together a Thing, in order that he might shew openly how he had performed his tasks.

This was done, and the queen, and the king, and other great folk were assembled.

First, the tent was put forward, and nobody could find fault with it.

Secondly, the young king gave the wondrous healing water to his father; the queen was prayed to taste it, and to see if it was the right water, taken at the right time. She said that both things were as they should be.

Then said the old king: "Now the third and heaviest of all the tasks is left; come, and have it off your hands quickly."

Then the young king summoned the king with one eye. And, as he appeared on the Thing, he waxed so hideous, that all the people were struck with fright and horror, and most of all the old king. When this ugly monarch had shewn himself for a while there, he thrust his staff against the breast of the queen, and tilted her up into the air, on the top of it, and then thrust her against the ground with such force, that every bone in her body was broken. She turned at once into the most monstrous troll ever beheld.

After this, the one-eyed king rushed away from the Thing, and the people thronged round the old king, in order to help him, for he was in the very jaws of death from fright. The healing water was sprinkled on him, and refreshed him.

After the death of his queen, who was killed of course when she turned into a troll, the king confessed that all the tasks which he had given his son to perform were undeserved, and that he had acted thus, egged on by the queen. He called his son to him, and humbly begged his forgiveness for what he had done against him. He declared he would atone for it, by giving up into his hand all that kingdom, while he himself only wished to live in peace and quiet for the rest of his days. So the young king sent for his queen, and for the courtiers whom they loved the most.

And, to make a long story short, they gave up their former kingdom to the king with one eye, as a reward, for his lifetime; but governed the realm of the old king to a high age, in great glee and happiness.

The Story of Thorsteinn, the King's Son

THERE WAS ONCE a king and queen, in their realm, who had a son named Thorsteinn. He was early a youth of great growth, and very hopeful was he. Everybody loved him for his amiable disposition, and his liberality. But his love of giving away money, soon passed all measure, and his mother used often to chide him for squandering his means.

She did all she could to check his prodigality, as she called it, but he went on his own way, giving money on all sides, as far as he could. When his mother died, he thought he could now give away, without being chided, and was glad to be rid of her grumblings. Thorsteinn was firm in the belief that his father would approve of his way of spending his money, as he had never blamed him, in the least, for it, hitherto. But things took quite another turn. For, now the king continued chiding his son, where the queen had left off. He tried to shew the youth, by reasoning, how unbecoming such prodigality was, and that thereby, he must become poor sooner than he expected, as there was nothing within his reach, that he did not wish to squander away. But reasoning was here out of place. Thorsteinn was the same and continued the same as formerly, and gave everything away, as soon as he became owner of it.

Now the time came, when his father died. Being left to his own designs, the prince thought he could act delightfully, being checked by no bonds, and having only to yield to his own pleasure, – that of giving money away. So, now, he gave money to anyone who liked to have it; and many a one was found who liked it. Therefore, albeit the wealth he had come into, on his father's death, was great, it must needs lessen with his prodigality. And, to tell a long story in few words, it came at last to that pass, that all Thorsteinn's property was squandered away, and he had the kingdom left on his hands, with no money to govern it. Now, Thorsteinn wanted to get a purchaser for the kingdom, that he might have some money,

– which would be easier to manage than a whole kingdom, – to give away. At last, he found a buyer, and got for his realm, a horse loaded with gold and silver.

When Thorsteinn had made his bargain, his friends began to diminish in number. They all turned their backs to him, when they saw that there was not a fat pig to flay, where he was. Now Thorsteinn saw how matters stood, and thought that the best thing would be, to leave these fellows for good. He therefore went away, with all his property, which was easily carried on one horse. He himself rode on his chestnut, a horse with which he never would part, on account of his many good qualities: but of these no mention is made in this story.

Now, Thorsteinn travelled about, for a long time, through heaths and wildernesses, without knowing, in the least, whither he went; nor did he much care which direction he took. Wherever he found a clump of grass, growing in the wildernesses, he grazed his horses thereupon. But no other delay had he there.

Once, when he was baiting his horses, there came over him a deep gloom and sadness, for he thought that he should lose his life on this journey. However, he saw that there was nothing to be done, but to go on, whatsoever he might encounter on the road, since he had already begun his journeying. At last, on the road, he found a farmhouse. Thereat was he very glad, as he had neither seen nor encountered anybody, for a long time. He asked for shelter, and was taken, at once, into the family-room, where he slept the night through. But when he awoke in the morning every soul was out of the farmhouse. This startled him somewhat, for he thought there might be some trick in it. He got up in all haste, and when he was dressed, ran out. He then saw that the farmer was, with all his household, knocking eagerly on a mound in the field. Thorsteinn, not a little astonished at this madman's proceeding, asked the farmer what this foolish conduct meant. The farmer said that it was no wonder he did this, for, in the mound was buried a man, who had owed him two hundred rix-dollars when he died. Now the prince tried, by reason, to persuade the farmer that, by these means he was not very likely to get his debt paid; on the contrary, he said, he wasted yet more, in the time it took him to perform this foolish job. The farmer said he cared not a snap of the finger for that; his only satisfaction was to leave the dead no rest or repose in the grave, and he would never, as long as he lived, break off what he had once made his custom. Then the king's son asked if the farmer would not find it enough, should someone happen to pay the debt for the dead man. The farmer said: "Yes." Thereupon, the prince paid him all the money, and the farmer left off thumping the mound, promising never to do it more.

After this, the king's son asked the farmer to shew him the way to places thickly peopled. This the farmer did, telling him that when he had followed the road for a while, straight from the house, he would come to where the paths branched one from the other, and begged him not to take the path that went to the east, but the other which went to the west.

But when the prince had gone some distance along the left path, he thought it might be good sport, to try if any danger loomed on the other. He therefore returned to the place where the road branched, and thence went on eastward, till he came to a farm, consisting of lofty buildings. This place was strongly guarded both by nature and the hand of man. He found, however, a pass leading to the houses, and, leaving his horses behind, went through into the farm. He walked into one of the houses that chanced to be open, but nobody was to be seen out of doors. When the prince came in, he saw seven beds, all very large in size, but one of them was far the biggest. In the middle of the floor was standing a table, the whole length of the house, but with a passage at each end, and plate was standing in rows on it. But no living being did Thorsteinn see in the house. He now went to look after his horses, intending to take up his night-quarters there, although he found it rather awful. He therefore took the packs and saddles of his horses, and drove them on to pasture, and then put the baggage where he thought fittest. But his sword he kept with him, being the thing on which he set most store, next to his chestnut horse. When all this was done, he returned to the farmhouse, and going in, entered every building and every room to which he found access possible. In one of the rooms he found good and plenty of provisions. He took a goodly portion of them, which he put in each plate on the table, and afterwards made the beds, as nicely and as neatly as he could. Although he thought he had done here as much good as it was possible for him to do, he did not dare to be in a place where he could be easily discovered and surrounded, therefore he would find for himself some dark nook, to hide himself in, and at last he managed to thrust himself into an opening behind a door, between the doorpost and a panel.

A short while after, Thorsteinn heard a great rumbling noise outside, and then the door of the house was thrust open and someone heard to enter the room. Immediately afterwards, he heard someone say: "Someone has been here: let us cut short his hours!"

Then answered another: "That shall not be; I take him under my protection, for here I have so much to say, that I have power to save one man's life. Besides, he has, of his own accord, done us a service, made our beds, and spread our table, and done everything well. If he appears he shall take neither hurt nor harm."

At these words, the king's son plucked up spirit, and appeared. He found the fellows very great-grown, and more like trolls than men, but their leader was the most strikingly trollish in look of them, and giantlike withal. Thorsteinn stayed with them through that night. Next morning, they bade him stay a week with them, telling him he should have nothing to do, but cook for them and make their beds. To this the king's son agreed, and was thus with them through that week, and they were mutually satisfied. After the lapse of this week, the farm-dweller entreated the prince to stay with them for a year. This he promised to do, albeit he found this home a very dull one. The big giant promised Thorsteinn high wages for his work, and gave him all his keys but one. Every day, the prince went through all the houses and rooms at the farm, except that one whereof the big giant kept the key, none of the keys he had fitting the lock of it. Once he tried to pick the lock, but unavailingly. But Thorsteinn observed that the great carl went into it, every evening and every morning. When he had been here for a while, he asked the giant why he had given him keys to all the rooms but that one; saying further that, as he was faithful with that which had been already entrusted to his charge, so would he also be, with whatever might be in that room.

"In this room," said the giant, "there is nothing, as you may judge from my having trusted you with many things of great value." And here the matter dropped.

Now we may here relate shortly, that the prince stayed in this place for four years running, and had very high wages for it. He had, by that time, quite given up mentioning the room that interested him, and that amongst other things served to make him more beloved by the giants, every day.

But, what chiefly tempted the prince to stay so long, was that he was for ever watching a chance, to find out if nothing was in this wonderful room.

One morning, he was thinking of this as usual, and hit upon a plan. He knocked violently at the door, and came running into the house, with his heart in his shoes, feigning the greatest fright. He had in his hand a piece of dough, which he was kneading. He asked the giants if they had heard nothing. "Yes," they said, and that they fancied it had been some noise made by himself. He said it was far from that, adding that he had not dared to go to the door, but was sure that someone had knocked at it. They said he was quite right in not going out; and rushing from their beds (for they were not up yet), they flew to the door, half-dressed. In his hurry, the big giant had left the key by his pillow, and the prince at once took a mould of it, in the dough. Now the giants came in, worse than ashamed of their disappointment, as they, naturally enough, had seen nobody at the door. They charged Thorsteinn with having done this in order to make fools of them, but he excused himself and denied their charges, saying at last, that it must have been some spirit. And that was the end of the matter.

But after this, the prince used, in the daytime, to make himself a key after the mould in the dough. For a long while, this was a work of great difficulty, but, at last, he succeeded. He now opened the room, but nothing save thick darkness was, at first, to be seen. He lighted a candle, and found, on looking round, a maiden hung up by her hair. His first work was to unfasten her and take her down, and next he asked her about her family and origin, and found that she was a king's daughter, whom the big giant had stolen, and would force, against her will, to marry him. But as she was not to be persuaded by any means, he tortured her in this way. She was now little more than mere bone, for the giant also starved her. The prince gave her food, but, before evening, he fastened her up by the hair as formerly, so that nothing out of the way should be observed. After this, he came to her every day, and brought her food enough, but fastened her up every night, before the giant came home; no change, therefore, was to be traced in the dark room, and nobody had the least suspicion of the prince's doings.

When the fifth year was past, Thorsteinn said he must indeed go away, but the giants would make any sacrifice to persuade him to stay. He then said to the big giant that, if he wanted to keep him yet one year, he must give him as his wages for the year, that which was in the locked room, which he was not allowed to enter, whatever it might be. The giant prayed him not to ask for what was nothing, as it would be far better for him to receive his wages as usually. No! That was not the prince's will; he said he would have nothing but what he had asked for, should it be loss or gain to him, and about this they disputed hard, till the giant promised him the wages he demanded.

How Thorsteinn treated the princess this year, we need not tell. But when the year was over, the giant opened the room, for the king's son was by no means to be persuaded to stay longer. The giant went into the darkness, and soon came back with the princess, and wondered at her being so fat and well-looking; but, paying no further attention to this, he gave her to Thorsteinn. Now Thorsteinn prepared for departure, fetched his horses, over which he had kept a sharp watch, and tied up his package. But, what with his wages, all his baggage had swollen up to such a mighty bulk, that he could scarcely get away with it all. The king's daughter bade him be watchful, for the giant would attack him on the way. He was, therefore, always in his armour, and kept at hand his own good sword. What the princess had said, soon came true, for, on their way, when they had only travelled a short way from the farm, they were overtaken by three of the giants, who in trollish fury flew upon Thorsteinn, but he defended himself so gallantly, that he left them all dead on the field. After that, he took breath. But a short while after, there came two others of the giants, whom Thorsteinn also managed to kill. Now two were left, the big giant and his brother. They came in a mighty rage, and made a violent onset upon Thorsteinn. First he managed to kill the brother. Then the big giant, utterly losing his temper, flung away his weapon, and rushed wildly upon the prince, and seized him in his arms. Now the king's son could do nothing to defend himself, and fell to the earth with the giant on the top of him. When the princess saw into what straits the prince was brought, she seized an axe which had belonged to one of the others, and stabbed the big giant with it.

Afterwards she aided the prince in throwing off the giant's body, but Thorsteinn was now so weary, that he could not continue the journey. They therefore turned back to the abode of the giants, and though they found it dull and wearisome, they determined to wait there a while, to see if some vessel might not appear in the neighbourhood of the shore, or even anchor there, the farm being close to the sea. After some time, there came a vessel, and they went to the shore and talked to the folk on board. The master of the ship was hight Raudr, and was the minister of the princess's father. The king had promised him his daughter, if he could find her and bring her to him. The crew received Thorsteinn and the king's daughter, and brought all their property, which they had taken from the giant-farm, and which was very great, on board the vessel. After this, they went on board and left the country. But when the vessel was some distance from the shore, Raudr had a boat hauled overboard, and put the king's son into it, alone. He then made the crew swear that they would not mention the name of Thorsteinn, but would say that he had himself killed the giants, and delivered the king's daughter from them. This they swore, but the king's daughter refused to do so, in spite of Raudr's threats and coaxing. Raudr thought, however, that he had done a good job, and sailed home.

But of Thorsteinn it is told that, when the boat, oarless and rudderless, began to toss and roll about on the waves, he waxed mighty fearful. Then he heard a voice say to him: "Be not afraid of drifting about in the main; I shall help you." Thereupon, the boat sped forward through the sea, as if it were dragged or pushed, as swiftly as the vessel which carried Raudr, and came to the right shore at the same time as the ship, but in another place. And he who brought the boat safely to shore, was the dead man for whom Thorsteinn had formerly paid the debt. He now appeared, and told Thorsteinn that he had arrived in the kingdom where the father of the princess lived, and that he should go and be the king's stableman, and have what was under the manger in this stable. Thorsteinn's chestnut horse had been brought over on the ship, and was added to the number of the king's chestnuts. This horse nobody could approach or touch, save the king's daughter and the new groom.

When the king saw his daughter, he was more glad than we can tell, and had a great feast to welcome her, and at that feast it was determined that Raudr should marry her. She, however, would not have the wedding performed, until the stableman had told the story of his life. This the king granted, and then all the truth came out. Raudr was killed and the crew tortured, but his daughter the king gave to Thorsteinn, yielding him up, at the same time, the half part of his kingdom. Now, under the manger in the stables, Thorsteinn found heaps of all kinds of gems; and, after the king's death, he had the whole kingdom. He lived both long and well, and was found to be a most excellent king, and was beloved by everybody, till the day of his death, at a high age.

Sigurdr, the King's Son

THERE WAS ONCE a king and queen, who ruled over a country, and who had four daughters, all of them hopeful and fair; but the youngest of them was most the darling of her father. One day, the king went a-hunting with his men, and they had not ridden long before they met a hind.

They pursued the animal a good part of the day, and, at last, all the men were left behind, but the king, who had the swiftest horse. He chased the hind, until he was in the thickest part of the wood, where he entirely lost it, and with it, his way, and he rode at random through the forest, not knowing whither to go. At length, in the evening, he came to a house, the door of which he found ajar. The king entered the house, and found an open room, with meals and wine on the table. He saw there too, a bed, already made, but no sign of people; a brown-coloured dog lay on the floor. The king went out again, and found an open stable, big enough to take in one horse, and a crib with food enough for one. Having stabled his horse there, the king returned to the house, in order to wait till the landlord came home. But, as midnight passed without any signs of him, the king waited no longer, and, having refreshed himself from the meals on the table, went forthwith to bed. He soon fell sound asleep, and did not wake till broad daylight next morning. He got up, and finding all sorts of eatables and wine on the table, refreshed himself, and then went out to look after his horse, which he found well provided with food. The brown dog was still lying on the floor. When the king had refreshed himself, he took his horse and went away. After he had ridden for a while, he came to a knoll, where he was overtaken by the brown dog, who looked snappish and wild. The dog said: "You are indeed an ungrateful king; last night I have given you shelter, and bed, and meals, and wine, and provided for your horse to boot, and yet off you go without saying one word of thanks. I am going to tear you to death, unless you will promise to give me whatever you first meet on your return home." This promise the king gave, as he preferred saving his life. The dog said he would come for the fulfilment of the vow, in three days. After that, the king went home.

Now we must tell how all the court in the palace were much concerned about the king, who did not return from the chase; and most of all, his youngest daughter was filled with sorrow. Next day she mounted a high tower in the palace, to look out for her father, and when she saw him approaching, she ran down into the fields, in order to be the first to welcome him. The king was very sad at his dearest daughter's being the first thing he met; but they went home together to the palace, and everybody rejoiced to see the king return in full safety. When the king had sat down to table, he told all that had happened to him, and also what vow he had been forced to make, but added that he was not in the least going to fulfil it. On the third day, there was a knock at the palace door. A servant, having been sent to the door, returned, saying that he had seen nothing but a brown dog. Now people knew what this meant, and the king's daughter wanted, by all means, to go to the door herself, but the king said that that should never be. So a servant-maid was sent to the door. As she appeared, the dog said: "Art thou sent to me?" The servant was silent, and the dog put her on his back, and ran with her into the wood. On a mound, the dog stopped, and let the servant dismount, and said: "What will the time be now, I wonder?" The maid answered that she did not know quite, but fancied it to be about the hour at which she was wont to sweep the king's palace. "Art thou then not the king's daughter?" asked the dog. "No," answered the servant, and the dog at once sprang upon her, and tore her to death.

Next day, there came again a knock at the palace door, and a man went out to see who was there. When he returned he said that he only had seen a brown and savage-looking dog. People knew what this meant, and the king's youngest daughter wanted to go out. But the king would not allow it, so another servant-maid went out. When she appeared at the door, the dog asked: "Art thou sent to me?" and making her sit on his back, ran off with her into the forest, until he came to the mound. Here he made her dismount, and said: "What will the time be now, I wonder?" The maid said she thought it was about the hour at which she was wont to get the king's table ready. "Art thou then not the king's daughter?" asked the dog. "No," answered the servant, and he fell upon her and tore her at once to death.

Next day, a third knock came to the door of the palace, and the man who went out, brought the news that it was once more the dog, who looked even fiercer than he had yet seen him. The king's daughter would go out, but the king forbade her, although she said that she should love nothing more than to save his life: and she went out, in spite of all the king's commands. When she was outside the door, where the dog lay, he said: "Art thou sent to me?" "Yes," she answered. So he made her sit on his back and went off with her. When he had reached the mound in the forest, he shook off his charge, and said: "What will the time be now, I wonder?" She answered: "I guess it is about the time at which I am wont to go in to my father's palace." "Then you are the king's daughter," said the dog. "I am," she replied. Now the dog made her sit on his back again, and carried her along till they came to a house, into which the dog took her, telling her that she was to dwell there. In the room were a table, a chair, and a bed, and all things she wanted, to make her comfortable. She should have alone, the management and full disposition of everything around her, the dog said. Now time passed away, and she never saw a human being, save, every night, a man, who slept in her bed. Morning and evening, the dog was to be seen, but in the day-time, he was often away. After a while, the king's daughter was with child, and the dog once told her, that her child should be taken from her, as soon as she was delivered of it. "But you must try," said he, "to avoid shedding a tear, as that is of great importance to me; if, however, you should shed tears, you must let them fall into this cloth;" and, with these words, he gave her a silken cloth, and walked off. Soon the princess gave birth to a child, a little girl of great beauty. She bathed and swaddled the baby, and then put it close to her in the bed, kneeling over it, with a tender mother's love and warm prayers. While she knelt thus over her child, there passed a shadow across the window of the house, and in a moment afterwards a vulture came in, and seizing up the child in its claws, flew away with it. The king's daughter was deeply grieved at her loss, but did not weep. After this, the dog, who was called Mori, (being brown,) came to her and looked mild and friendly. He brought her a golden comb, and told her that she should have it for her steadfastness and courage. Again, a long time passed, till, one day, Mori came to the king's daughter, and said that a prince had come to her father, in order to marry one of her sisters, and he asked her, as the wedding-day was drawing near, if she would like to be present at her sister's marriage, which she said she gladly would.

Now the dog took her, and brought her to the mound in the forest, where he had been wont, heretofore, to rest himself, as we have said, and shewed her the way thence, home to her father's palace. He gave her two splendid state-dresses, one for herself, and the other to give her sister, who should wear it on the day of honour. When they parted, he prayed her to say nought about her way of life, and to be no longer away than three days; after which time she should come again to the mound.

Now the king's daughter came home to the palace, and was received with great delight and rejoicing. She was present at her sister's marriage, and gave her the beautiful dress, which was greatly admired by everyone.

In spite of all enquiry, she told nothing of her way of life, save that she was well and happy.

On the third day she returned to the mound, where the dog was waiting for her and brought her home from the mound to the house.

Now, after some while, the king's daughter was, for the second time, with child. The dog Mori came to her and said: "You must try, with all your strength, to shed no tears, for much depends for me thereupon. Keep, however, the cloth at hand, in case you should weep, for the pang at the child's loss will come more sharply home to you than at the first time."

He then went away. The king's daughter gave birth to a female child of great beauty. She bathed it, wrapped it up in swaddling-clothes, and laid it at her side in the bed, and knelt down over it, in all a tender mother's love and warmth of prayer. Soon, she saw a dark cloud pass across the window, and knew what she had to expect. She therefore turned her from the baby towards the wall, as she had no strength to bear the sight of her child stolen away from her. The vulture came in through the window, and catching the child in his claws, flew away with it. In spite of her loss and sorrow, the king's daughter did not, even yet, shed a tear. After this, the dog Mori came to her, looking very mild and friendly, and gave the princess a gold necklace, with jewels, saying that she should have this for her courage.

Time passed away, until the dog said that another prince had visited her father, in order to marry her second sister. She might, he said, go to the wedding, if she would; and that she would gladly. He gave her fine state-attire for her sister and for herself; accompanied her to the mound, and told her not to be more than three days away, nor to divulge aught concerning her way of life

The king's daughter now came home to the palace, and was welcomed as heartily as ever. She gave her sister the fine clothes, and stayed over the marriage; but, of her life, she only told that she was well and happy. On the third day, she returned to the mound, where Mori waited for her, and took her and brought her home to the house.

After some while, the king's daughter was with child, for the third time, and when the hour of her deliverance was at hand, the dog Mori came, and told her that the child to whom she was about to give birth, would be taken away from her, like the others. He begged her, as before, to avoid weeping, as much as lay in her power; but, if she should not be able to restrain herself, – as the loss of this child would come more painfully home to her than the loss of the other two, – to take great care to shed every tear into the cloth he had given her, as upon this much depended for him.

Now the king's daughter was delivered of a comely male child. Having bathed her son, wrapped him in swaddling clothes, and laid him by her side in the bed, she knelt over the child, in all a tender mother's love and warmth of prayer. But soon, a shadow moved across the window, and she at once turned away from the child and held the cloth before her face. Then the same vulture as before, came in, and seizing the child in its claws, flew away with it. From the eye of the princess there fell one tear, into a corner of the cloth, and she at once tied that corner into a knot. After this, Mori came to her, looking rather sad, and said that somewhat had now befallen, for which he grieved. He gave her a mirror, bordered with gold, which, he said, she should have for her constancy.

Some time after this, he told her that yet another prince had come to her father, in order to marry her third sister. He gave her two precious state-dresses, one for herself and the other for her sister, with leave to go to her sister's marriage, whereof she was glad. He went with her as far as the mound, and begged her to tell nothing about her life, and to return in three days. She went home and was received heartily by the kinsfolk. She gave her sister one of the beautiful dresses, but in the other she clad herself. She stayed there three days, and told nothing of her life, save that she was well and happy. On her leaving, her mother accompanied her, and asked her very closely after her way of life. But all the princess told her was that a man slept with her every night, whom she had never yet seen.

The queen then gave her a stone, telling her to hold it over the man's face while he slept, by which means she would be able to behold him. After this, they parted, and when the king's daughter came to the mound, there was Mori waiting, who took her home with him. Next night, when her bed-fellow had fallen asleep, she held over him the stone, and saw that he was young and very fair of look; but, by ill-chance, just as she was gazing at his beauty, he awoke, and was greatly grieved when he saw what she had done. He told her that this was the greatest of mishaps, as they would now be forced to part, perchance for ever. He told her too, that he was a king's son, by name Sigurdr; his father had lost his wife, and fallen into deep grief at his loss. But once it had chanced that he had gone with his father into the forest for their pleasure, and there they found a silken tent, in which two ladies were sitting, one young, but the other elderly and of sad look: both were handsome, and his father had questioned them about their life. The elder had answered that she was the wife of a certain king, and that this was her daughter. Enemies, she said, had invaded her husband's realm, who had fallen in battle, while she had fled with her daughter away from the country, and had at last arrived here. "Their condition," the youth continued, "called forth my father's pity, and he bade them to his palace, and, soon after, married the elder lady. I felt always an unavoidable dislike for my step-mother, and the more she wished me to marry her daughter, the less I felt inclined towards her. At this time, my father went on an expedition, in order to claim the taxes from his lands; then came my step-mother to me, and pressed me, with fresh earnestness, to marry her daughter, but I gave her, once for all, a decided refusal. Hereupon, she waxed fearfully wroth, and laid magic spells upon me, so that I vanished into the forest, and have been compelled to wear a dog's shape by day, taking my own again by night. This spell should remain in force for ten years, at the end of which time, I should return home and marry her daughter, willing or no, since I would not do so freely, at first, – unless, meanwhile, some king's daughter of wondrous virtue should become my wife, and bear me three children, without ever seeing me, or knowing who I was, or trying to run away from me; but all her children were to be cruelly taken from her, directly after their birth, and if she shed tears thereat, those tears should be so many clouds on her children's eyes, which nothing could remove but the very tears themselves. "I found myself," he continued, "then, in this house, and, by this time, I had only one month to remain under this fearful spell, but now I must return to my father's court, and undergo the worst fate of all, marriage with my step-mother's daughter; and there is no way whereby you can save me from this strait, however much you may yearn to do so."

He, however, went on to tell her, that he had three uncles, who, for his sake, had forfeited their homes, wealth and honours, and two of whom had taken up their abode in poor huts in his neighbourhood, in order to escape from his step-mother, and also to aid him; for it was they who had provided him with everything he had for his living and pleasure, while under this heavy curse.

"That one," he said, "who lives nearest to me, was no other than the hind that enticed your father into the thicket, once on a time. My uncles are the only men, of whom I know, able to help you in these straits. Go from the house, along the brook that runs by, and, after a while, you will find the hut of one of my uncles. Take care now, I entreat you, of the cloth, into which fell your tear, and never part with it; neither shall you part with the precious things which I have given you, save compelled by great need."

After this, he gave her a large purse of gold, praying her to be liberal in rewarding his uncles' services, if she should meet with them and receive aid from them, for they were very poor.

Then he vanished, but she remained behind, alone in the house, in deep grief. She now prepared herself for leaving the house, and walked along the brook, till in the evening, she came to a cottage, outside the door of which stood an old man, poorly clad, with a slouch-brimmed hat on his head. She greeted him, but he received her greeting mighty coldly. She asked for a night's shelter, but he said that he was, in no way, fond of guests, and, as to her, she would, he was sure, bring small luck into the house. But she begged and entreated him, and put into his hand a goodly portion of her gold, whereat his brows were somewhat lightened, and he consented to house the king's daughter; so she stayed there through the night. Now, she stated to the old man her whole case, and asked him for his help, that she might once again be joined to the prince. This, the man said, was so full of difficulties, that he was not the man to help her through them. That would be the task of his brother, who lived at a great distance from him, under this same spur of the mountain; and he offered to shew her the way thither.

Next morning, as she left the hut, the old man told her how to keep by the mountain-slope, in order that she might reach his brother's hut. In the evening she came to a cottage, at the door of which she knocked. There came out an old man, with an ugly face and fearful mien; he was dressed in a black tunic, and had a hat on his head, with a mighty broad brim. The king's daughter prayed him to give her shelter for the night;

but, said he, it would scarcely be a gain to anyone to house her, as surely she did not look as if she brought good luck with her. But she begged him for a night's shelter, and gave him unstinted gold from her purse, so that he waxed somewhat milder, and asked her to step in. There, on the dais, was a woman sitting, with a child in swaddling-clothes in her lap, and two other children played on the floor. This woman received the king's daughter kindly, bade her sit down, and was courteous to her. In their talk they chanced upon the matter of the children, and the old woman said, when the princess had admired them greatly, that it was a pity that the boy in her arms should have a cloud upon his eyes, and she grieved that she had no cure for it. The princess thought this sad indeed, as the boy was so comely. When the good-wife would go down to get ready some meals for her guest, she dropped the matter, and gave the boy to the princess; who, when she was alone with the child, bethought her, all at once, that perchance her tear might heal other clouded eyes than those of her own lost child; and, undoing the knot in the cloth, into which the tear had fallen, she placed it on the eye of the child, and the cloud at once passed away from before it. When the woman came in, and saw what had happened, she was exceeding glad, and thanked the king's daughter much for her good deed.

After this, meals were brought in to the princess, and she stayed there through the night. She repeated to the old man all the tale of her troubles and mischances. He listened to her with much pity, and told her that, much as he grieved for her and shared her sorrow, he found the difficulties, in the way of helping her, great indeed, and the time short, inasmuch as the prince would hold his wedding-feast the next day, and marry his step-mother's daughter; and, moreover, the way to him would be long, if she took the road round the mountain. He said, too, that she would certainly be too late, if she chose that road, but that there was another and a shorter path, which lay straight over the mountain, but that that was well-nigh impassable, owing to the spells and witchcraft of the queen, who would, by all means, hinder the coming of the princess.

"However," he said, "I must try to help you to get over the mountain by the shortest way." So then he went with her to the mountain, and before she began to scale it, furnished her with shoes, in whose soles were sharp iron points, in order that she might be able to mount some part of the path, which was very steep, and as slippery as glass. He also wrapped her head up in a cloth, that she might neither hear nor be bewildered by the wonders with which the queen would beset the path. At last, he warned her strongly, never to look back. At the foot of the mountain, on the other side, he said lived his friend, with whom he told her to take up her quarters during the night, and to get him to guide her to the king's court, while he himself should see that she was not recognized by the queen. Now the king's daughter bade farewell to the old man, and went on her way over the mountain, clinging closely to the rules he had given her. She never looked back, in spite of all the roaring sounds and fearful wonders she both saw and heard; and the head-cloth proved of great service to her.

In the evening, she came to the hut wherein the old man's friend lived; it was a small but neatly built cottage. She was well received, and remained there through the night. She asked her host to guide and accompany her to the king's palace, which he was the more willing to do, as he was going, so he said, thither himself, in order to be present at the wedding-feast of the king's son. When they arrived at the palace, the prince's wedding-feast was going on, in all kingly splendour. The princess went up to the door of the palace, and saw the king, the queen, the king's son, and his bride (the step-mother's daughter), gay and happy, always save the prince himself, who shewed much sadness. No one recognized the princess, not even the king's son, her lover. She stayed there all the day, looking at the folk, till in the evening, the bride and bridegroom were guided to their bed-chamber. The king's daughter was full of sorrow, and utterly despaired of her affair; but, suddenly the idea came to her, that her precious things would never be better used than now, if only to some avail.

It was night; the moon shone brightly, and the princess sat down beneath the window of the sleeping-room, and began combing her hair with the golden comb. It chanced, that the bride looked out; and catching a glance of the golden comb, glittering in the moonlight, she went down and asked the owner to exchange for hers, her golden comb. This, the king's daughter declared herself quite unwilling to do. Then the bride wanted to buy it, as it was more befitting for a princess than for a cottage lass. The king's daughter declared herself unwilling to sell it. Then the bride asked if there was nothing for which she would part with it: the other answered that she would give it up only on condition that she might sleep with the prince that night; and this they, at last, agreed upon.

The bride gave the king's son a sleep-draught, and, having so done, left him, and let in the princess, who tried in vain, all night long, to wake him. She repeated to him, in loud lamentations, her love and misfortunes, but nothing could move him, till, in the morning, the bride herself came, and having ordered the princess to be off at once, roused him again.

This same day, the king's daughter was even more sorrowful than before, but remained, nevertheless, in the palace, without being known.

When the bride and bridegroom had gone to their room in the evening, she made another attempt to allure the bride, choosing, this time, her beautiful necklace, as a bait for her. Their bargaining finished just as it did the last time, and the king's daughter failed, as before, in her attempts at waking the bridegroom, for the prince remained asleep the whole night through. She bewailed her lot, and mourned loudly over her misfortune, when she was forced to leave her beloved chosen one, in the morning, as dead-asleep as he had been in the night.

But the bride, as soon as she came in, woke him easily, and he got up, and they went to the palace, where the princess saw, to her deep grief, the loving demeanour of the king's son to his bride.

This same day, it chanced that one of the prince's three uncles, of whom we have before spoken, went on the sly, up to the prince, and had a secret talk with him. This uncle of his lived in the palace, and it so happened, that his bedroom was next that of the prince.

He asked the prince: "Who is that lady, who watches over you every night, in tears and sorrowful bewailings? It is a thing that seems strange to me, and not void of some wondrous mystery."

The prince answered that he knew of no woman there, besides his own wife.

The other asked: "Why is this woman so full of grief and sorrow?"

That, the prince said, he did not know, for he was, all the night, asleep.

The other asked, furthermore; "Why is it that you sleep so soundly all night? Is it, perchance," he continued, "because your wife gives you any drink at eventide?"

The king's son said that, in truth, she did so.

His uncle then went on to say: "Let that drink, be spilt into your clothes tonight, and make believe to fall asleep thereafter, in order to see if you can find any clue to this mystery."

So that day passed away, till evening, and mighty long it seemed to the mournful princess, who tried, much as her sorrow cast her down, to keep up her courage, fixing her last hopes in her last precious thing.

When the prince and princess had retired to their bedroom, she took, once more, her stand at the window, holding her mirror in her hand. The bride, as she was wont, was attracted by the glittering gold, and agreed with the king's daughter upon the bargain, that she should, for the glass, be with the prince that night.

Now the bride gave the prince his sleep-draught, and he made as if he drank it, whereas he let it all fall into his clothes. After this, he made believe to drop to sleep. The princess now entered the bed, and strove to awake her lover, as before, but still he made as if he were fast asleep. She then recounted to her sleeping lover all her griefs, and sorrows, and sufferings on his account, and bewailed herself loudly. She entreated him to awake, to remember their former life, and their union, and to listen at last to her, who was here broken-hearted with her despairing search for him. At last she said: "All the precious things you gave me I have parted with, in order only to get an interview with you, that you might recognize me, unfortunate and forsaken as I am."

Owing to the step-mother's magic spells, it was as if the prince dreamt all this, and yet was awake; but, at last the trance broke, and he came to himself, and what was his delight to recognize and remember his love, the king's daughter. The first thing that he did, was to give her all the consolation and comfort that he possibly could, and he told her that now they had gained the victory, and that their ill-luck was all over. In the morning, when the bride came, the prince prayed the princess to go to his uncle's room, hard by, while he himself made believe to be asleep.

In the morning, when the bride came, she drove the king's daughter away, and roused the prince, and they went to the palace together. This day, as the greatest bustle and joy reigned in the palace, and everybody was drinking, the king and queen being on one throne, the prince and his bride on another, three men were seen entering the palace. They were the king's three brothers. One of them carried two female children on one of his arms; with the other hand he led a woman, who carried one child; while the other two brothers had each a round piece of wood in his hand, and all of them, stepped before the prince's throne. He who led the woman said to the prince: "Do you not recognize this lady and the three children who are with her?"

The prince replied that he did so.

Hereupon his step-mother and her daughter were suddenly changed, and swelled out into trollish size, and would have spoken, when the king's brothers stuffed the blocks of wood into their mouths, and sixteen folk, whom they had hidden under the tables, rushed forth at once, and seized those two ladies, eight to each, and bound them with cords and chains.

At first, the king was mightily startled hereat, but when he saw of what race the dames were, he rejoiced at the turn things had taken, and congratulated heartily his son and the princess, his former bride.

Then the prince's father-in-law and mother-in-law were sent for, and in great joy the marriage of the prince and princess was celebrated without delay, after that the trolls had been put to death as they deserved.

Soon after, the king died, and his son was made king in his stead over all the realm the other had ruled over. He and his queen were wise and well-loved rulers, and were unfeignedly fond, one of the other, all their lives. The new king made his uncles all earls of different parts of his realm, and they proved brisk and wise rulers too, strengthening the king's sway, and keeping his friendship until death.

And this is the end of the story of Sigurdr, the King's Son.

The Story of Hermódr and Hádvör

ONCE THERE WERE a king and queen who had a daughter, by name Hádvör. She was both fair of look, and beautiful of mien, and being an only child, was right-born to the crown.

The king and queen had, too, a foster-son, by name Hermódr. He was of about the same age as Hádvör, fair of look, and accomplished in all things. Hermódr and Hádvör often played together when they were young, and such love they felt one for the other, that they vowed secretly eternal faith, even in their early youth.

Now time passed on, till the queen fell ill, and, as she felt that her illness would be deadly, she called the king to her. When he came, she said that, most likely, she had but few hours to live, wherefore she would ask one favour of him, namely, that he would promise her that, if he were ever going to marry again, he would, for her word's sake, marry no other than the queen of Hetland the Good. This the king promised, and then the queen died. But when time went on, the king, being tired of a single life, fitted out a ship, and put to sea. On this voyage, a thick fog surrounded him, so that he lost his course and became bewildered as to his whereabouts. After much ado, he found land before him, and steered his vessel thither, and entering a harbour, went ashore. When he had walked a while, a forest lay in his way. He went a short way into it, and stopped walking, for he heard strains of sweet music, and having listened, he went on again in the direction from which the sound was heard, till he came to an open lawn in the wood, whereon he saw sitting three women, one of whom was on a golden chair, in splendid attire, holding a harp in her hand, and very sad of look. The second of the ladies was younger-looking than this one; she was also very richly dressed, but her seat was not of such fine workmanship as that of the first. The third woman, standing by them, was cleanly-looking, and wore a green mantle over her dress, and was plainly the others' servant. When the king had gazed at them for a while, he stepped forward, and greeted them. She who sat on the golden chair asked who he was and whither he meant to go. He told her the whole story, that he was a king, had lost his queen, and had meant to sail to Hetland the Good, in order to engage the queen of that country. She answered: "Wonderfully has fate brought all this about. Hetland was invaded by Vikings, who killed my husband, the king, in a battle. Then I left the country in haste, sad in mind, and, after a long struggle, got hither. I am therefore the queen you are seeking, but these women I have with me are my daughter and my handmaid."

The king, therefore, lost no time in engaging her, and she returned a gentle answer, became glad in manner, and gave her consent at once to his wooing. After a short stay, they all embarked on board the vessel, and nothing is told of their travels, till they came home to the kingdom. The king then had a great feast prepared, and married the bride. For a while all was quiet. Hermódr and Hádvör paid little attention to the queen or her daughter. But Olöf, the queen's maid, and Hádvör soon became attached to one another, and Olöf used often to visit Hádvör in her castle. Before a long time had gone by, the king fitted out an expedition of war, and when he was gone, the queen came one day to Hermódr, and said to him: "It is my plan that you should marry my daughter."

Hermódr answered straightforwardly that that could never be. At this the queen grew angry, and declared that, for the first thing, Hermódr and Hádvör should no longer be allowed to enjoy one another's company; "for," she said, "I lay this curse upon you, that you shall retire to a desert island, and be a lion by day, but a man at night, in order that you may ever remember Hádvör to your greatest torment. From this spell you shall not be delivered, until Hádvör has burnt the lion's shape you wear, which will be late."

When the queen had finished raving in this way, Hermódr answered: "Whenever I am delivered from your spell, I will lay this curse upon yourself and your daughter, that one shall be changed into a rat and the other into a mouse, and shall continue fighting in the palace till I kill you both with my own sword."

After this, Hermódr vanished, nobody knowing what had become of him. The queen had a search made after him, but he was nowhere to be found.

Once, when Olöf happened to be in the castle with Hádvör, she said to her: "Do you know what has become of Hermódr?" At these words Hádvör grew sad, and said: "Alas! I do not, indeed, know it." Olöf then said she would tell it her, as she knew it quite well. She said that Hermódr had vanished away, by the deed of the queen, who was a troll, and her daughter no less so, but they had managed to change their looks as they had done. But when Hermódr had refused to agree to her proposal that he should marry her daughter, she had laid upon him the spell of becoming a lion by day, and a man again at night, away in a desert island, where he should remain until Hádvör had burnt his lion's shape. She furthermore said that a match was held in view for Hádvör; for the queen had a brother in the under-earth world, a three-headed giant, whom she meant to change into the shape of a beautiful king's son, and thus make him marry Hádvör. She declared, too, that these were not the first or newest of the queen's tricks. She had stolen Olöf away from the home of her father and mother, and forced her to serve her, but had never prevailed by her tricks against her, for the green cloak she wore preserved her against any hurt intended by the foul troll. Hádvör became sorrowful and sad in mind about her intended marriage, and begged Olöf to give her, by all means, some good advice. Olöf said: "I fancy the bridegroom will appear from below, up through the floor of your castle. But when you hear the underground din, and when the floor begins to burst, and a yawning pit opens in it, you shall have at hand, ready for use, a pot full of boiling pitch; this you shall pour unsparingly into the yawning rift, and it will prove enough to kill him."

At this time, the king returned from his expedition, and found it rather awkward not to get any information about Hermódr's disappearance.

But the queen used all her powers of comforting, and managed to appease him at last about it.

Now the story returns to Hádvör, who sat in her castle, and made all due preparations to receive her suitor hinted at by Olöf. Not long afterwards it happened that, one night, there was heard a great underground din and rumbling, beneath the castle foundations. Hádvör knew what would be the cause of this, and called upon her maids to yield her their best aid. The rumbling and the din increased as it drew nearer to the castle, and now the floor began to burst up. Hádvör ordered forth the tar-pot, and poured its contents unsparingly into the hole; and thereupon the rumbling gradually grew less, and at last all was still.

Early the next morning, the queen said she must get up, and the king allowed her to do so. When she was dressed, she walked outside the gate of the town, and found there the giant, her brother, dead. The queen went to him, and said: "I lay the spell on thee that thou takest the shape of the most handsome prince, that Hádvör may have no excuses to make when I accuse her."

At once the body of the giant was turned into that of the handsomest of princes. After that, the queen returned home to the king, and said she found his daughter not of such lady-like virtue as she ought to be. She further declared that her brother had come thither in order to woo the princess, but that Hádvör had simply murdered him, and this, she said, she knew, for she had found his body lying outside the town. Then the king went with his queen to look at the body, and found all this a wonderful story, and said that such a beautiful prince had certainly been a good enough match for Hádvör, and that he himself would have been the first to consent to the marriage. Now the queen asked the king to let her have her own will in fixing the punishment Hádvör should have for her crime; to this he willingly agreed, as he said he could not fix his own daughter's punishment. In this case, therefore, the queen decided that the king should have a large cairn raised over her brother, and that Hádvör should he buried alive in the barrow with him. This the king deemed a good rede and a just sentence.

Now the story turns to Olöf, who knew well enough all this plot of the queen's. She therefore went to the castle of the king's daughter, telling her what plots were being hatched against her. Hádvör then begged her, by all means, to give her anything in the shape of advice. Olöf said: "First of all, you shall have a wide cloak over your clothes, when you go into the cairn. The giant is sure to be re-quickened, when you are first both together in the cairn, and will have by him two dogs. He will ask you to cut a slice of flesh out of your calves, to give to the dogs; but this you shall refuse to do, unless he tell you where Hermódr is, and how to find him out. But when you leave the cairn, the giant will put you on his shoulder, making believe to lift you up; he will, however, try to deceive you, by grasping at your cloak. Have it therefore loose on your shoulders, that he may only clutch it and not you." Now the cairn was ready, the body laid in it, and Hádvör obliged to go into it too, not being able to defend herself against the queen's charges. When they were both inside, all went on as Olöf had said. The prince came to life, and became the giant he had been before. Two dogs were with him, and he asked Hádvör to cut bits out of her calves for them, but she refused to do so unless he told her where Hermódr was, and how to get to him. The giant then told her that Hermódr was on a certain desert island, which he named to her; but she could not get thither, unless she flayed the soles of her feet, and made shoes for herself out of the skin; and these shoes, when made, would be of such a nature, that they would take her through the air, or over the water, as she liked. After this Hádvör did as the giant had asked, – cut pieces out of her calves, and threw them to the dogs. Then she flayed the skin off the soles of her feet, and made shoes for herself out of it, and said to the giant that now she wished to go. The giant said she must needs get on to his shoulders: she did so, and thus got out of the cairn. But as she leapt up through the cairn she was grappled at by the cloak, in an unsparing manner. She had remembered well, however, to have it loose; wherefore the giant kept it empty in his hand, but Hádvör escaped. And now she went the shortest way, towards the sea, in the direction of the desert island, Hermódr's dwelling-place. She got well over the sea, for the shoes buoyed her up. When she had landed in the island, she saw that all round the coast there ran a sandy beach, but that this was bounded landwards by high and sheer cliffs; wherefore, seeing no way to get up them, and being sad in mind and overwhelmed with weariness, she lay down and fell asleep. Then she had a dream, that a woman of great size came to her, and said: "I know that you are Hádvör, the king's daughter, on a search for Hermódr. He is here on the island, but hard, I deem, will it be for you to manage to meet him; for if you act by yourself, and of your own power, you will not be able to mount the cliffs. I have therefore let down a rope, which will hold well; by this rope you can climb up, and get to the upper-island. As the island is very large, you will, most likely, have a long search before finding the dwelling of Hermódr; therefore, I have placed a ball of thread by your side. You have only to hold the end of the thread attached to it, and the ball will run on before you, and thus shew you the way. Furthermore, I put at your side a belt, which you shall buckle round your waist when you awake, and then you will never faint with hunger."

After this, the woman disappeared, and Hádvör saw that she had been true-dreaming in all that she had seen in her sleep. The rope hung over the rocks, and by her side lay the belt and the ball. Having clasped the belt round her, she hauled herself up by the cable, and thus mounted the rocks. After this, she took the thread-end of the ball, which now rolled away before her, never stopping till she came to the door of a cave not over-large. She went into the cave, and saw there a lowly and lair-like bed, under which she crept and lay down. In the evening, she heard abroad some under-walking, and next could distinguish the sound of steps, and soon became aware that the lion was at the door of the cave, where it shook itself violently. Then she heard a man walk in to the bed. She was soon left without any doubt as to who the man was, as she heard him speaking to himself of his former state, repeating the loved name of Hádvör, together with many a memory of their bygone life. Hádvör took good heed not to move, but waited patiently till he was fast asleep. Then, knowing that his slumber was sound and fast, she crept out from beneath the bed, and taking the lion-shape which he had left outside, burnt it. After that, she went into the cave and roused Hermódr from his sleep, and now a meeting of great love and joy ensued. In the morning, when planning their departure, they were mighty anxious as to how to make their escape good. Hádvör told Hermódr her dream, and said she thought that on the island there was someone who would be able to help them. Hermódr said he knew that there was a she-troll, the most faithful troll possible, and that their only chance was to go and see her. So they sought for the cave of the she-troll, and found it. She was there, surrounded by her fifteen young sons. The lovers asked her to help them in getting away. She answered that many things were easier than that, for the giant with whom Hádvör had been in the cairn would be in their way, for he had changed himself into a great evil whale, intending to attack them as they passed over to the land. The troll said, however, that she would lend them a boat, and that if they should happen to see the whale, and deem their lives at stake, they might call out her name. They thanked her with many fair words for her promises and aid, and then put to sea from the island. On the sea, they saw an evil whale coming towards them, with much bustle and surf, and as they thought that no time for calling out the troll's name would be better than now, they called it aloud. No sooner was this done, than they saw coming towards them another whale of monstrous size, followed by fifteen smaller ones. All this shoal swam past the boat in which were Hermódr and Hádvör, against the evil whale. Now a great whale-fight began, and the sea was so troubled, that the boat could scarcely be kept safe from the surf rising round the whales. Soon after, when the fight had lasted some while, Hermódr and Hádvör saw that the sea was blood-coloured, and the good whale and her young ones went away, but the lovers got all safe to shore.

Now turns the story to the king's palace, where a strange thing had taken place. The queen and her daughter had disappeared; but a rat and a mouse were always fighting there. Many would divide these disgusting combatants, but to no avail. Thus a good time passed. The king was in a sad state on account of his lost queen, and also because these hideous animals disturbed the peace of the court.

One evening, while all the folk sat thus in the palace, filled with loathing and disgust, Hermódr suddenly entered it, with his sword in his belt, and greeted the king, who received him with the greatest joy and happiness, deeming that he had indeed recovered him from the dead. But before Hermódr took any seat in the hall, he stepped towards the mouse and rat, and cut both asunder with his sword. All were astonished then at seeing, instead of a rat and a mouse, two trolls lying dead on the floor, and they were at once burnt to cold cinders. After that, Hermódr told the king the whole story, and the king, in his surprise, never could come to an end of wishing his son joy, upon being saved from the evil ones.

Then Hermódr asked his father's leave to marry Hádvör, which the other readily granted, and their marriage was speedily performed. The king, being old, gave up the crown and realm to his son, who was at once elected king. Olöf married a nobleman, and had a good husband. And thus ends this story.

Carl's Son, Little, Trittle and the Birds

THERE WERE ONCE a king and queen in their palace, and an old man and woman in the nook of the garden wall. The king had a daughter of whom he was very fond. But, to his distress, his daughter was lost, and nowhere could she be found,

in spite of a diligent search being made for her. Then the king made a vow, that whosoever found her, and brought her to him, should have her for a wife. But, although many tried to gain such a match, the king's daughter was not found, and searchers came empty-handed home, as they had left.

Now it must be told of the old man, that he had three sons. He made much of the two eldest, but the youngest was treated as an elbow-child, both by his father and his brothers. When the carl's sons were of age, the eldest brother once said to his father, that he would go abroad in search of fame and wealth. His parents gave their consent to this, and he left home with provisions and new shoes, and walked long, long, and far. At last he came to a mound. There he sat down to rest, and took forth his knapsack and began to eat. Soon after, there came to him a tiny old carl, and asked him for something to eat. The youth refused to give him anything, and drove him off as he had come. Afterwards, he went on, a long, long way, till he came to another mound, where he sat down to eat. And while he was eating, there came to him a queer, little, wee old man, and asked him for something to eat. But the carl's son refused him, and drove him off with foul words. Yet again walked on the youth, till he came to an open space in a wood, where he sat down to eat. And while he was eating there, there came to him a large flock of birds, quite close up to him. He waxed angry with the birds, and drove them away from him. He went on still farther yet, till he came to a large cave, into which he went, but saw no human being. He then made up his mind to wait until the cave-dwellers came in. In the later part of the day, a fearfully large she-troll came into the cave. He asked her for shelter for that night. She said she would give it, if he would perform, on the morrow, the work which she would give him to do.

He said, "Yes." Thus he was in the cave through the night. In the morning, the troll bade him shovel out the cave, and have the work finished in the evening; if not, she said she would kill him. And thereupon she went away.

Now the cottager's son seized the spade, and began to shovel, but when he put it down for the first time, it became fixed to the cave-floor, so that he could not move it. In the evening, when the troll returned home, the cave was unshovelled, as you may fancy; without making any ado, she instantly took the carl's son and killed him; and therefore, henceforth, he is out of the story.

Now turns the tale home, to the old couple's cottage, the second son next asked them to give him leave to go abroad, in search of fame and wealth. He said he could not be content with staying longer in his dull home, when his brother had already, most likely, risen to some high post, in some king's service. His parents allowed him to go away, and provided him with all things needful for the journey.

To cut his story short, he fared in every way as his brother had fared before him.

Now the youngest of the brothers was yet left. But he was in no favour with his parents for being left alone with them. He asked therefore their leave to go away. "I am not going in search of fame and wealth," he said, "but only in order to find something to do for my support, that I may no longer be a burden to you, as I now am."

The old man and woman, his parents, consented to this, and gave him a tolerably good store of provisions, and new shoes, but all his outfit was far from being as good as that of his brothers. Now he went away, and chanced to take the same road as his brothers had before trodden, on leaving home. He came to the first mound and said: "Here my brothers have rested themselves, and I shall do so too." He then sat down to eat, and the little, tiny old man came to him, and asked him for something to eat. The youth received him well, and bade him sit down and eat as he lusted. When they had eaten enough, the tiny old man said: "Call me when you are in some tiny need; my name is Trittle." And so saying the little manikin toddled away and disappeared. The carl's son went on till he came to the other mound. Then said he: "Here my brothers have rested themselves, and I shall do so too." He began eating, and while he was eating, a wee, little old man came to him and asked him for something to eat. The carl's son answered well his wish, and bade him sit down and eat with him, as much as he wanted. When they had eaten enough, the carl said : "Call me when you are in some little need; my name is Little." And so saying, he toddled away and disappeared. Now the carl's son went on, till he came to the open space in the wood. Then he said: "My brothers have rested here before, and

I will do so too." Thereupon he sat down, and began to eat. Then came to him a mighty large flock of birds, who behaved round him most starvingly. He rubbed a piece of bread between his hands, and strewed the crumbs amongst the birds, who picked them up and ate them. When they had finished the breadcrumbs, one of the birds said: "Call us when you are in some little strait, and call us your birds." And thereupon they flew away and disappeared. But the carl's son went on, till he came to the cave, as his brothers had done before him. He went in, but saw no living being there, only the dead bodies of his brothers hanging from the roof of the cave, a little way within the door. This he thought no over pleasant sight, but made up his mind, nevertheless, to wait for the cave-dweller. A short time passed until a huge troll, the owner of the cave, of whom we have spoken before, came in. The carl's son asked for a shelter, for the night. She said he should have it, if he would do whatsoever she bade him do. He agreed to this, and thus he was in the cave, through the night. Next morning the troll bade him shovel out the cave, and if he had not finished his work in the evening, when she came back, she said she would kill him, at once, on her return. Then she strode away. The carl's son seized the shovel, and was beginning to shovel out the cave, but no sooner had he thrust the spade down to the floor, than it stuck fast in it, and was not to be moved. Now the youth was in despair, and called out in his trouble: "My Trittle, come hither!" At the same moment Trittle came in, and asked the carl's son what he wanted. The other told him into what straits he was brought. Then Trittle said: " Stick, mattock! Shovel out, spade!" Then the mattock stuck and the spade shovelled, and, in a short time, the cave was well shovelled and neatly cleaned. This done, Trittle went away. But in the evening, when the she-troll came home, and saw all that had been done, she said to the carl's son: "You are not alone at work, carl, carl! Why, yes, let it be good!"

Now they slept quietly through that night. In the morning, she bade him air her bed-clothes, take all the feathers out of the beds, spread them in the sun to dry them, and then put them into the beds again. But if one single feather was wanting in the evening, she said she would most assuredly kill him. She then left him. The carl's son spread out the bed-clothes. In the troll's bedstead there were three feather-beds, and as the weather was perfectly calm, he ripped the seams of them, and spread out the feathers in the sun. But, when he least looked for it, a gust of a whirlwind came, and whirled all the feathers into the air, so that he saw not one feather of them left. This, the carl's son did not quite enjoy, and in his trouble he cried: "My Trittle, my Little, and all my birds, come hither!" Then came Trittle, and Little, and all the flock of birds, bringing all the feathers with them. And Trittle, and Little, and all the birds aided the carl's son in putting the feathers into the beds, and in sewing them together again. They took one feather from each bed, and bound them together, and told the carl's son that he should stick them into the troll's nose, if she missed them. Then Trittle, Little, and the birds left him. When the troll came home in the evening, she flung herself down on to the bed so heavily, that all the whole cave cracked. Then she handled the beds, and turned to the carl's son, saying: "Now will I kill you, for from each bed there is one feather missing." He therefore took forth from his pocket the three feathers, and stuck them into her nose, and said: "There! Take them, they are all there." The troll took them, and said: "You are not alone at work, carl, carl! Why, yes, let it be good as it is."

Now the carl's son passed that night also in the cave. In the morning, the troll said to him that, today he should slaughter her ox, cook the entrails, shave the hide, and make spoons out of the horns ; and have all this done by her return in the evening. She said that she had fifty oxen, but only wanted one of them killed, and that he must tell for himself which of them that was. "If you have finished all this ere nightfall," quoth the hag, "you may go to any quarter of the land you like, for all that I care, and besides, choose out of my property any three things you like. But, if anything happens to be undone, or if you take the wrong ox, I shall kill you." When the troll had thus spoken to the carl's son, she went away, and left him to his own despair, and he stood there, not knowing, in the least, what to do.

However, he called out loud, in his troubles: "My Trittle, my Little, come ye both!" He then saw the tiny old men coming towards him, leading between them a huge ox. They killed it immediately, and the carl's son set himself to cook the entrails, Little to make the spoons, and Trittle to shave the hide. The work went off quickly, and in due time was all done. The carl's son told the tiny old men what the troll had promised him, if he should have finished the work by the evening. The old fellows then said that he could choose what was above her bed, the chest that she had standing at the side of her bed, and whatever stood under the wall of the cave. This the carl's son promised to do. After this, the old men went their way, and the youth bade them farewell with many thanks. In the evening, when the troll came home, and saw that the carl's son had done everything to her satisfaction, she said: "You are not alone at work, carl, carl! Why, yes, let it be good as it is." Then she paid him the reward. That which was above the bed was the king's lost daughter. The great chest at the bedside was full of gold and precious things. But that which stood under the cave-wall was a ship, thoroughly fitted out, with rigging and all, which had the strange power of going of its own accord, whithersoever one liked.

When the troll had given this reward to the carl's son, she took leave of him, saying that he would be the luckiest of men, and then went off as she was wont. The carl's son now carried the chest on board the ship, and went himself on board, together with the king's daughter. He gave the sails to the wind, and sailed home to the king, the princess's father. He restored his daughter to the king, and told him all about his travels. The king much marvelled at the strange adventures of the carl's son, and received his daughter with great joy, as one may fancy. The king held a great welcome-banquet for his daughter and her deliverer, and the banquet ended with the marriage of the king's daughter to the carl's son, who first became the king's commander and first-minister. But after the death of his father-in-law, he inherited all the kingdom, and governed it afterwards, both long and well, till the date of his death. And there is our story at an end.

The Story of Frithiof the Bold

Chapter I – Of King Beli and Thorstein Vikingson and their Children

THUS BEGINNETH THE TALE telling how that King Beli ruled over Sogn-land; three children had he, whereof Helgi was his first son, and Halfdan his second, but Ingibiorg his

daughter. Ingibiorg was fair of face and wise of mind, and she was ever accounted the foremost of the king's children.

Now a certain strand went west of the firth, and a great stead was thereon, which was called Baldur's Meads; a Place of Peace was there, and a great temple, and round about it a great garth of pales: many gods were there, but amidst them all was Baldur held of most account. So jealous were the heathen men of this stead, that they would have no hurt done therein to man nor beast, nor might any man have dealings with a woman there.

Sowstrand was the name of that stead whereas the king dwelt; but on the other side the firth was an abode named Foreness, where dwelt a man called Thorstein, the son of a Viking; and his stead was over against the king's dwelling.

Thorstein had a son by his wife called Frithiof: he was the tallest and strongest of men, and more furnished of all prowess than any other man, even from his youth up. Frithiof the Bold was he called, and so well beloved was he, that all prayed for good things for him.

Now the king's children were but young when their mother died; but a goodman of Sogn, named Hilding, prayed to have the king's daughter to foster: so there was she reared well and needfully: and she was called Ingibiorg the Fair. Frithiof also was fostered of goodman Hilding, wherefore was he foster-brother to the king's daughter, and they two were peerless among children.

Now King Beli's chattels began to ebb fast away from his hands, for he was grown old.

Thorstein had rule over the third part of the realm, and in him lay the king's greatest strength.

Every third year Thorstein feasted the king at exceeding great cost, and the king feasted Thorstein the two years between.

Helgi, Beli's son, from his youth up turned much to blood-offering: neither were those brethren well-beloved.

Thorstein had a ship called Ellidi, which pulled fifteen oars on either board; it ran up high stem and stern, and was strong-built like an ocean-going ship, and its bulwarks were clamped with iron.

So strong was Frithiof that he pulled the two bow oars of Ellidi; but either oar was thirteen ells long, and two men pulled every oar otherwhere.

Frithiof was deemed peerless amid the young men of that time, and the king's sons envied him, whereas he was more praised than they.

Now King Beli fell sick; and when the sickness lay heavy on him he called his sons to him and said to them: "This sickness will bring me to mine end, therefore will I bid you this, that ye hold fast to those old friends that I have had; for meseems in all things ye fall short of that father and son, Thorstein and Frithiof, yea, both in good counsel and in hardihood. A mound ye shall raise over me."

So with that Beli died.

Thereafter Thorstein fell sick; so he spake to Frithiof: "Kinsman," says he, "I will crave this of thee, that thou bow thy will before the king's sons, for their dignity's sake; yet doth my heart speak goodly things to me concerning thy fortune. Now would I be laid in my mound over against King Beli's mound, down by the sea on this side the firth, whereas it may be easiest for us to cry out each to each of tidings drawing nigh."

A little after this Thorstein departed, and was laid in mound even as he had bidden; but Frithiof took the land and chattels after him. Biorn and Asmund were Frithiof's foster-brethren; they were big and strong men both.

Chapter II – Frithiof Wooeth Ingibiorg of those Brethren

So Frithiof became the most famed of men, and the bravest in all things that may try a man.

Biorn, his foster-brother, he held in most account of all, but Asmund served the twain of them.

The ship Ellidi, he gat, the best of good things, of his father's heritage, and another possession therewith – a gold ring; no dearer was in Norway.

So bounteous a man was Frithiof withal, that it was the talk of most, that he was a man of no less honour than those brethren, but it were for the name of king; and for this cause they held Frithiof in hate and enmity, and it was a heavy thing to them that he was called greater than they: furthermore they thought they could see that Ingibiorg, their sister, and Frithiof were of one mind together.

It befell hereon that the kings had to go to a feast to Frithiof's house at Foreness; and there it happened according to wont that he gave to all men beyond that they were worthy of. Now Ingibiorg was there, and she and Frithiof talked long together; and the king's daughter said to him:

"A goodly gold ring hast thou."

"Yea, in good sooth," said he.

Thereafter went those brethren to their own home, and greater grew their enmity of Frithiof.

A little after grew Frithiof heavy of mood, and Biorn, his foster-brother, asked him why he fared so.

He said he had it in his mind to woo Ingibiorg. "For though I be named by a lesser name than those brethren, yet am I not fashioned lesser."

"Even so let us do then," quoth Biorn. So Frithiof fared with certain men unto those brethren; and the kings were sitting on their father's mound when Frithiof greeted them well, and then set forth his wooing, and prayed for their sister Ingibiorg, the daughter of Beli.

The kings said: "Not overwise is this thine asking, whereas thou wouldst have us give her to one who lacketh dignity; wherefore we gainsay thee this utterly."

Said Frithiof: "Then is mine errand soon sped; but in return never will I give help to you henceforward, nay, though ye need it ever so much."

They said they heeded it nought: so Frithiof went home, and was joyous once more.

Chapter III – Of King Ring and those Brethren

There was a king named Ring, who ruled over Ringrealm, which also was in Norway: a mighty folk-king he was, and a great man, but come by now unto his latter days.

Now he spake to his men: "Lo, I have heard that the sons of King Beli have brought to nought their friendship with Frithiof, who is the noblest of men; wherefore will I send men to these kings, and bid them choose whether they will submit them to me and pay me tribute, or else that I bring war on them: and all things then shall lie ready to my hand to take, for they have neither might nor wisdom to withstand me; yet great fame were it to my old age to overcome them."

After that fared the messengers of King Ring, and found those brethren, Helgi and Halfdan, in Sogn, and spake to them thus: "King Ring sends bidding to you to send him tribute, or else will he war against your realm."

They answered and said that they would not learn in the days of their youth what they would be loth to know in their old age, even how to serve King Ring with shame. "Nay, now shall we draw together all the folk that we may."

Even so they did; but now, when they beheld their force that it was but little, they sent Hilding their fosterer to Frithiof to bid him come help them against King Ring. Now Frithiof sat at the knave-play when Hilding came thither, who spake thus: "Our kings send thee greeting, Frithiof, and would have thy help in battle against King Ring, who cometh against their realm with violence and wrong."

Frithiof answered him nought, but said to Biorn, with whom he was playing: "A bare place in thy board, foster-brother, and nowise mayst thou amend it; nay, for my part I shall beset thy red piece there, and wot whether it be safe."

Then Hilding spake again:

"King Helgi bade me say thus much, Frithiof, that thou shouldst go on this journey with them, or else look for ill at their hands when they at the last come back."

"A double game, foster-brother," said Biorn; "and two ways to meet thy play."

Frithiof said: "Thy play is to fall first on the knave, yet the double game is sure to be."

No other outcome of his errand had Hilding: he went back speedily to the kings, and told them Frithiof's answer.

They asked Hilding what he made out of those words. He said:

"Whereas he spake of the bare place he will have been thinking of the lack in this journey of yours; but when he said he would beset the red piece, that will mean Ingibiorg, your sister; so give ye all the heed ye may to her. But whereas I threatened him with ill from you, Biorn deemed the game a double one; but Frithiof said that the knave must be set on first, speaking thereby of King Ring."

So then the brethren arrayed them for departing; but, ere they went, they let bring Ingibiorg and eight women with her to Baldur's Meads, saying that Frithiof would not be so mad rash as to go see her thither, since there was none who durst make riot there.

Then fared those brethren south to Jadar, and met King Ring in Sokn-Sound.

Now, herewith was King Ring most of all wroth that the brothers had said that they accounted it a shame to fight with a man so old that he might not get a-horseback unholpen.

Chapter IV – Frithiof Goes to Baldur's Meads

Straightway whenas the kings were gone away Frithiof took his raiment of state and set the goodly gold ring on his arm; then went the foster-brethren down to the sea and launched Ellidi. Then said Biorn: "Whither away, foster-brother?"

"To Baldur's Meads," said Frithiof, "to be glad with Ingibiorg."

Biorn said: "A thing unmeet to do, to make the gods wroth with us."

"Well, it shall be risked this time," said Frithiof; "and withal, more to me is Ingibiorg's grace than Baldur's grame."

Therewith they rowed over the firth, and went up to Baldur's Meads and to Ingibiorg's bower, and there she sat with eight maidens, and the newcomers were eight also.

But when they came there, lo, all the place was hung with cloth of pall and precious webs.

Then Ingibiorg arose and said:

"Why art thou so overbold, Frithiof, that thou art come here without the leave of my brethren to make the gods angry with thee?"

Frithiof said: "Howsoever that may be, I hold thy love of more account than the gods' hate."

Ingibiorg answered: "Welcome art thou here, thou and thy men!"

Then she made place for him to sit beside her, and drank to him in the best of wine; and thus they sat and were merry together.

Then beheld Ingibiorg the goodly ring on his arm, and asked him if that precious thing were his own. Frithiof said Yea, and she praised the ring much. Then Frithiof said:

"I will give thee the ring if thou wilt promise to give it to no one, but to send it to me when thou no longer shalt have will to keep it: and hereon shall we plight troth each to other."

So with this troth-plighting they exchanged rings.

Frithiof was oft at Baldur's Meads a-night time, and every day between whiles would he go thither to be glad with Ingibiorg.

Chapter V – Those Brethren Come Home Again

Now tells the tale of those brethren, that they met King Ring, and he had more folk than they: then went men betwixt them, and sought to make peace, so that no battle should be: thereto King Ring assented on such terms that the brethren should submit them to him, and give him in marriage Ingibiorg their sister, with the third part of all their possessions.

The kings said Yea thereto, for they saw that they had to do with overwhelming might: so the peace was fast bound by oaths, and the wedding was to be at Sogn whenas King Ring should go see his betrothed.

So those brethren fared home with their folk, right ill content with things. But Frithiof, when he deemed that the brethren might be looked for home again, spake to the king's daughter:

"Sweetly and well have ye done to us, neither has goodman Baldur been wroth with us; but now as soon as ye wot of the kings' coming home, spread the sheets of your beds abroad on the Hall of the Goddesses, for that is the highest of all the garth, and we may see it from our stead."

The king's daughter said: "Thou dost not after the like of any other: but certes, we welcome dear friends whenas ye come to us."

So Frithiof went home; and the next morning he went out early, and when he came in then he spake and sang:

"Now must I tell
To our good men
That over and done
Are our fair journeys;
No more a-shipboard

Shall we be going,
For there are the sheets
Spread out a-bleaching."

Then they went out, and saw that the Hall of the Goddesses was all thatched with white linen. Biorn spake and said: "Now are the kings come home, and but a little while have we to sit in peace, and good were it, meseems, to gather folk together."

So did they, and men came flocking thither.

Now the brethren soon heard of the ways of Frithiof and Ingibiorg, and of the gathering of men. So King Helgi spake:

"A wondrous thing how Baldur will bear what shame soever Frithiof and she will lay on him! Now will I send men to him, and wot what atonement he will offer us, or else will I drive him from the land, for our strength seemeth to me not enough that we should fight with him as now."

So Hilding, their fosterer, bare the king's errand to Frithiof and his friends, and spake in such wise: "This atonement the kings will have of thee, Frithiof, that thou go gather the tribute of the Orkneys, which has not been paid since Beli died, for they need money, whereas they are giving Ingibiorg their sister in marriage, and much of wealth with her."

Frithiof said: "This thing only somewhat urges us to peace, the good will of our kin departed; but no trustiness will those brethren show herein. But this condition I make, that our lands be in good peace while we are away." So this was promised and all bound by oaths.

Then Frithiof arrays him for departing, and is captain of men brave and of good help, eighteen in company.

Now his men asked him if he would not go to King Helgi and make peace with him, and pray himself free from Baldur's wrath.

But he answered: "Hereby I swear that I will never pray Helgi for peace."

Then he went aboard Ellidi, and they sailed out along the Sognfirth.

But when Frithiof was gone from home, King Halfdan spake to Helgi his brother: "Better lordship and more had we if Frithiof had payment for his masterful deed: now therefore let us burn his stead, and bring on him and his men such a storm on the sea as shall make an end of them."

Helgi said it was a thing meet to be done.

So then they burned up clean all the stead at Foreness and robbed it of all goods; and after that sent for two witch-wives, Heidi and Hamglom, and gave them money to raise against Frithiof and his men so mighty a storm that they should all be lost at sea. So they sped the witch-song, and went up on the witch-mount with spells and sorcery.

Chapter VI – Frithiof Sails for the Orkneys

So when Frithiof and his men were come out of the Sognfirth there fell on them great wind and storm, and an exceeding heavy sea: but the ship drave on swiftly, for sharp built she was, and the best to breast the sea.

So now Frithiof sang:

"Oft let I swim from Sogn
My tarred ship sooty-sided,
When maids sat o'er the mead-horn
Amidst of Baldur's Meadows;
Now while the storm is wailing
Farewell I bid you maidens,
Still shall ye love us, sweet ones,
Though Ellidi the sea fill."

Said Biorn: "Thou mightest well find other work to do than singing songs over the maids of Baldur's Meadows."

"Of such work shall I not speedily run dry, though," said Frithiof. Then they bore up north to the sounds nigh those isles that are called Solundir, and therewith was the gale at its hardest.

Then sang Frithiof:

"Now is the sea a-swelling,
And sweepeth the rack onward;
Spells of old days cast o'er us
Make ocean all unquiet;
No more shall we be striving

Mid storm with wash of billows,
But Solundir shall shelter
Our ship with ice-beat rock-walls."

So they lay to under the lee of the isles hight Solundir, and were minded to abide there; but straightway thereon the wind fell: then they turned away from under the lee of the islands, and now their voyage seemed hopeful to them, because the wind was fair awhile: but soon it began to freshen again.

Then sang Frithiof:

"In days foredone
From Foreness strand
I rowed to meet
Maid Ingibiorg;
But now I sail
Through chilly storm
And wide away
My long-worm driveth."

And now when they were come far out into the main, once more the sea waxed wondrous troubled, and a storm arose with so great drift of snow, that none might see the stem from the stern; and they shipped seas, so that they must be ever a-baling. So Frithiof sang:

"The salt waves see we nought
As seaward drive we ever
Before the witch-wrought weather,
We well-famed kings'-defenders:
Here are we all a-standing,
With all Solundir hull-down,
Eighteen brave lads a-baling
Black Ellidi to bring home."

Said Biorn: "Needs must he who fareth far fall in with diverse hap."

"Yea, certes, foster-brother," said Frithiof. And he sang withal:

"Helgi it is that helpeth
The white-head billows' waxing;
Cold time unlike the kissing
In the close of Baldur's Meadow!
So is the hate of Helgi
To that heart's love she giveth.
O would that here I held her,
Gift high above all giving!"

"Maybe," said Biorn, "she is looking higher than thou now art: what matter when all is said?"

"Well," says Frithiof, "now is the time to show ourselves to be men of avail, though blither tide it was at Baldur's Meadows."

So they turned to in manly wise, for there were the bravest of men come together in the best ship of the Northlands. But Frithiof sang a stave:

"So come in the West-sea,
Nought see I the billows,
The sea-water seemeth
As sweeping of wild-fire.
Topple the rollers,
Toss the hills swan-white,
Ellidi wallows
O'er steep of the wave-hills."

Then they shipped a huge sea, so that all stood a-baling. But Frithiof sang:

"With love-moved mouth the maiden
Mepledgeth though I founder.
Ah! Bright sheets lay a-bleaching,
East there on brents the swan loves."

Biorn said: "Art thou of mind belike that the maids of Sogn will weep many tears over thee?"

Said Frithiof: "Surely that was in my mind."

Therewith so great a sea broke over the bows, that the water came in like the in-falling of a river; but it availed them much that the ship was so good, and the crew aboard her so hardy.

Now sang Biorn:

"No widow, methinks,
To thee or me drinks;
No ring-bearer fair
Biddeth draw near;
Salt are our eyne
Soaked in the brine;
Strong our arms are no more,
And our eyelids smart sore."

Quoth Asmund: "Small harm though your arms be tried somewhat, for no pity we had from you when we rubbed our eyes whenas ye must needs rise early a-mornings to go to Baldur's Meadows."

"Well," said Frithiof, "why singest thou not, Asmund?"

"Not I," said Asmund; yet sang a ditty straightway:

"Sharp work about the sail was
When o'er the ship seas tumbled,
And there was I a-working
Within-board 'gainst eight balers;
Better it was to bower,
Bringing the women breakfast,
Than here to be 'mid billows
Black Ellidi a-baling."

"Thou accountest thy help of no less worth than it is?" said Frithiof, laughing therewith; "But sure it showeth the thrall's blood in thee that thou wouldst fain be awaiting at table."

Now it blew harder and harder yet, so that to those who were aboard liker to huge peaks and mountains than to waves seemed the sea-breakers that crashed on all sides against the ship. Then Frithiof sang:

"On bolster I sat.
In Baldur's Mead erst,
And all songs that I could
To the king's daughter sang;
Now on Ran's bed belike
Must I soon be a-lying,
And another shall be
By Ingibiorg's side."

Biorn said: "Great fear lieth ahead of us, foster-brother, and now dread hath crept into thy words, which is ill with such a good man as thou."

Says Frithiof: "Neither fear nor fainting is it, though I sing now of those our merry journeys; yet perchance more hath been said of them than need was: but most men would think death surer than life, if they were so bested as we be."

"Yet shall I answer thee somewhat," said Biorn, and sang:

"Yet one gain have I gotten
Thou gatst not 'mid thy fortune,
For meet play did I make me
With Ingibiorg's eight maidens;
Red rings we laid together
Aright in Baldur's Meadow,
When far off was the warder
Of the wide land of Halfdan."

"Well," said he, "we must be content with things as they are, foster-brother."

Therewith so great a sea smote them, that the bulwark was broken and both the sheets, and four men were washed overboard and all lost.

Then sang Frithiof:

"Both sheets are bursten
Amid the great billows,
Four swains are sunk
In the fathomless sea?"

"Now, meseems," said Frithiof, "it may well be that some of us will go to the house of Ran, nor shall we deem us well sped if we come not thither in glorious array; wherefore it seems good to me that each man of us here should have somewhat of gold on him."

Then he smote asunder the ring, Ingibiorg's gift, and shared it between all his men, and sang a stave withal:

"The red ring here I hew me
Once owned of Halfdan's father,
The wealthy lord of erewhile,
Or the sea waves undo us,
So on the guests shall gold be,
If we have need of guesting;
Meet so for mighty men-folk
Amid Ran's hall to hold them."

"Not all so sure is it that we come there," said Biorn; "and yet it may well be so."

Now Frithiof and his folk found that the ship had great way on her, and they knew not what lay ahead, for all was murk on either board, so that none might see the stem or stern from amidships; and therewith was there great drift of spray amid the furious wind, and frost, and snow, and deadly cold.

Now Frithiof went up to the masthead, and when he came down he said to his fellows: "A sight exceeding wondrous have I seen, for a great whale went in a ring about the ship, and I misdoubt me that we come nigh to some land, and that he is keeping the shore against us; for certes King Helgi has dealt with us in no friendly wise, neither will this his messenger be friendly. Moreover I saw two women on the back of the whale, and they it is who will have brought this great storm on us with the worst of spells and witchcraft; but now we shall try which may prevail, my fortune or their devilry, so steer ye at your straightest, and I will smite these evil things with beams."

Therewith he sang a stave:

"See I troll women
Twain on the billows,

Een they whom Helgi
Hither hath sent.
Ellidi now
Or ever her way stop
Shall smile the backs
Of these asunder."

So tells the tale that this wonder went with the good ship Ellidi, that she knew the speech of man.

But Biorn said: "Now may we see the treason of those brethren against us." Therewith he took the tiller, but Frithiof caught up a forked beam, and ran into the prow, and sang a stave:

"Ellidi, hail!
Leap high o'er the billows!
Break of the troll wives
Brow or teeth now!
Break cheek or jaw
Of the cursed woman,
One foot or twain
Of the ogress filthy."

Therewith he drave his fork at one of the skin-changers, and the beak of Ellidi smote the other on the back, and the backs of both were broken; but the whale took the deep, and gat him gone, and they never saw him after.

Then the wind fell, but the ship lay waterlogged; so Frithiof called out to his men, and bade bale out the ship, but Biorn said:

"No need to work now, verily!"

"Be thou not afeard, foster-brother," said Frithiof, "ever was it the wont of good men of old time to be helpful while they might, whatsoever should come after." And therewith he sang a stave:

"No need, fairfellows,
To fear the death-day;
Rather be glad,

Good men of mine:
For if dreams wot aught
All nights they say
I yet shall have
My Ingibiorg."

Then they baled out the ship; and they were now come nigh unto land; but there was yet a flaw of wind in their teeth. So then did Frithiof take the two bow oars again, and rowed full mightily. Therewith the weather brightened, and they saw that they were come out to Effia Sound, and so there they made land.

The crew were exceeding weary; but so stout a man was Frithiof that he bore eight men a-land over the foreshore, but Biorn bore two, and Asmund one. Then sang Frithiof:

"Fast bare I up
To the fire-lit house
My men all dazed
With the drift of the storm;
And the sail moreover
To the sand I carried;
With the might of the sea
Is there no more to do."

Chapter VII – Frithiof at the Orkneys

Now Earl Angantyr was at Effia whenas Frithiof and his folk came a-land there. But his way it was, when he was sitting at the drink, that one of his men should sit at the watch-window, looking weatherward from the drinking hall, and keep watch there. From a great horn drank he ever: and still as one was emptied another was filled for him. And he who held the watch when Frithiof came a-land was called Hallward; and now he saw where Frithiof and his men went, and sang a stave:

"Men see I a-baling
Amid the storm's might;

Six bale on Ellidi
Seven are a-rowing;
Like is he in the stem,
Straining hard at the oars,
To Frithiof the bold,
The brisk in the battle."

So when he had drunk out the horn, he cast it in through the window, and spake to the woman who gave him drink:

"Take up from the floor,
O fair-going woman,
The horn cast adown
Drunk out to the end!
I behold men at sea
Who, storm-beaten, shall need
Help at our hands
Ere the haven they make."

Now the Earl heard what Hallward sang; so he asked for tidings, and Hallward said: "Men are come a-land here, much forewearied, yet brave lads belike: but one of them is so hardy that he beareth the others ashore."

Then said the Earl, "Go ye, and meet them, and welcome them in seemly wise; if this be Frithiof, the son of Hersir Thorstein, my friend, he is a man famed far and wide for all prowess."

Then there took up the word a man named Atli, a great Viking, and he spake: "Now shall that be proven which is told of, that Frithiof hath sworn never to be first in the craving of peace."

There were ten men in company with him, all evil and outrageous, who often wrought berserks-gang.

So when they met Frithiof they took to their weapons.

But Atli said –

"Good to turn hither, Frithiof! Clutching ernes should claw; and we no less, Frithiof! Yea, and now may'st thou hold to thy word, and not crave first for peace."

So Frithiof turned to meet them, and sang a stave:

"Nay, nay, in nought
Now shall ye cow us.
Blenching hearts
Isle-abiders!
Alone with you ten
The fight will I try,
Rather than pray
For peace at your hands."

Then came Hallward thereto, and spake –

"The Earl wills that ye all be made welcome here: neither shall any set on you."

Frithiof said he would take that with a good heart; howsoever he was ready for either peace or war.

So thereon they went to the Earl, and he made Frithiof and all his men right welcome, and they abode with him, in great honour holden, through the wintertide; and oft would the Earl ask of their voyage: so Biorn sang:

"There baled we, wight fellows,
Washed over and over
On both boards
By billows;
For ten days we baled there,
And eight thereunto."

The Earl said: "Well nigh did the king undo you; it is ill seen of such-like kings as are meet for nought but to overcome men by wizardry. But now I wot," says Angantyr, "of thine errand hither, Frithiof, that thou art sent after the scat: whereto I give thee a speedy answer, that never shall King Helgi get scat of me, but to thee will I give money, even as much as thou wilt; and thou mayest call it scat if thou hast a mind to, or whatso else thou wilt."

So Frithiof said that he would take the money.

Chapter VIII – King Ring Weddeth Ingibiorg

Now shall it be told of what came to pass in Norway the while Frithiof was away: for those brethren let burn up all the stead at Foreness. Moreover, while the weird sisters were at their spells they tumbled down from off their high witch-mount, and brake both their backs.

That autumn came King Ring north to Sogn to his wedding, and there at a noble feast drank his bridal with Ingibiorg.

"Whence came that goodly ring which thou hast on thine arm?" said King Ring to Ingibiorg.

She said her father had owned it, but he answered and said –

"Nay, for Frithiof s gift it is: so take it off thine arm straightway; for no gold shalt thou lack whenas thou comest to Elfhome."

So she gave the ring to King Helgi's wife, and bade her give it to Frithiof when he came back.

Then King Ring wended home with his wife, and loved her with exceeding great love.

Chaper IX – Frithiof Brings the Tribute to the Kings

The spring after these things Frithiof departed from the Orkneys and Earl Angantyr in all good liking; and Hallward went with Frithiof.

But when they came to Norway they heard tell of the burning of Frithiof's stead.

So when he was gotten to Foreness, Frithiof said: "Black is my house waxen now; no friends have been at work here." And he sang withal:

"Frank and free,
With my father dead,
In Foreness old
We drank aforetime.
Now my abode
Behold I burned;
For many ill deeds
The kings must I pay."

Then he sought rede of his men what was to be done; but they bade him look to it: then he said that the scat must first be paid out of hand. So they rowed over the Firth to Sowstrand; and there they heard that the kings were gone to Baldur's Meads to sacrifice to the gods; so Frithiof and Biorn went up thither, and bade Hallward and Asmund break up meanwhile all ships, both great and small, that were anigh; and they did so. Then went Frithiof and his fellow to the door at Baldur's Meads, and Frithiof would go in. Biorn bade him fare warily, since he must needs go in alone; but Frithiof charged him to abide without, and keep watch; and he sang a stave:

"All alone go I
Unto the stead;
No folk I need
For the finding of kings;
But cast ye the fire
O'er the kings' dwelling,
If I come not again
In the cool of the even."

"Ah," said Biorn, "a goodly singing!"

Then went Frithiof in, and saw but few folk in the Hall of the Goddesses; there were the kings at their blood-offering, sitting a-drinking; a fire was there on the floor, and the wives of the kings sat thereby, a-warming the gods, while others anointed them, and wiped them with napkins.

So Frithiof went up to King Helgi and said: "Have here thy scat!"

And therewith he heaved up the purse wherein was the silver, and drave it on to the face of the king; whereby were two of his teeth knocked out, and he fell down stunned in his high seat; but Halfdan got hold of him, so that he fell not into the fire. Then sang Frithiof:

"Have here thy scat,
High lord of the warriors!
Heed that and thy teeth,
Lest all tumble about thee!

Lo the silver abideth
At the bight of this bag here,
That Biorn and I
Betwixt us have borne thee."

Now there were but few folk in the chamber, because the drinking was in another place; so Frithiof went out straightway along the floor, and beheld therewith that goodly ring of his on the arm of Helgi's wife as she warmed Baldur at the fire; so he took hold of the ring, but it was fast to her arm, and he dragged her by it over the pavement toward the door, and Baldur fell from her into the fire; then Halfdan's wife caught hastily at Baldur, whereby the god that she was warming fell likewise into the fire, and the fire caught both the gods, for they had been anointed, and ran up thence into the roof, so that the house was all ablaze: but Frithiof got the ring to him ere he came out.

So then Biorn asked him what had come of his going in there; but Frithiof held up the ring and sang a stave:

"The heavy purse smote Helgi
Hard 'midst his scoundrel's visage
Lowly bowed Halfdan's brother,
Fell bundling 'mid the high seat:
There Baldur fell a-burning.
But first my bright ring gat I.
Fast from the roaring fire
I dragged the bent crone forward."

Men say that Frithiof cast a firebrand up on to the roof, so that the hall was all ablaze, and therewith sang a stave:

"Down stride we toward the sea-strand,
And strong deeds set a-going,
For now the blue flame bickers
Amidst of Baldur's Meadow."

And therewith they went down to the sea.

Chaper X – Frithiof Made an Outlaw

But as soon as King Helgi had come to himself he bade follow after Frithiof speedily, and slay them all, him and his fellows: "A man of forfeit life, who spareth no Place of Peace!"

So they blew the gathering for the kings' men, and when they came out to the hall they saw that it was afire; so King Halfdan went thereto with some of the folk, but King Helgi followed after Frithiof and his men, who were by then gotten a-shipboard and were lying on their oars.

Now King Helgi and his men find that all the ships are scuttled, and they have to turn back to shore, and have lost some men: then waxed King Helgi so wroth that he grew mad, and he bent his bow, and laid an arrow on the string, and drew at Frithiof so mightily that the bow brake asunder in the midst.

But when Frithiof saw that, then he gat him to the two bow oars of Ellidi, and laid so hard on them that they both brake, and with that he sang a stave:

"Young Ingibiorg
Kissed I aforetime,
Kissed Beli's daughter
In Baldur's Meadow.
So shall the oars
Of Ellidi
Break both together
As Helgi's bow breaks."

Then the land-wind ran down the firth and they hoisted sail and sailed; but Frithiof bade them look to it that they might have no long abiding there. And so withal they sailed out of the Sognfirth, and Frithiof sang:

"Sail we away from Sogn,
E'en as we sailed aforetime,
When flared the fire all over
The house that was my fathers'.
Now is the bale a-burning

Amidst of Baldur's Meadow:
But wend I as a wild-wolf,
Well wot I they have sworn it."

"What shall we turn to now, foster-brother?" said Biorn.

"I may not abide here in Norway," said Frithiof: "I will learn the ways of warriors, and sail a-warring."

So they searched the isles and out-skerries the summer long, and gathered thereby riches and renown; but in autumn-tide they made for the Orkneys, and Angantyr gave them good welcome, and they abode there through the winter-tide.

But when Frithiof was gone from Norway the kings held a Thing, whereat was Frithiof made an outlaw throughout their realm: they took his lands to them, moreover, and King Halfdan took up his abode at Foreness, and built up again all Baldur's Meadow, though it was long ere the fire was slaked there. This misliked King Helgi most, that the gods were all burned up, and great was the cost or ever Baldur's Meadow was built anew fully equal to its first estate.

So King Helgi abode still at Sowstrand.

Chapter XI – Frithiof Fareth to See King Ring and Ingibiorg

Frithiof waxed ever in riches and renown whithersoever he went: evil men he slew, and grimly strong thieves, but husbandmen and chapmen he let abide in peace; and now was he called anew Frithiof the Bold; he had gotten to him by now a great company well arrayed, and was become exceeding wealthy of chattels.

But when Frithiof had been three winters a-warring he sailed west, and made the Wick; then he said that he would go a-land: "But ye shall fare a-warring without me this winter; for I begin to weary of warfare, and would fain go to the Uplands, and get speech of King Ring: but hither shall ye come to meet me in the summer, and I will be here the first day of summer."

Biorn said: "This counsel is naught wise, though thou must needs rule;

rather would I that we fare north to Sogn, and slay both those kings, Helgi and Halfdan."

"It is all naught," said Frithiof; "I must needs go see King Ring and Ingibiorg."

Says Biorn: "Loth am I hereto that thou shouldst risk thyself alone in his hands; for this Ring is a wise man and of great kin, though he be somewhat old."

But Frithiof said he would have his own way: "And thou, Biorn, shalt be captain of our company meanwhile."

So they did as he bade, and Frithiof fared to the Uplands in the autumn, for he desired sore to look upon the love of King Ring and Ingibiorg. But or ever he came there he did on him, over his clothes, a great cloak all shaggy; two staves he had in his hand, and a mask over his face, and he made as if he were exceeding old.

So he met certain herdsmen, and, going heavily, he asked them: "Whence are ye?" They answered and said: "We are of Streitaland, whereas the king dwelleth."

Quoth the carle: "Is King Ring a mighty king, then?"

They answered: "Thou lookest to us old enough to have cunning to know what manner of man is King Ring in all wise."

The carle said that he had heeded salt-boiling more than the ways of kings; and therewith he goes up to the king's house.

So when the day was well worn he came into the hall, blinking about as a dotard, and took an outward place, pulling his hood over him to hide his visage.

Then spake King Ring to Ingibiorg: "There is come into the hall a man far bigger than other men."

The queen answered: "That is not such great tidings here."

But the king spake to a serving-man who stood before the board, and said: "Go thou, and ask yon cowled man who he is, whence he cometh, and of what kin he is."

So the lad ran down the hall to the newcomer and said: "What art thou called, thou man? Where wert thou last night? Of what kin art thou?"

Said the cowled man: "Quick come thy questions, good fellow! But hast thou skill to understand if I shall tell thee hereof?"

"Yea, certes," said the lad.

"Well," said the cowl-bearer, "Thief is my name, with Wolf was I last night, and in Grief-ham was I reared."

Then ran the lad back to the king, and told him the answer of the newcomer.

"Well told, lad," said the king; "but for that land of Grief-ham, I know it well: it may well be that the man is of no light heart, and yet a wise man shall he be, and of great worth I account him."

Said the queen: "A marvellous fashion of thine, that thou must needs talk so freely with every carle that cometh hither! Yea, what is the worth of him, then?"

"That wottest thou no clearer than I," said the king; "but I see that he thinketh more than he talketh, and is peering all about him."

Therewith the king sent a man after him, and so the cowl-bearer went up before the king, going somewhat bent, and greeted him in a low voice. Then said the king: "What art thou called, thou big man?"

And the cowl-bearer answered and sang:

"Peace-thief they called me
On the prow with the Vikings;
But War-thief whenas
I set widows a-weeping;
Spear-thief when I
Sent forth the barbed shafts;
Battle-thief when I
Burst forth on the king;
Hel-thief when I
Tossed up the small babies:
Isle-thief when I
In the outer isles harried;
Slains-thief when I
Sat aloft over men:
Yet since have I drifted
With salt-boiling carls,
Needy of help
'Ere hither I came."

Said the king: "Thou hast gotten thy name of Thief from many a matter, then; but where wert thou last night, and what is thy home?"

The cowl-bearer said: "In Grief-ham I grew up; but heart drave me hither, and home have I nowhere."

The king said: "Maybe indeed that thou hast been nourished in Grief-ham a certain while; yet also maybe that thou wert born in a place of peace. But in the wild-wood must thou have lain last night, for no goodman dwelleth anigh named Wolf; but whereas thou sayest thou hast no home, so is it, that thou belike deemest thy home naught, because of thy heart that drave thee hither."

Then spake Ingibiorg: "Go, Thief, get thee to some other harbour, or in to the guest-hall."

"Nay," said the king, "I am old enow to know how to marshal guests; so do off thy cowl, newcomer, and sit down on my other hand."

"Yea, old, and over old," said the queen, "when thou settest staff-carles by thy side."

"Nay, lord, it beseemeth not," said Thief; "better it were as the queen sayeth. I have been more used to boiling salt than sitting beside lords."

"Do thou my will," said the king, "for I will rule this time."

So Thief cast his cowl from him, and was clad thereunder in a dark blue kirtle; on his arm, moreover, was the goodly gold ring, and a thick silver belt was round about him, with a great purse on it, and therein silver pennies glittering; a sword was girt to his side, and he had a great fur hood on his head, for his eyes were bleared, and his face all wrinkled.

"Ah! Now we fare better, say I," quoth the king; "but do thou, queen, give him a goodly mantle, well shapen for him."

"Thou shalt rule, my lord," said the queen; "but in small account do I hold this Thief of thine."

So then he gat a good mantle over him, and sat down in the high-seat beside the king.

The queen waxed red as blood when she saw the goodly ring, yet would she give him never a word; but the king was exceeding blithe with him and said: "A goodly ring hast thou on thine arm there; thou must have boiled salt long enough to get it."

Says he, "That is all the heritage of my father."

"Ah!" says the king, "maybe thou hast more than that; well, few salt-boiling carles are thy peers, I deem, unless eld is deep in mine eyes now."

So Thief was there through the winter amid good entertainment, and well accounted of by all men; he was bounteous of his wealth, and joyous with all men: the queen held but little converse with him; but the king and he were ever blithe together.

Chapter XII – Frithiof Saves the King and Queen on the Ice

The tale tells that on a time King Ring and the queen, and a great company, would go to a feast. So the king spake to Thief: "Wilt thou fare with us, or abide at home?"

He said he had liefer go; and the king said: "Then am I the more content."

So they went on their ways, and had to cross a certain frozen water. Then said Thief: "I deem this ice untrustworthy; meseemeth ye fare unwarily."

Quoth the king: "It is often shown how heedful in thine heart thou wilt be to us."

So a little after the ice broke in beneath them, and Thief ran thereto, and dragged the wain to him, with all that was therein; and the king and the queen both sat in the same: so Thief drew it all up on to the ice, with the horses that were yoked to the wain.

Then spake King Ring: "Right well drawn, Thief! Frithiof the Bold himself would have drawn no stronger had he been here; doughty followers are such as thou!"

So they came to the feast, and there is naught to tell thereof, and the king went back again with seemly gifts.

Chapter XIII – The King Sleeps Before Frithiof

Now weareth away the mid-winter, and when spring cometh, the weather groweth fair, the wood bloometh, the grass groweth, and ships may glide betwixt land and land. So on a day the king says to his folk: "I will that ye come with us for our disport out into the woods, that we may look upon the fairness of the earth."

So did they, and went flock-meal with the king into the woods; but so it befell, that the king and Frithiof were gotten alone together afar from other men, and the king said he was heavy, and would fain sleep. Then said Thief: "Get thee home, then, lord, for it better beseemeth men of high estate to lie at home than abroad."

"Nay," said the king, "so will I not do." And he laid him down therewith, and slept fast, snoring loud.

Thief sat close by him, and presently drew his sword from his sheath and cast it far away from him.

A little while after the king woke up, and said: "Was it not so, Frithiof, that a many things came into thy mind e'en now? But well hast thou dealt with them, and great honour shalt thou have of me. Lo, now, I knew thee straightway that first evening thou earnest into our hall: now nowise speedily shalt thou depart from us; and somewhat great abideth thee."

Said Frithiof: "Lord king, thou hast done to me well, and in friendly wise; but yet must I get me gone soon, because my company cometh speedily to meet me, as I have given them charge to do."

So then they rode home from the wood, and the king's folk came flocking to him, and home they fared to the hall and drank joyously; and it was made known to all folk that Frithiof the Bold had been abiding there through the winter-tide.

Chapter XIV – King Ring's Gift to Frithiof

Early of a morning-tide one smote on the door of that hall, wherein slept the king and queen, and many others: then the king asked who it was that called at the hall door; and so he who was without said: "Here am I, Frithiof; and I am arrayed for my departure."

Then was the door opened, and Frithiof came in, and sang a stave:

"Have great thanks for the guesting
Thou gavest with all bounty;

Dight fully for wayfaring
Is the feeder of the eagle;
But, Ingibiorg, I mind thee
While yet on earth we tarry;
Live gloriously! I give thee
This gift for many kisses."

And therewith he cast the goodly ring towards Ingibiorg, and bade her take it.

The king smiled at this stave of his, and said: "Yea, forsooth, she hath more thanks for thy winter quarters than I; yet hath she not been more friendly to thee than I."

Then sent the king his serving-folk to fetch victuals and drink, and saith that they must eat and drink before Frithiof departed. "So arise, queen, and be joyful!" But she said she was loth to fall a-feasting so early.

"Nay, we will eat all together," said King Ring; and they did so.

But when they had drank a while King Ring spake: "I would that thou abide here, Frithiof; for my sons are but children and I am old, and unmeet for the warding of my realm, if any should bring war against it." Frithiof said: "Speedily must I be gone, lord." And he sang:

"Oh, live, King Ring,
Both long and hale!
The highest king
'Neath heaven's skirt!
Ward well, O king,
Thy wife and land,
For Ingibiorg now
Never more shall I meet."
Then quoth King Ring:
"Fare not away,
O Frithiof, thus,
With downcast heart,
O dearest of chieftains!
For now will I give thee

For all thy good gifts,
Far better things
Than thou wottest thyself."

And again he sang:

"To Frithiof the famous
My fair wife I give,
And all things therewith
That are unto me."

Then Frithiof took up the word and sang:

"Nay, how from thine hands
These gifts may I have,
But if thou hast fared
By the last way of fate."

The king said: "I would not give thee this, but that I deem it will soon be so, for I sicken now. But of all men I would that thou shouldst have the joy of this; for thou art the crown of all Norway. The name of king will I give thee also; and all this, because Ingibiorg's brethren would begrudge thee any honour; and would be slower in getting thee a wife than I am."

Said Frithiof: "Have all thanks, lord, for thy goodwill beyond that I looked for! But I will have no higher dignity than to be called earl."

Then King Ring gave Frithiof rule over all his realm in due wise, and the name of earl therewith; and Frithiof was to rule it until such time as the sons of King Ring were of age to rule their own realm. So King Ring lay sick a little while, and then died; and great mourning was made for him; then was there a mound cast over him, and much wealth laid therein, according to his bidding.

Thereafter Frithiof made a noble feast, whereunto his folk came; and thereat was drunken at one and the same time the heritage feast after King Ring, and the bridal of Frithiof and Ingibiorg.

After these things Frithiof abode in his realm, and was deemed therein a most noble man; he and Ingibiorg had many children.

Chapter XV – Frithiof King in Sogn

Now those kings of Sogn, the brethren of Ingibiorg, heard these tidings, how that Frithiof had gotten a king's rule in Ringrealm, and had wedded Ingibiorg their sister. Then says Helgi to Halfdan, his brother, that unheard of it was, and a deed over-bold, that a mere hersir's son should have her to wife: and so thereat they gather together a mighty army, and go their ways therewith to Ringrealm, with the mind to slay Frithiof, and lay all his realm under them.

But when Frithiof was ware of this, he gathered folk, and spake to the queen moreover: "New war is come upon our realm; and now, in whatso wise the dealings go, fain am I that thy ways to me grow no colder."

She said: "In such wise have matters gone that I must needs let thee be the highest."

Now was Biorn come from the east to help Frithiof; so they fared to the fight, and it befell, as ever erst, that Frithiof was the foremost in the peril: King Helgi and he came to handy-blows, and there he slew King Helgi.

Then bade Frithiof raise up the Shield of Peace, and the battle was stayed; and therewith he cried to King Halfdan: "Two choices are in thine hands now, either that thou give up all to my will, or else gettest thou thy bane like thy brother; for now may men see that mine is the better part."

So Halfdan chose to lay himself and his realm under Frithiof's sway; and so now Frithiof became ruler over Sogn-folk, and Halfdan was to be Hersir in Sogn and pay Frithiof tribute, while Frithiof ruled Ringrealm. So Frithiof had the name of King of Sogn-folk from the time that he gave up Ringrealm to the sons of King Ring, and thereafter he won Hordaland also. He and Ingibiorg had two sons, called Gunnthiof and Hunthiof, men of might, both of them.

And so here endeth The Story of Frithiof the Bold.

The Story of the Farmer's Three Daughters

NOT VERY FAR from a town, where dwelt the king, lived, once upon a time, a farmer. He was well to do, and had three daughters ; the eldest was twenty years of age, the other two younger, but both marriageable. Once when they were walking outside their father's farm, they saw the king coming riding on horseback, with two followers, his secretary and his bootmaker. The king was unmarried, as were also these two men. When they saw him, the eldest of the sisters said: "I do not wish anything higher than to be the wife of the king's shoemaker."

"And I the wife of his secretary," said the second. Then the youngest said: "I wish then that I were wife of the king himself." Now the king heard that they were talking together, and said to his followers: "I will go to the girls yonder, and know what it is they were talking about. It seemed to me that I heard one of them say, "The king himself."

His followers said that what the girls had been chattering about could hardly be of much importance. The king did not heed this, however, but declared that they would all go to the girls and have a talk with them. This they did. The king then asked what they had been talking about, a moment ago, when he and his men passed them. The sisters were unwilling to tell the truth, but, being pressed hard by the king, did so at last. Now as the damsels pleased the king, and he saw that they were both handsome and fair-spoken, particularly the youngest of them, he said that all should be as they had wished it. The sisters were amazed at this, but the king's will must be done.

So the three sisters were married, each to the husband she had chosen.

But when the youngest sister had become queen, the others began to cast on her looks of envy and hatred, and would have her, at any cost, dragged down from her lofty position. And they laid a plot for the accomplishment of this their will. When the queen was going to be confined for the first time, her sisters got leave to act as her midwives. But, as soon as the child was born, they hid it away, and ordered it to be thrown into a slough into which all the filth was cast. But the man to whom they had entrusted this task could not bring himself to do it, so put the child on the bank of the slough, thinking that someone might find it and save its life. And so it fell out; for an old man chanced to pass the slough soon afterwards, and finding a crying child on the bank, thought it a strange find, took it up, and brought it to his home, cherishing it all he could.

The queen's sisters took a whelp, and shewed it to the king as his queen's offspring. The king was grieved at this tale, but being as fond of the queen as of his own life, he restrained his anger, and punished her not.

At the second and third confinement of the queen, her sisters played the same trick: they exposed the queen's children, in order to have them drowned in the slough. The man, however, always left them on the bank, and it so happened that the same old carl always passed by, and took up the children, and carried them home, and brought them up as best he could.

The queen's sister said that, the second time the queen was confined, she had given birth to a kitten, and the third time, to a log of wood. At this the king waxed furiously wroth, and ordered the queen to be thrown into the house where he kept a lion, as he did not wish this monster to fill his kingdom with deformities. And the sisters thought they had managed their boat well, and were proud of their success. The lion, however, did not devour the queen, but even gave her part of its food, and was friendly towards her; and thus the queen lived with the lion a wretched enough life, without anybody's knowing anything about it.

Now the story turns to the old man who fostered the king's children. The eldest of these, a boy, he called Vilhjálmr; the second, also a boy, he called Sigurdr. The third child was a girl, and her name is unknown.

All that came to him or with whom he met, the old man would ask if they knew nothing of the children he had found on the bank of the slough. But no one seemed to have the faintest notion about their birth or descent. As the children grew up, they were hopeful and fine-looking. The carl had now waxed very old, and expecting his end, he gave the children the rede, – always to ask everyone to whom they spoke, for news of their family and birth, in order that they might perchance be able at last, to trace out the truth. He himself told them all he knew about the matter. After this the old man died, and the children followed closely his advice.

Once there came to them an old man, of whom they asked the same questions as of all others. He said he could not give them any hints on the matter himself, but that he could point out one to them who was able to do so. He told them that a short way from their farm, was a large stone, whereupon was always sitting a bird which could both understand and speak the tongue of men. It would be best for them, he went on, to find this bird; but there was a difficulty in the matter, to be got over first, for many had gone there but none had ever returned. He said that many king's children had gone to this bird, in order to know their future fate, but they had all come short in the very thing needed. He told them that whosoever wanted to mount the stone, must be so steady as never to look back, whatever he might hear or see, or whatever wonders seemed to take place around the rock. All who did not succeed in this were changed into stones, together with everything they had with them. This steadiness no one had had yet, but whosoever had it could easily mount the rock, and having once done so would be able to quicken all the others who had been turned to stone there. For the top of the rock was flat, and there was a trap-door on it, whereon the bird was sitting. Underneath the trap-door was water, the nature of which was that it would turn all the stones back to life again. The old man ended by saying: "Now he who succeeds in getting to the top is allowed by the bird to take the water and sprinkle the stone-changed folk, and call them to life again, just as they were before."

This the king's children thought no hard task. The brothers, however, were the most outspoken about the easiness of the thing. They thanked the old man much for his story, and took leave of him.

Not long after this, Vilhjálmr, the eldest brother, went to the rock. But before he left, he said to his brother, that if three drops of blood should fall on his knife at table, while he was away, Sigurdr should come at once to the rock, for then it would be sure that he had fared like the others. So Vilhjálmr went away, following the old man's directions, and nothing farther is told of him for a while. But after three days, or about the time when his brother should have reached the stone, three drops of blood fell upon Sigurdr's knife, once, while at table. He was startled at this, and told his sister that he must needs leave her, in order to help his brother. He made the same agreement with his sister, as Vilhjálmr had before made with him. Then he went away, and, to make the story short, all came to the same issue with him as with his brother, and the blood-drops fell on his sister's knife, at the time when Sigurdr should have reached the stone.

Then the damsel went herself, to see what luck she might have. She succeeded in finding the rock, and when she came there she was greatly struck with the number of stones that surrounded it, in every shape and position.

Some had the form of chests, others of various animals, while some again were in other forms. She paid no heed to all this, but, going straight forward to the great rock, began climbing up it.

Then she heard, all of a sudden, behind her, a loud murmur of human voices, all talking, the one louder than the other, and amongst the number she heard those of her brothers. But she paid no heed to this, and took good care never to look back, in spite of all she heard going on behind her. Thus she got at last to the top of the rock, and the bird greatly praised her steadiness and constancy, and promised both to tell her anything she chose to ask of him, and to assist her in every way he could. First, she would have the surrounding stones recalled to their natural shapes and life. This the bird granted her, pointing to one of the stones, and saying: "Methinks you would free that one from his spell, if you knew who he was." So the king's daughter sprinkled water over all the stones, and they returned to life again, and thanked her for their release with many fair words. Next, she asked the bird who were the parents of herself and her brothers, and to whom they might trace their descent. The bird said that they were the children of the king of that country, and told her how the queen's sisters had acted by them at their birth, and last of all told her how her mother was in the lion's den, and how she was nearer dead than alive from sorrow and want of good food and comfort.

The stone which the bird had pointed out to the princess was a king's son, as noble as he was handsome. He cast affectionate looks to his life-giver, and it was plain that each loved the other. It was he who had brought the greater part of the chest-shaped stones thither, the which were coffers full of gold and jewels. When the bird had told to everyone what each wanted to know, all the company of the disenchanted scattered, the three children and the wealthy prince going together. When they came home, the first thing they did was to break into the lion's den. They found their mother lying in a swoon, for she had lost her senses on hearing the house broken into. They took her away, and she soon afterwards recovered. Then they dressed her in fitting attire, and taking her to the palace, asked audience of the king. This granted, Vilhjálmr, Sigurdr and their sister declared to the king that they were his children, and that they had brought with them their mother from the lion's den. The king was amazed at this story and at all that had happened. The sisters of the queen were sent for and questioned, and having got into scrapes by differing in accounts, confessed at last their misdeed and told the truth. They were thrown before the same lion that the queen had been given to, and it tore them to pieces immediately, and ate them up, hair and all.

Now the queen took her former rank, and a banquet was held in joy at this happy turn of affairs, and for many days the palace resounded with the glee of the feast. And at the end of it, the foreign prince wooed the king's daughter, and gained easily her hand, and thus the banquet was begun afresh, and became the young people's marriage-feast. Such glee has never been witnessed in any other kingdom. After the feast, the strange prince returned to his home with his bride, and became king after his father. Vilhjálmr also married and took the kingdom after his father. Sigurdr married a king's daughter abroad, and became king after the death of his father-in-law; and all of them lived in luck and prosperity. And now is the story ended.

History of Líneik and Laufey

IN THE DAYS of yore, a king and his queen ruled over a great and wealthy realm. Their names have not been recorded, but it is told that they had two children, a son and a daughter, both of whom were of age when this tale begins. The king's son was hight Sigurdr, and his daughter, Líneik. They were mighty well endowed and accomplished children in every way, and you would have to go far to find any of their own age, to match them. The children loved each other so deeply, that they never would part, so the king had a bower built for them, fine and costly, and gave them their own servants, as many as they wanted.

Now time passed on without anything notable happening, until the queen was thrown on to a sick-bed, by a fever. She called the king to her, and told him that she feared this would be her bane. "I have two things to ask of you," said the queen, "before I die, which I hope you will bear in mind, as they are my last wishes. The first is that, if you marry again, you will not choose a wife from small towns or lone islands, but in large cities and great nations, and then she will prove a good one to you. The other thing is, that you will take all possible pains in bringing up our children, for I deem that hereafter they will afford you the greatest pleasure and consolation." Having thus spoken, the queen died.

The king's grief was deep and true, and little regard did he pay thenceforth to the ruling of his kingdom.

Some time after this, it happened one day, that the king's first-minister came to him and told him that the people were grumbling and wroth that the whole government went astray, as the king paid no heed to his duties, on account of his grief and regret for the late queen. "It is surely more king-like," said the first-minister, "to pluck up some spirit, and banish grief from your mind, and to search for a wife, with whom you could live in honour and happiness."

"This is a matter of great difficulty," answered the king; "but, as you have once made mention of it, I think it best to throw upon you the honour and carrying out of it. I therefore give you the command, to choose a fit wife for me; but I must warn you not to seek for her in small towns, or in lone islands."

Now the first-minister made ready and was equipped in fine style, and given a good suite, and then put to sea. But when he had sailed for a while, he was surrounded by such a fog that he lost his course, and knew not where he was, or whither he went. After a month's aimless wanderings, he, one day, suddenly saw land before him, but knew not at all the coast. He found a fine harbour and went ashore, and there pitched his tent. No living beings did his suite find, and all of them thought that this must be a desert island.

When the others had gone to rest, the minister went out into the country, and before he had gone far, he heard such sweet music that he thought he had never heard the like of it before. He walked towards the sound, and wandered on, till he came to an open space in the forest. Here he found a woman sitting, so noble and fine-looking, that he thought he never had seen such a beauty, and on her footstool was sitting a beautiful young girl, who sang to the music.

The minister saluted the woman courteously, and she nobly returned his greeting, and looked on him with a gentle face.

The woman then asked the minister how he was faring and what his errand was. He told her truly what was his errand, and what in the king's life had brought about this sending.

Then the lady said: "How like is the king's lot to mine! I was married to a good king that ruled over this country, but Vikings made an in-raid into his realms, and killed him, and conquered the land, but I fled away with this young maiden, my daughter."

As the young damsel heard these last words, she said to the lady: "Dost thou tell truth, now?"

But the other only dealt her a goodly slap on the ear, and said: "Remember what thou hast promised." The minister now asked the lady's name, and she said it was Blávör, but that of her daughter, Laufey.

The first-minister had a long talk with this lady, and finding her clever and wise, thought within himself, that he might never have a fairer chance of securing a wife for his king. He therefore wooed her on behalf of his king. He had no trouble in gaining her consent, nor had he to wait long for her to get ready, for she said she was alboun to go with him at once.

"For," said she, "I have all my precious things with me, but, as to followers, I care for none save my daughter Laufey."

And, without delay, they went with the minister to the beach, and he gave orders to strike the tents, and hoist the sails, and put to sea in all haste. As they sailed away, the fog cleared up, and they saw that they had been upon a desert rock surrounded by steep cliffs, but paid no further heed to it. A fair breeze too sprang up, and when they had sailed for six days they saw land ahead, and soon knew it for their own, and that they were sailing straight up to the capital, where their king lived.

Having gained the harbour, they let fall the anchor, and the minister sent messengers home into the city to tell their arrival. The king was very glad, and dressing in his state robes, went out with a splendid suite to receive his bride. But as the king approached, and was midway between the town and the shore, he was met by the prime-minister leading the ladies, one on each side, dressed in the gayest way possible. When the king saw all this richness and beauty, he was filled with joy; and when he saw the elder lady, who was far lovelier even than the younger, he thought he tasted the bliss of heaven. He welcomed the minister and the ladies with the greatest gladness, and forgot, from sheer joy, to ask from what country they came. He took them home to the palace and had the richest apartments prepared for them. Then a great wedding-feast was got ready, and all the great people were bidden; but it is not told that the king's children, Líneik and Sigurdr, were there. They had neither of them yet come to welcome Blávör; and the king, who did nothing but talk with his bride, had pretty well forgotten all about them. Now the wedding-feast passed brightly and joyously, and at the end of it, the guests were honoured with fine parting-gifts; but the king, as soon as the feast was over, began to busy himself quietly about the affairs of his country. The queen shared in the government with the king, and folk thought that she spoilt more than she mended; and thus some time passed on.

The queen waxed very ambitious and tyrannical, insomuch that the king began to see that his wife would be less profitable to him than he had at first thought.

The queen paid no heed whatever to the royal children, Sigurdr and Líneik, who dwelt in their bower, night and day.

Not a long time after all this, when the queen had taken in hand the government of the realm, in company with her husband, the king's courtiers began, in a strange way, to vanish, one by one, nobody knowing what became of them. But the king paid no heed to this, further than that he took new courtiers in place of the lost ones.

One day, the queen went to the king, saying that it was already time for him to go and gather the taxes of his lands. "Go, and do this," she said, "and meanwhile I will take the lead of the government." The king was rather amazed at this, but said nothing, as he scarcely dared do aught but obey his queen, who had by this time become harsh and hard to deal with.

The king fitted out a fleet, of some few ships only, and was very sad in his mind.

When he was alboun, he went to his children's bower, and greeted them, and was heartily welcomed by them. He sighed heavily and said: "If it should so happen that I do not return from this journey, I fear you will have little safety here, and I would that you should take secretly to flight as soon as you despair of my ever returning home. You shall go eastward till you come to a great and steep mountain, up which you must try to climb; and when you are over it, you will see a long arm of the sea. At the end of this bay stand two trees, one green and the other red; they are both hollow within, in such a wise that no one can see the opening from outside. You shall then get, each of you, into one of the trees, and so nothing will ever hurt you."

After this, the king said farewell to his children, hoisted sail, and sailed away out of the country. But when he had sailed for a while, such a hurricane arose, that nothing could save the ships from being wrecked; and with the hurricane there were such wondrous thunders and lightnings that none had ever seen the like; and, to make short the tale, the king and all his men found their death in the waves, and all the ships sank.

The same night, Sigurdr, the king's son, had a dream, in which his father came all wet into the bower, and took off his crown and laid it at Sigurdr's feet, and then silently departed. Sigurdr told Líneik his sister, the dream, and they felt sure of what fate their father had met with, and busked forthwith for departure, taking all their precious things and clothes with them, but no guide.

Then they went out of the town, disguised and took the way their father had pointed out. But when they had reached the foot of the mountain, they looked back, and lo! there was their step-mother coming after them with great strides, and looking hideously trollish.

Skirting the foot of the mountain where they now were, was a forest which they had just come through, and they hit upon the plan of setting fire to it, so that, when Blávör approached it, it was all in flames.

Thus far, therefore, and no farther could Blávör manage to get, this being a bar between her and the flying children, who now continued to scale the mountain, with great difficulty, and reached the top. Once over this, they at last found the trees which their father had spoken of to them, and took up their abode in the hollow trunks, which were so contrived, that they could see one another, and talk together for their pleasure.

And now the story turns, for a while, to other doings.

At this time, Greece was governed by a great and mighty king, whose name, however, is not mentioned.

He also had two children by his queen, neither of whose names have come down to us. These children were both fair of look and accomplished beyond all of their age.

When the king's son was of age, he went out sea-faring, to acquire honour and wealth. He led a Viking life through the summer, but in the winter remained at home in Greece.

On his expedition, he often heard the name of Líneik, mentioned, and that she was above all other women, in beauty and virtues. He therefore at once made up his mind to sail away for the purpose of wooing Líneik.

When he came to the shore, Blávör's magic knowledge told her who was come thither, and wherefore he was come. She therefore dressed herself and her daughter in the most brilliant and rich attire, and walked to the shore, in order to meet the king's son.

He greeted them right courteously, and asked them of everyone's health. The queen told him, with a show of great sorrow, that her husband had been lost, with all his followers, when he had gone to gather the taxes of his lands. All this she told him, with a mightily sad and cast-down air.

Then the prince asked for Líneik. The queen answered that the lady by her side, was none other. But the prince, instead of bursting out into praises of her beauty, said that he had imagined Líneik to be far lovelier than this damsel.

The queen answered, that it was no wonder, for she had been quite otherwise formerly, and had waxed pale and sad-looking, from sorrow at losing her father and brother at once.

This the prince thought true enough, and forthwith wooed Laufey, and easily got the queen's consent to their marriage, for both mother and daughter approved well of his suit. Now the king's son made ready, in all haste, to go back to his own country, taking with him his bride, whom he thought to be Líneik. The queen would go with him, but to this the prince would by no means yield, and he must needs have his will.

When he had sailed but a short way from the shore, he lost his course in a fog, and knew not whither the ships were driving, till he came into a long and broad firth. He launched a boat into the sea, and went ashore. At the end of the bay, he saw standing two trees, whose like in beauty he had never seen before. He had these trees felled and brought on board his vessel, and when this work was done, the fog had cleared away. And he at once hoisted sails, and made for Greece.

He took his affianced bride home to the city and bade every mark of honour to be shewn to her. He gave her his own bed-chamber to live in by day, but at night she retired to her bower.

Now the prince was so delighted with the beauty of the trees, that he had one set up at the head, and the other at the foot of his bed. This done, folk began to look for the wedding feast.

The prince gave Laufey, whom he took for Líneik, stuffs to make three suits of clothes for him, one blue, the other red, and the third green, with the command to her to have them all ready before the time of the wedding feast came. First she was to do the blue suit, then the red, and lastly the green: "For," said the prince, "I am going to wear them on our wedding day." Laufey took the stuff, and the prince left the room.

Now Laufey fell to weeping grievously, for old Blávör had not taught her much in the way of needlework, and she had never in her life set her hand to work so fine as this which she was now called upon to do. She thought it pretty sure that the prince would shew her the door, in disgust and scorn, if she did not get through her task, and even, perhaps, take her life away. All these thoughts gave her great pain and grief.

The king's children, Sigurdr and Líneik, were sitting all this while, in their trees, and saw all that passed in the prince's bed-chamber, and heard Laufey's lamentations. They so touched Sigurdr, that he called to his sister, and said:

"Líneik, Líneik, little sister;
Laufey weepeth bitterly.
Mend hem and border, to assist her,
If thou canst work better than she."

Líneik answered:

"Dost thou not, brother, call to mind
Yon mountain towering higher and higher,
And how there roared and raved, behind,
The mighty force of fire?"

But Sigurdr so managed to prevail upon Líneik, that she slipped out from her tree and began sewing with Laufey. Thus they finished the first suit of the prince's clothes, and Laufey was mighty glad to see how neatly and highly they were finished. Líneik stepped into her tree again, and Laufey gave the clothes to the prince.

When he saw them he said: "Never saw I clothes so fine and so well finished as these are. Begin now making the red clothes, and make them the better, the costlier the stuff is." Laufey went again to the room and sat down weeping, until Sigurdr, the king's son, called out to his sister, in the same words as before, saying:

"Líneik, Líneik, little sister;
Laufey weepeth bitterly.

Mend hem and border, to assist her,
If thou canst work better than she."

And Líneik answered:

"Dost thou not, brother, call to mind
Yon mountain towering higher and higher,
And how there roared and raved, behind,
The mighty force of fire?"

At last, however, she came out from her tree, as before, and began sewing. Now she made these clothes far handsomer than the first suit; they were all broidered with gold and jewels, and when they were quite finished, Líneik gave them to Laufey, in order that she should take them to the prince, but she herself returned to her tree.

Laufey went to the prince, and shewed him the clothes. He looked at them and said: "Far too well are these clothes made for it to be likely that you have made them alone; methinks that more folk have handled them than I ken of. Go now, and make the third suit, and have it ready within three nights; this last suit you must have so highly finished, that it be to the others what gold is to brass. I shall wear them on the day of our wedding."

Laufey went to the room, and sat down and wept. Sigurdr, pitying her much, spoke to his sister as he had formerly done, and, after a while, Líneik stepped out from the tree, and began sewing as before, and this time she loaded the clothes with beautiful handiwork and embroidery, so as to leave scarce a place in the cloth, that was not covered with gold or gems.

The third day, as Líneik and Laufey were sewing their hardest, they were all of a sudden startled by seeing the prince, unlooked for, open the door and hurry in.

Líneik was most alarmed of the two, and was going to rush into her tree, when the prince caught her by her robe, and holding her at his side, said: "I have long suspected a trick in this game; tell me your name."

Líneik told him truly, as also of what family she was.

Then the prince looked to Laufey in great anger, and said she deserved to be tortured to death with the dreadest of tortures for her slyness and falsehoods. Laufey knelt at the prince's feet, and, asking his pardon, said: "I have used no other craft towards you, prince, than conceal from you the maker of the clothes, and that I did, because Líneik bade me strictly to do so. And remember that I have never pretended to be Líneik, the king's daughter; the only one who has deceived you is the queen, who is called my mother."

As they were thus talking, Sigurdr, the king's son, stepped out from his tree, and there was a meeting of great joy between them all. And, in short, the Prince of Greece wooed Líneik, who said she would be betrothed to none, until her step-mother was got rid of.

Now Laufey had a tale to tell about Queen Blávör: She was the foulest of trolls, and had governed the island where she was when the minister came and found her; she had lived in a cave on the island, in company with a lot of other hideous trolls. "But I am," said Laufey, "a king's daughter, from this neighbourhood. Blávör stole me away and said she would kill me, if I did not confess all her words to be true, and I chose to promise her this, instead of losing my life. She called me her daughter, in order to make it look more likely that she was a queen. Blávör has caused the death of your father, Sigurdr and Líneik! it was she, too, who caused the great loss of his courtiers, for she used, as trolls' wont is, to seize them during the night and eat them. And her plan is to destroy every man in your country, and then to people it with her trollish pack."

Now the two princes gathered, in all haste, people together, and fitted out an expedition.

Nothing is told of their journey, till they came to the town over which Blávör now held sway. They appeared quite unlooked for, and met with but few of the townspeople, as Blávör had killed the greatest part of them, and others had fled away from her trollish rule.

Blávör had little means of defence, and was, therefore, soon made prisoner. Then her face took a grim and threatening look, but they stoned her to death, and afterwards gave her body to the flames.

After this they returned home to Greece, and a grand wedding-feast was held, and many nobles and great folk were bidden.

At this feast, Sigurdr wooed the Greek king's daughter, who at once agreed to the union, and thus two wedding-feasts were held at one time.

After the feasts, the guests were sped on their ways with good gifts and farewells. Sigurdr now took the crown of his bride's kingdom, and the prince of Greece, that of Líneik's inheritance; and all rejoiced that the king's offspring was again in power where Blávör had disturbed the succession. Laufey went with Líneik, and married into a princely family, and was, afterwards, her father's heiress, he having meanwhile died of sorrow for her loss.

All these kings governed ever afterwards their realms, in peace and good luck: and so end we our tale.

Honour & Adventure

FROM THE TIMES of the earliest settlement, Iceland has abounded with tales of elves, goblins, trolls and supernatural beings of every description, as will be at once acknowledged by anyone who is conversant with the sagas. These tales are closely coherent with, and have risen, and grown in the company of, the historical sagas.

When times are dark and superstition gloomy, we find tales of goblins and witchcraft to be most prevalent. But on the dawning of brighter days, the quaint and elegant stories of elves become the objects of popular poetry. In this chapter all of these themes cross over; the stories here exploring honour that can only truly be understood in the context of history and tradition, and the adventure that inevitably ensues.

Hildur, Queen of the Elves

ONCE, IN A MOUNTAINOUS DISTRICT there lived a certain farmer, whose name and that of his farm have not been handed down to us; so we cannot tell them. He was unmarried, and had a housekeeper named Hildur, concerning whose family and descent he knew nothing whatever. She had all the indoor affairs of the farm under her charge, and managed them wondrous well. All the inmates of the house, the farmer himself to boot, were fond of her, as she was clean and thrifty in her habits, and kind and gentle in speech.

Everything about the place flourished exceedingly, but the farmer always found the greatest difficulty in hiring a herdsman; a very important matter, as the well-being of the farm depended not a little on the care taken of the sheep. This difficulty did not arise from any fault of the farmer's own, or from neglect on the part of the house-keeper to the comforts of the servants, but from the fact, that no herdsman who entered his service lived more than a year, each one being without fail found dead in his bed, on the morning of Christmas Day. No wonder, therefore, the farmer found herdsmen scarce.

In those times it was the custom of the country to spend the night of Christmas Eve at church, and this occasion for service was looked upon as a very solemn one.

But so far was this farm from the church, that the herdsmen, who did not return from their flocks till late in the evening, were unable to go to it on that night until long after the usual time; and as for Hildur, she always remained behind to take care of the house, and always had so much to do in the way of cleaning the rooms and dealing out the rations for the servants, that the family used to come home from church and go to bed long before she had finished her work, and was able to go to bed herself.

The more the reports of the death of herdsman after herdsman, on the night of Christmas Eve, were spread abroad, the greater became the difficulty the farmer found in hiring one, although it was never supposed for an instant that violence was used towards the men, as no mark had ever been found on their bodies; and as, moreover, there was no one to suspect. At length the farmer declared that his conscience would no longer let him thus hire men only in order that they might die, so he determined in future to let luck take care of his sheep, or the sheep take care of themselves.

Not long after he had made this determination, a bold and hardy-looking man came to him and made him a proffer of his services. The farmer said:

"My good friend, I am not in so great need of your services as to hire you."

Then the man asked him, "Have you, then, taken a herdsman for this winter?"

The farmer said, "No; for I suppose you know what a terrible fate has hitherto befallen everyone I have hired."

"I have heard of it," said the other, "but the fear of it shall neither trouble me nor prevent my keeping your sheep this winter for you, if you will but make up your mind to take me."

But the farmer would not hear of it at first; "For," said he, "it is a pity, indeed, that so fine a fellow as you should lose your chance of life. Begone, if you are wise, and get work elsewhere."

Yet still the man declared, again and again, that he cared not a whit for the terrors of Christmas Eve, and still urged the farmer to hire him.

At length the farmer consented, in answer to the man's urgent prayer, to take him as herdsman; and very well they agreed together. For everyone, both high and low, liked the man, as he was honest and open, zealous in everything he laid his hands to, and willing to do anyone a good turn, if need were.

On Christmas Eve, towards nightfall, the farmer and all his family went (as has been before declared to be the custom) to church, except Hildur, who remained behind to look after household matters, and the herdsman, who could not leave his sheep in time. Late in the evening, the latter as usual returned home, and after having eaten his supper, went to bed. As soon as he was well between the sheets, the remembrance struck him of what had befallen all the former herdsmen in his position on the same evening, and he thought it would be the best plan for him to lie awake and thus to be ready for any accident, though he was mighty little troubled with fear. Quite late at night, he heard the farmer and his family return from church, enter the house, and having taken supper, go to bed. Still, nothing happened, except that whenever he closed his eyes for a moment, a strange and deadly faintness stole over him, which only acted as one reason the more for his doing his best to keep awake.

Shortly after he had become aware of these feelings, he heard someone creep stealthily up to the side of his bed, and looking through the gloom at the figure, fancied he recognized Hildur the housekeeper. So he feigned to be fast asleep, and felt her place something in his mouth, which he knew instantly to be the bit of a magic bridle, but yet allowed her to fix it on him, without moving. When she had fastened the bridle, she dragged him from his bed with it, and out of the farmhouse, without his being either able or willing to make the least resistance. Then mounting on his back, she made him rise from the ground as if on wings, and rode him through the air, till they arrived at a huge and awful precipice, which yawned, like a great well, down into the earth.

She dismounted at a large stone, and fastening the reins to it, leaped into the precipice. But the herdsman, objecting strongly to being tied to this stone all night, and thinking to himself that it would be no bad thing to know what became of the woman, tried to escape, bridle and all, from the stone. This he found, however, to be impossible, for as long as the bit was in his mouth, he was quite powerless to get away. So he managed, after a short struggle, to get the bridle off his head, and having so done, leapt into the precipice, down which he had seen Hildur disappear. After sinking for a long, long time, he caught a glimpse of Hildur beneath him, and at last they came to some beautiful green meadows.

From all this, the man guessed that Hildur was by no means a common mortal, as she had before made believe to be, and feared if he were to follow her along these green fields, and she turn round and catch sight of him, he might, not unlikely, pay for his curiosity with his life. So he took a magic stone which he always carried about him, the nature of which was to make him invisible when he held it in his palm, and placing it in the hollow of his hand, ran after her with all his strength.

When they had gone some way along the meadows, a splendid palace rose before them, with the way to which Hildur seemed perfectly well acquainted. At her approach a great crowd of people came forth from the doors, and saluted Hildur with respect and joy. Foremost of these walked a man of kingly and noble aspect, whose salutation seemed to be that of a lover or a husband: all the rest bowed to her as if she were their queen. This man was accompanied by two children, who ran up to Hildur, calling her mother, and embraced her. After the people had welcomed their queen, they all returned to the palace, where they dressed her in royal robes, and loaded her hands with costly rings and bracelets.

The herdsman followed the crowd, and posted himself where he would be least in the way of the company, but where he could catch sight easily of all that passed, and lose nothing. So gorgeous and dazzling were the hangings of the hall, and the silver and golden vessels on the table, that he thought he had never, in all his life before, seen the like; not to mention the wonderful dishes and wines which seemed plentiful there, and which, only by the look of them, filled his mouth with water, while he would much rather have filled it with something else.

After he had waited a little time, Hildur appeared in the hall, and all the assembled guests were begged to take their seats, while Hildur sat on her throne beside the king; after which all the people of the court ranged themselves on each side of the royal couple, and the feast commenced.

When it was concluded, the various guests amused themselves, some by dancing, some by singing, others by drinking and revel; but the king and queen talked together, and seemed to the herdsman to be very sad.

While they were thus conversing, three children, younger than those the man had seen before, ran in, and clung round the neck of their mother. Hildur received them with all a mother's love, and, as the youngest was restless, put it on the ground and gave it one of her rings to play with.

After the little one had played a while with the ring he lost it, and it rolled along the floor towards the herdsman, who, being invisible, picked it up without being perceived, and put it carefully into his pocket. Of course all search for it by the guests was in vain.

When the night was far advanced, Hildur made preparations for departure, at which all the people assembled showed great sorrow, and begged her to remain longer.

The herdsman had observed, that in one corner of the hall sat an old and ugly woman, who had neither received the queen with joy nor pressed her to stay longer.

As soon as the king perceived that Hildur addressed herself to her journey, and that neither his entreaties nor those of the assembly could induce her to stay, he went up to the old woman, and said to her:

"Mother, rid us now of thy curse; cause no longer my queen to live apart and afar from me. Surely her short and rare visits are more pain to me than joy."

The old woman answered him with a wrathful face.

"Never will I depart from what I have said. My words shall hold true in all their force, and on no condition will I abolish my curse."

On this the king turned from her, and going up to his wife, entreated her in the fondest and most loving terms not to depart from him.

The queen answered, "The infernal power of thy mother's curse forces me to go, and perchance this may be the last time that I shall see thee. For lying, as I do, under this horrible ban, it is not possible that my constant murders can remain much longer secret, and then I must suffer the full penalty of crimes which I have committed against my will."

While she was thus speaking the herdsman sped from the palace and across the fields to the precipice, up which he mounted as rapidly as he had come down, thanks to the magic stone.

When he arrived at the rock he put the stone into his pocket, and the bridle over his head again, and awaited the coming of the elf-queen. He had not long to wait, for very soon afterwards Hildur came up through the abyss, and mounted on his back, and off they flew again to the farmhouse, where Hildur, taking the bridle from his head, placed him again in his bed, and retired to her own. The herdsman, who by this time was well tired out, now considered it safe to go to sleep, which he did, so soundly as not to wake till quite late on Christmas morning.

Karly that same day the farmer rose, agitated and filled with the fear that, instead of passing Christmas in joy, he should assuredly, as he so often had before, find his herdsman dead, and pass it in sorrow and mourning. So he and all the rest of the family went to the bedside of the herdsman.

When the farmer had looked at him and found him breathing; he praised God aloud for his mercy in preserving the man from death.

Not long afterwards the man himself awoke and got up.

Wondering at his strange preservation the farmer asked him how he had passed the night, and whether he had seen or heard anything.

The man replied, "No; but I have had a very curious dream."

"What was it?" asked the farmer.

Upon which the man related everything that had passed in the night, circumstance for circumstance, and word for word, as well as he could remember. When he had finished his story everyone was silent for wonder, except Hildur, who went up to him and said:

"I declare you to be a liar in all that you have said, unless you can prove it by sure evidence."

Not in the least abashed, the herdsman took from his pocket the ring which he had picked up on the floor of the hall in Elf-land, and showing it to her said:

"Though my dream needs no proof, yet here is one you will not doubtless deem other than a sure one; for is not this your gold-ring, Queen Hildur?"

Hildur answered, "It is, no doubt, my ring. Happy man! May you prosper in all you undertake, for you have released me from the awful yoke which my mother-in-law laid, in her wrath, upon me, and from the curse of a yearly murder."

And then Hildur told them the story of her life as follows:

"I was born of an obscure family among the elves. Our king fell in love with me and married me, in spite of the strong disapproval of his mother. She swore eternal hatred to me in her anger against her son, and said to him, 'Short shall be your joy with this fair wife of yours, for you shall see her but once a year, and that only at the expense of a murder. This is my curse upon her, and it shall be carried out to the letter. She shall go and serve in the upper world, this queen, and every Christmas Eve shall ride a man, one of her fellow-servants, with this magic bridle, to the confines of Elf-land, where she shall pass a few hours with you, and then ride him back again till his very heart breaks with toil, and his very life leaves him. Let her thus enjoy her queenship.'

"And this horrible fate was to cling to me until I should either have these murders brought home to me, and be condemned to death, or should meet with a gallant man, like this herdsman, who should have nerve and courage to follow me down into Elf-land, and be able to prove afterwards that he had been there with me, and seen the customs of my people. And now I must confess that all the former herdsmen were slain by me, but no penalty shall touch me for their murders, as I committed them against my will. And as for you, O courageous man, who have dared, the first of human beings, to explore the realms of Elf-land, and have freed me from the yoke of this awful curse, I will reward you in times to come, but not now.

"A deep longing for my home and my loved ones impels me hence. Farewell!"

With these words Hildur vanished from the sight of the astonished people, and was never seen again.

But our friend the herdsman, leaving the service of the farmer, built a farm for himself, and prospered, and became one of the chief men in the country, and always ascribed, with grateful thanks, his prosperity to Hildur, Queen of the Elves.

Katla's Dream

A CERTAIN CHIEF named Már, lived, long ago, at Reykhólar. His wife, who was of noble family, was called Katla. Once, as was his custom, Már had ridden to the Diet, leaving his wife at home.

One morning, during his absence, Katla, feeling tired and heavy, went to bed, not very long after she had risen from it, and fell into a deep sleep. At noon her attendants went to her to call her, but, try as they would, could not wake her; so, fearing that she was dead, they called her foster-father, who lived in the house, and told him of her state. He went to the side of her bed, and himself endeavoured to rouse her, but quite in vain. Then, looking attentively at her, he said, "She is not dead: the flame of life is still flickering in her bosom, but I am no more able to wake her than you were." And, with these words, he sat down beside her couch, and kept close watch over her for four whole days and nights.

On the fifth day Katla awoke, and seemed to be overcome with sorrow; but no one dared to ask her what was the cause of it.

Soon after this her husband came back home from the Diet; but his wife was no longer the same that he had left behind him. She was changed. She neither went to meet him, as she was wont to do, nor when he came did she say "Welcome" to him, nor salute him with her usual love, nor show joy to see him safe.

Wondering and grieved at her strange manner, he asked her attendants apart what had befallen her, and why she behaved thus; but they could only tell him that she had slept unceasingly for four days and four nights, and on awaking had shown this sorrow, without ever telling anybody the reason of it, or what ailed her. On hearing this, Már took Katla herself apart, and urged her to tell him what ailed her – whether aught had befallen her in her long sleep, assuring her that she would lighten her load of sorrow in thus giving him the half of it. At last, yielding to her husband's prayers, she spoke as follows: "As you know, my husband, I fell into a deep sleep early one morning while you were away. I had not slept long, when there came to my bedside a beautiful lady, richly dressed, who spoke sweetly to me, and telling me that she lived at the farm Thverá, not far hence, begged me to go back with her some part of the way thither. As soon as I rose to comply with her wish, she placed her gloves in my bed, saying, 'These shall take your place while you are away. Then we went out, and came soon to a large lake, as clear and as smooth as glass, upon which, near the shore, a gaily-painted boat was moored. Here I would part from the lady, and wished her God-speed; but she, thanking me for having come so far with her, held out her hand, as if to bid me farewell, crying, 'Will you not say farewell to Alvör?'

"No sooner had I stretched forth mine in return, than she grasped it tightly, and leaping from the shore into the skiff with me, rowed it swiftly to a small island which stood in the midst of the lake. Now, indeed, I felt only too well that she had all power over me, and that I was unable to resist her. She saw that I was filled with dread, and tried to calm my fears, showing me every kindness and courtesy, and assuring me that it was Fate alone which had compelled her to treat me thus. 'I will,' she said, 'soon take you safely home again.'

"When we had come to the island, I saw that there stood upon it a castle, more beautiful than anything I had ever seen or heard of before. 'This is mine,' said Alvör; and leading me into it by the hand, she took me to her own room, where many ladies were sitting. There she made me enter a bath of sweet water, and when I had bathed, she took me to a beautiful bed which stood in the room, covered with curtains of the richest stuff, and filled with soft down. In this I fell asleep after I had drunk a cup of some rare wine which was handed me. When I awoke, I found on a couch near me a mantle worked richly in gold, which the lady who sat by my side bade me put on, together with an embroidered dress which she gave me. When I was dressed, she threw also over me her own mantle, which was daintily wrought in gold and lined with fur. Besides all this, she gave me five rings of red gold, a golden band for my hair, and a costly belt, begging me to keep them all as gifts. After I had thus attired myself, she bade me follow her to the dining hall, and we went there with her, eight ladies in all.

"All the walls of the room were hung with cloth of woven gold, and the tables were crowded with silver vessels and flagons, and with inlaid gold horns; and round the table sat many handsome men, splendidly attired. At the high table stood a throne, and near this I saw a man, dressed in rich silk, lying asleep on a couch. Alvör went up to him and woke him, and I heard that she called him Kári.

"He started up from his slumber, and said to her, 'Why have you broken my rest? Have you aught of good tidings to tell me? or, perchance, have you brought Katla hither?'

"As soon as he saw that I was in the hall, he came to me, and taking me by the hand, led me to the throne, where he made me sit, and sat beside me. Then the Lady Alvör pointed to us, and cried out to the guests, 'See! the bride and bridegroom!' Whereupon they shouted, as with one voice, and drank and made merry till nightfall. And through all this din of revel, Alvör told me that for that night I was to share the couch of Kári; but I, full wroth, withdrawing myself from her side, said:

"'Never will I do this thing! Far too dearly do I love my husband to share the love of any other.'

"The lady answered, 'If you say nay, bale and bann will cling to you for ever: be wise, therefore, and consent.'

"Wretched that I was, I knew not what to do, or whither to turn myself, for neither comfort nor aid was near, and I was as a lamb in the midst of a herd of wolves. They led me to the couch in which I had slept before, and then Kári came to me, and offered me all he had, if I would only love him. I told him that his love was hopeless, but he would not hear me. Then he brought me a horn of wine; and after he had tasted it himself first, made me drink of it, saying:

"'Rather would I struggle with Helja than see sorrow in your eyes. Be comforted; you shall soon return to your home.'

"With these words he lay beside me; and whether it were the force of his entreaties, or the beauty of his presence, or the weight of the wine upon my soul, I cannot tell, but I no longer opposed his love, though the while my heart was filled with grief.

"And so, in sorrow passed two days and nights; nor could all the kindness of the attendants, and of all around me, comfort me. At last, Kári said to me, 'Call the son whom you shall bear to me by my name, and give him from his father, whom he shall never see, this belt of wrought gold, and this knife with the haft of cunning workmanship, and let them be heirlooms in his family.' And he bade me place the belt and knife, together with the embroidered garments and costly ornaments which I had worn while with him, in a sack, and take them home with me.

"'Show them,' he said, 'to your husband Már, and tell him the whole truth, though it be a grief and woe to your heart to do so; for it is but just, and your duty. Let him aid you in building a farm at Thverá, where you shall see two small hillocks, which shall be your money mounds. In that place you shall found a great and noble family. Now I must leave you, and you will never see me again, for,' said he sadly, 'the hours of my life are numbered.'

"When he had finished speaking, Alvör the lady took my hand and led me out; and as I left the hall I heard a loud and echoing sound, and turning my head to see whence it came, behold Kári lay dead, for his heartstrings had broken with exceeding love and sorrow. So the lady rowed me again in the boat across the lake and brought me home, and took the gloves out of my bed.

"As she left me she said, 'May it fare well with you, though you have caused but sorrow to me in breaking my son's heart for love and anguish. Enjoy all the wealth you have, and be happy.' So saying, she was no more with me.

"This is the end of my dream. Therefore, my husband, as you are a just and true man, weigh my fault against its causes, and forgive me. Truly my love for you has not one whit departed."

So she showed Már all the beautiful and costly things that she had brought with her from Alvör's castle.

In the summer she gave birth to a son, a lovely child, and exceeding all other children in mind and form, whom she called, as she had promised his father, Kári. But she never loved the boy with a true mother's love; though on the other hand Már doted upon him as if he had been his own son. Soon after, they built a new farm at Thverá, where they found the two money mounds, as Kári had promised, and, unestranged by Katla's dream, dwelt there happy and prosperous to a ripe old age.

Gold-brow

LONG AGO a certain woman named Audur the wealthy lived at a farm called Hvammur, in the west country. The farm stood on the bank of a river, on the opposite side of which were rich cornfields. But Audur had forbidden any seed to be sown on a particular spot where the land happened to be best, nor did she

allow her servants to graze any cattle there, and if by chance any cows had been there, she forbade them to be milked the next day.

Once it happened that when Audur was very old, a young and handsome woman came to Hvammur, who declared her name to be Gold-brow, but nobody knew either whence she came or who she was. The only person she could find to speak to was the superintendent, but Audur herself she did not see. The woman asked him why a particular spot in the field was not sown with corn, nor grazed, and the superintendent answered that Audur had forbidden it to be so. At this Gold-brow laughed heartily, and asked him to sell her the ground.

"For," she said, "I will give more for a single hillock of that land than, for all the great farm of Hvammur. I have a certain foreboding that on that ground a custom will be introduced, and that sort of house built, of which I have the greatest dread and dislike. Sell me, therefore, the spot of ground without asking Audur about it."

With these words she took out a large purse filled with coin.

When the manager saw the glitter of her gold he said to himself, "Audur is old and has but little to do with the management," and forthwith sold the land to Gold-brow.

But when Audur came to know what had been done, she was exceedingly wroth, and sent her manager away, saying to him, "You will never fatten on this gold. I suspect the woman who paid it to you to be the most evil of witches, and knew long ago what would happen to that ground... No harm, however, can come home to Hvammur, for a good spirit watches over it." Then the steward thought that he would pacify the old lady by giving her some of the contents of the purse he had just received. So he undid the strings, and lo! instead of gold out poured from it a heap of worms which smelt so horrible that the man forthwith went mad and died. After this the man and his purse were buried in a little hollow of that spot of ground which Gold-brow had purchased, which is called to this day "worm hollow."

Audur did not endeavour to reclaim from Gold-brow the ground which she had bought, but destroyed all the cornfields round it from the sea to a rocky river-gulf in one direction, and from the mountain to the river in the other. She also set up three crosses where the gulf joined the mountain (whence its name Cross-gulf), and said, "During my life Gold-brow shall never cross this boundary." And this came true, for during the life of Audur, Gold-brow neither brought her sheep and cattle to graze anywhere near the crops nor approached them herself. Now Gold-brow built on her piece of ground a farm and a large temple, where she made great offerings, and performed all sorts of witchcraft. It is told as a curious thing, that whenever she was using her incantations, and happened to look either towards Hvammur, or the crosses by the mountains, all her spells went wrong, which she declared was because at each of these points she always saw a light, whose rays were so dazzling as to make her forget at once all her magic words and signs.

Audur, who was a Christian, died shortly after all this and was buried in some ground which she had caused, in her lifetime, to be consecrated, by the sea, not far from the land belonging to Gold-brow, who found herself now in a sort of prison, what with the sacred remains of Audur on one side and the crosses on the other. So she sold her piece of ground to the heathen successor of Audur, at Hvammur, and purchased another in a dark and dismal valley, over which the sun seldom shone in summer and never in winter, and in the darkest and gloomiest recess intended to take up her abode. But when it came to passing out of her old property to go to her new one, by the road which led near the crosses, she found herself nearly powerless, and going into her temple was compelled to use the strongest charms to strengthen herself; and then ordering her servants to bind her eyes so that she should not see, she took from the temple a large chest of gold, on to which she had fastened a ring from the temple door, mounted her horse, holding the chest in front of her, and caused the horse to be led quickly along the path. She particularly commanded her servants to avoid looking toward the crosses. But when they came to the Cross-gulf, one of them looked in the forbidden direction, and, being frightened, caused the horse to stumble, so that the chest of gold burst away from its ring and fell to the ground. Gold-brow being astonished at this, tore the bandage from her eyes, and looked to see what had become of it, but in so doing happened to see the crosses not far off. At this she shrieked aloud, and declaring that their brightness was greater than she could bear, bade her servants hurry on as quickly as possible, and bring the chest after her. Then looking at her hand she saw the ring from which the box had fallen, and flung it away in a rage, saying, "All my life will I repent of having brought you with me. Different, indeed, to the purpose for which I intended you, and most hateful to me will be the use to which you will be put."

As soon as she had passed the gulf, a fierce and burning pain seized her eyes, so that before she had reached her new abode she was perfectly blind. In this gloomy valley she lived no long time, suffering perpetual tortures till she died.

On her death-bed, she told her servants to bury her in a deep and precipitous gulf, where neither was the sun ever seen, nor church-bells ever heard. In the gulf she pointed out, there was a vast waterfall, and under the waterfall a cave, and the water at the foot of the fall was very deep and its eddying awful. To this cave Gold-brow was carried, and in it buried, with her head upon the chest of gold. Long afterwards her ghost haunted all the mountains round, so that neither man nor beast was safe after twilight, and much mischief was done.

At this time a farmer lived at Hvammur, named Skeggi, who was a heathen, and addicted to witchcraft. This man suffered much from the persecutions of the goblin Gold-brow, who killed his herdsmen and his sheep for him one after the other. Skeggi became more wroth with her every day, and in proportion to his anger increased his desire to become possessed of her golden treasures under the waterfall, for he considered that her gold would be of infinitely more use to a living man than to a dead witch. With this idea in his head, he one day started off for the waterfall; but so long was the way that it was evening before he arrived there. He commanded his two servants whom he had brought with him, to let him down into the gulf with a rope. They did so, and he disappeared into the cave under the waterfall. The two men who held the end of the rope, heard, after a little while, the sound of heavy blows and loud shrieks beneath the water, and it was plain that some fearful struggle was going on there. At last, they became so horrified as to be on the point of taking flight, when Skeggi gave them the sign to pull up the rope. When they did so they found the chest full of gold fastened to the end of it. They had scarcely pulled it up to the edge of the gulf before they saw the whole valley filled with a strange and spectral fire, whose flames flared higher than the very mountains, and letting go of the rope in their fright, took to their heels, while the chest fell down again into the abyss. Skeggi came home some time afterwards very weary, and covered with bruises and blood, but bringing on one of his arms, a kettle full of gold which he had managed to take out of the chest of Gold-brow, and climb with up the rope. But though he had fought hard with the ghost of the troll, he had been unable to subdue her, and she became now more dangerous than ever, killing his sheep and his herdsmen, till at last he could get no servants at all. Skeggi from this time became a changed man, and was so affected by the constant loss of his servants, that he fell ill and took, for a long while, to his bed.

At last one day, after his recovery, being without any herdsman, he went out himself as if to watch the flocks. But he did not return either that night or the next. On the third day, however, he came back, more dead than alive, bearing on his back Gold-brow's treasure-chest.

He said, "You will not see much more either of the troll or of me."

And after these words took to his bed, whence he never rose again.

Before he died, he ordered that the gold contained in the kettle should be expended in timber for building a church at Hvammur.

"For," he continued, "the first time I went to the waterfall and struggled with the ghost of Gold-brow, I called upon Thor to aid me, but he deceived me and played me false. The last time I fought with her, in my despair and anguish I called upon Christ the God of the Christians to aid me, promising to build a church to him. Suddenly a bright beam of light struck full into the eyes of the phantom-troll, and she became a stone in the midst of the gulf."

But in spite of all this, Skeggi died a heathen, and refused to be buried in the consecrated ground of the church which he had commanded to be built. So they buried him in the open country, and under his head placed the chest of Gold-brow. Whether he slept more calmly upon this pillow than the troll had done, this tale saith not.

The Story of Jón Asmundsson

IN THE DISTRICT of Boyarfjördur, once lived a poor married couple. The man's name was Asmundur. They had many children, whose names have not been handed down to us, except that of the eldest, and he was called Jón. At this time, so severe a season was prevailing, that Asmundur was obliged to leave his home and his children, who were scattered about the country and brought up, one here and one there, at the houses of various farmers.

Now there lived at Reykjavík a priest, named Christján, and he it was that took Jón into his house, and brought him up as his own son. Jón grew into a fine and handsome lad, and was stronger than any of his fellows. But he was always very quiet, and seldom opened his mouth, unless first spoken to. He was, moreover, hardworking and willing, and became before long a great favourite, not only with the priest himself, but with every member of the household.

One summer, according to yearly custom, a trading vessel arrived at Reykjavík. Its owner was a foreign merchant, who carried on a large business at this season; but of his name no mention is made. Among other people with whom he had dealings was Christján, the priest. One day while Christján was on board the ship, it fell out that they came to talk about strong men. The merchant, being himself well-built and powerful, went up to where four barrels of rye lay bound together, and, seizing them by the rope which was round them, lifted them all together as high as his knee. When he had put them down again, he said, "There! Let anyone prove himself my match in lifting, and I will give him three half-pounds of gold by weight."

When the priest returned home, he told his foster-son what he had seen, and how the merchant had promised three half-pounds of gold by weight to any man that should match him in lifting, and encouraged the boy to make the trial. To this Jón agreed without wasting many words. So they went together to the ship, and Christján told the captain that the lad would like to try his strength. The merchant pointed out the rye barrels to Jón, who, going up to them, lifted them on to his shoulder as if they were but a handful of feathers, and when he had walked with them to and fro upon the deck, put them down again in their place.

When he saw this, the merchant changed colour, but weighed out the three half-pounds of gold, and paid them over to Jón, begging him, as he took leave, to come and pay him one more visit on board the ship before he sailed away. This Jón promised to do.

One day, shortly before the time the merchant had fixed for sailing, the priest came to Jón, and reminded him of his promise to visit the ship. Accordingly Jón went, and Christján with him, and the merchant received them with all due honour, begging Jón to come with him into the cabin for a few words he wished to say in his ear.

But when he saw that the priest was going to make one of their party, he turned round to him, and said, "Friend, you can stay up here a while; we have no need of you."

Christján, however, was not to be put off, but assuring the merchant that he would not disturb them, or be in their way, followed them down into the cabin.

Then the merchant said to Jón, "You have not yet done with me; for next year I shall bring with me a boy for you to wrestle with, and if you get the better of him in that game, I will weigh you out five pounds of gold."

Jón agreed to this, and when he and Christján had taken leave, the merchant sailed away.

For some time everything went on quietly, and the winter set in. One day the priest asked Jón whether he remembered the agreement he had made with the foreign merchant before his departure.

Jón answered, that it was so slight a matter that he had never yet given it a thought. But the priest said, "Indeed it is no such child's play as you think; for the boy that this merchant will bring for you to wrestle with, is none other than a fiendish and monstrous black man, and get the better of you he surely will, unless you employ craft against him. I will find out speedily some means for gaining you the victory, for 'ere three weeks of the summer be over the merchant-ship will come into harbour."

Jón nodded, but said nothing, and seemed in no way troubled by the news; nor did he give himself the least pains about it till the time came.

Before three weeks of the summer were over, as Christján had foretold, a vessel was seen making for the harbour of Reykjavík from the open ocean. It was no sooner in sight than the priest went to Jón, and, warning him of what he now might expect, dressed him in a peasant's frock of black wool, and clasped a belt round his waist; when he had thus equipped him, he gave him a little, bright, sharp-edged dagger, which he bade him keep ready to his hand, hidden in the sleeve of the woollen frock. He further told Jón, not to attempt to resist the negro's attacks, as the latter would fling him easily over his shoulder.

"I," said he, "will take good care that you fall on your feet. But, after a while, challenge the negro to take off his shaggy mantle, and do you make ready in your hand the dagger, that when he rushes upon you a second time you may thrust it into his chest."

The anchor was scarcely dropped before a boat sped from the vessel, and set on shore a black man of giant's build, dressed in a shaggy mantle, who, directly he saw the priest and the lad standing close to the sea, rushed at Jón, and, seizing him in his arms, flung him like a pebble over his head, high into the air. But the boy fell on his feet, and forthwith challenged the black to fight without his woolly mantle, that they might the more easily try their skill in wrestling. To this the negro consented; but while he was doffing his cloak, Jón made ready in his right hand the sharp-edged dagger which thc priest had given him, and when the other ran blindly upon him, thrust it into his breast once and again. But yet, they wrestled together for a while, and assuredly even now Jón would have got the worst of it, were it not that his black woollen frock served him as armour against the heavy blows of the negro.

At last the fight came to an end, and Jón slew his enemy.

Then he and Christján went on board the vessel, where they found the merchant, and saluted him.

"Well," said the latter, "and how went the fight?"

The priest answered, "If you will look towards the shore, you will see the negro lying dead close to the waves. That is how the fight went."

Then the merchant was exceeding wroth, and said, "Aha! You have not acted like brave and true-hearted men. This lad has but fought by craft and with steel."

"But," replied the priest, "however that may be, he has deserved fairly the prize; for, whereas you promised to bring a lad to wrestle with him, you have brought an evil-souled, giant-built black."

To this the merchant had no answer ready, so, as needs must be, paid into Jón's hand the five pounds of weighed-out gold, which he had promised to the winner in the wrestling. Then, smoothing his angry brows, he begged Jón to come and see him once more before the ship sailed, which would be in the latter end of the summer.

Everything went on as usual till a short time before the merchant had determined to sail from Reykjavík, and then the priest reminded Jón of his promise to visit the merchant before his departure, offering at the same time to accompany him, and be present during the interview. They went, therefore, to the vessel and greeted the merchant, who received them with great politeness, but, as before, begged Jón to go a little aside with him, as he had something particular to tell him. Christján, however, followed close upon their heels, and the merchant, seeing him, said, "You need not trouble yourself to come so close; what we speak about has nought to do with you."

But the priest was not to be put off so, and saying, "I will neither leave the side of my foster-son, nor will I interrupt your converse," kept still close to them.

Then the merchant said to Jón, "Next summer I will bring with me a little whelp against which you shall try your strength, and if you get the best of the fight, I will weigh out into your hand seven-and-a-half pounds of good gold."

Upon this they parted; Jón and Christján returning on shore, and the merchant sailing away.

Now the summer passed away, and a great part of the winter passed away without Jón making any preparations for, or saying a word about, the next visit of the merchant.

One day the priest asked him whether or no he remembered the merchant's words and promise.

"Not I," replied Jón.

"But," said the priest, "this visit of his will bring almost as much difficulty as his last one. The whelp he promised to match against you, ere half a month of the summer be past, is nothing less than a large and cruel deer-hound, and to get the best of the fight we must devise some wile, for your strength will be as nothing."

But Jón only answered, "Devise, then, for me," and there he let the matter rest, occupying himself no further about it.

Ere half a month of the summer was over, a vessel appeared in sight, sailing from the open sea towards Reykjavík.

Then the priest went to Jón and said, "The merchant will now soon be in harbour, and you must be ready for him." And he made him put on again the black woollen frock which he had now woven through and through with links of iron. He gave him, at the same time, a spear, with moveable barbs, which would spread out, and tear the flesh into which they had been thrust, and, placing on the point of this a piece of meat, bade Jón watch his chance and thrust it with all his strength down the dog's throat.

When he had thus equipped him he led him down to the shore.

Scarcely was the anchor dropped, when a boat sped from the vessel, and placed upon the beach a large and evil-eyed deer-hound, who, directly he saw Jón advancing towards him, rushed at him with mad fury, and would have torn him to pieces on the spot had not the frock, with its links of mail, saved Jón from his teeth. Over and over again the brute rushed upon him, each time with greater rage and strength. But Jón, who escaped unscathed from each attack, watched his chance, and keeping the piece of meat always before the dog till the beast opened its mouth to snap at it, thrust it with all his force down its throat, till, in a short while, it lay dead at his feet.

Then they went out to the ship and saluted the merchant, who received and returned their greeting surlily enough. But feign and conceal as he would, he could not hide from them the wrathful red blood that filled his cheek and brow and swelled his lip.

"We have come to claim the gold," said the priest; "my foster-son has fairly earned it."

"Fairly, forsooth!" replied the merchant. "He has fought like a brave man in truth, by wile and craft and steel. He has no claim to the gold, he has not kept to our agreement."

"Neither have you," the priest returned, "for you promised to bring a whelp, and have brought a wild beast to match it against this lad." So the merchant, who could not deny this, put the smoothest face he could upon the matter and weighed into Jón's hand the gold. Just before Jón and the priest left the ship, the merchant begged the former to come once more to see him before he weighed anchor and sailed away at the summer's end. Jón promised to come.

Now the time came round at which the merchant had fixed to sail, and Christján reminded Jón of his promise to go once more and visit him, saying, at the same time, that he himself would take good care to be present at their meeting. Accordingly they went on board the ship, whose anchor was even now being weighed. Just as before, the merchant begged Jón to come down with him into the cabin, as he had something particular to say to him, and when he saw Christján following them, turned round to him with a fierce look and cried, "Stand back, and meddle not where nothing concerns you."

"I do not wish to meddle," said the priest, "but I will not leave my foster son." And as he seemed firm about this the merchant said no more; so they went all three down to the cabin.

Then the merchant took down from one of the shelves a book, out of which he pulled a leaf and waved it quickly before Jón's eyes, as if to prevent the priest from seeing its contents. But Christján caught a glance of some of the words written upon it, without the merchant's knowledge. Then he returned the leaf to the book and the book to its place, saying to Jón, "If you do not bring me next summer, when I come back here, the book from which this leaf was taken, I will brand you as a fool and a faint heart; but if you bring the book I will weigh you out fifteen full pounds of good gold."

With these words they parted, Jón and Christján going home, and the merchant putting at once to sea.

When one week of the summer was still left, the priest asked Jón whether he had yet given a thought to the task with which the merchant had charged him for the next year.

Jón answered that it had never entered his head.

Then the other asked him whether he had known the leaf that the merchant had shown him, but Jón said, "No."

"No wonder," answered Christján, "for it was none other than a leaf from the devil's manual, which the merchant has bidden you bring him, and this is surely no slight or easy matter. But I have a brother who is a priest in the worlds below, and who is the only man that can help you to procure this book. Make yourself ready, therefore, at once for the journey, for you must spend with him in the lower regions the whole winter, from the first day to the last."

So Jón addressed himself to his journey, and when he was all ready for starting, the priest gave him a letter to his brother down below, and a ball of thread which would run before him and guide him. When he wished him God-speed, he warned him most strictly never once to look back on the way, and never to utter a single word the whole winter through. The youth promised, saying, he thought this surely easy enough.

Bidding his friend and foster-father, Christján, farewell, he flung down on the ground the ball of thread, keeping one end in his hand, and it ran quickly along before him, he following and never looking back. After a while they came to a mountain which lay north of Reykjavík, and in which appeared a passage leading deep into the earth. Into this the ball ran. Soon it became so dark, and the passage so rough and difficult, that more than once Jón stopped, doubting whether to go any further or to turn back. But every time he paused the ball pulled so hard that he was encouraged to go on, and still followed it in spite of difficulties. Thus, for a long way, they went on, till all at once the place became light, and Jón saw lying before him a vast and charming green plain over which the ball still rolled till it came to a farm as big as a town, and stopped at the door of one of the houses, where Jón picked it up from the ground. At this door Jón knocked, and a girl came out, neatly and plainly dressed, and of modest mien, and, as Jón thought, the most winsome he had ever seen. Jón nodded to her, and gave her the letter, which she took without speaking, as well as the ball of thread, and went with them into the house, leaving Jón standing at the door. In a few minutes she came back, and with her another girl younger than herself, who looked hard at Jón, and turned back into the house. But the other took him by the hand and led him through some passages into a room, where stood one small table, one chair, a bench, and a bed.

In this room Jón lived for a long time, till he thought the winter must be far advanced. He saw no one but the young girl, who came every day into the room, brought him his meals, and made his bed, but never spoke to him, nor did he, the whole time, hear the sound of a human voice.

One day, however, there entered the room a tall and handsome man, dressed in a long black cassock. This was the brother of Christján, the priest in the infernal world. He bade Jón good-day in a sweet and courteous voice, but Jón merely nodded in reply.

Then the other asked him if he knew how long he had, by this time, remained in the worlds below.

But Jón was still silent, and only shook his head.

The priest then said to him, "You have done well to keep so long and so firmly silent. But you may speak now, as the winter is over, and this is the first day of summer. Your task is accomplished, for here is the book you came to seek. Take care of it, and give it safely into my brother's hands. You must start hence to-day, as the merchant will arrive before a week of the summer be fully past. The owner of this book will miss it just about the same time, and claim it first from the merchant's hands. Therefore bid my brother buy every scrap of the merchandise on board the ship, and beware to land it before he delivers the volume into the captain's hands. Be bearer, too, of my love to my brother. My daughter shall go with you to point out the way." And with these words he took leave of him.

Then the girl who had served Jón all the winter, came to him and led him from the house, and they walked on sadly, holding one another by the hand. What they talked about now that Jón's tongue was loosed, nobody knows. However, at last the girl stopped and said she could go no further, as it was now easy enough for him to find his own way home. And these were her last words, "Now we must part, though it go nigh to break our hearts for sorrow. We cannot live together, for neither can you dwell here below, nor I in the world above. But, in the course of some months, I shall bear you a child. If it be a boy, I will send it you when it is six years old; but if a girl, when it is twelve. I pray you, receive it well." She then gave him the ball of thread. And when she had embraced him, with many tears, left him.

He, sad at heart, flung down the ball, which rolled before him, leading him this time, not through dark and difficult caverns, but along such a smooth and smiling country, that Jón knew not when he had left the one world and entered the other. Towards the close of the first week in summer he arrived at Reykjavík and was received joyfully by Christján, to whom he gave the book, and his brother's love and message.

The very next day the merchant arrived in harbour, and he had no sooner dropped anchor than the priest hurried on board and saluted him, but their greetings were just about as warm and cordial as the north-east wind. These over, the priest told him that, as a harsh and severe season had just prevailed and provisions were scant all through the near country, he wished to buy the whole stock that lay on board, and land it at once. They soon came to an agreement, and in a few days all the merchandise was landed.

No sooner was the last bale on shore than Christján and Jón went on board the vessel. When they had saluted, the merchant immediately asked Jón how he had succeeded in fulfilling the task wherewith he had been charged.

"Pretty well," said Jón.

Then Christján gave the book to the merchant, in the name of Jón, and mightily astonished the man was when he saw that it was the right one, but paid out the gold at the priest's request without saying any more about it. This Jón took, and after they had bidden adieu to the merchant, he and Christján jumped into their own boat and rowed quickly to shore.

But they had no sooner stepped out on to the beach, than the sea became, all at once, rough and stormy, and when they looked towards the merchant's vessel, lo! It was no more to be seen. The devil had claimed his manual.

After this they returned to the priest's house, where no small wealth was now stored up, and Jón stayed there for another half-year. Always quiet and reserved, he was ten-fold more so since his return from the lower worlds. At the end of that time the priest, who had noted the youth's melancholy, taxed him with having fallen in love with one of the daughters of his brother, the priest in the subterranean world. But to this Jón made no reply. Then Christján went on to offer him one of his own daughters (he had three, whose names we know not), whichever he loved the best, as a wife, thinking that this would perhaps free him from the thrall of his sadness, Jón chose the youngest of the three, and the priest married them, and giving his daughter no mean marriage present, settled them in a neighbouring farm, which could boast of the best land for many a long mile round.

Here they lived for many years in unbroken love and great prosperity, and had not a few children, but never the whole time did Jón bate one jot of his sadness.

At the end of twelve years, it happened one day that, as all the household were assembled in the family-room, a knock was heard at the door. Jón sent one of his sons, a lad about six years old, to the door to see who was there. The child returned, saying that there stood outside a little girl of wonderful beauty, who had asked him sweetly to say in the house that she wished to speak to her father.

At these words, it was as if a ray of sunshine had passed across Jón's face. He rose from his seat and ran eagerly to the outer door. The little girl, directly she saw him, ran up to him, and throwing her arms round his neck, kissed him fondly, calling him her own dear father. Jón returned her embrace with the greatest joy and love. She told him that her mother, the daughter of the priest in the worlds below, had sent her to him, bearing her sweetest love. Jón took the child by the hand and led her in to his wife, to whom he told the whole story of her parentage, begging her at the same time, as she loved him, so to treat the little girl as one of her own. The woman, being of true heart, welcomed the child with open arms and became a fond mother to her, from that day forth. They called her Sigrídur, and she grew up among them, a sister to the other children, and was lovelier by far and by far more accomplished than any girl of her own age, round about for many a stretch of long miles.

At the end of three years, Sigrídur, whose beauty was in everybody's mouth, asked her father's leave to pay her mother a visit in the worlds below. Jón granted it willingly, telling her that, if she would, she might stay a whole year with her mother, and making her the bearer of his sweetest love.

The year over, Sigrídur came back and was welcomed with delight by her father and all the family. She told Jón that she brought him her mother's dying farewell, together with the message that he himself had but one month more to live. Far from being grieved by this news, Jón seemed glad, and for the whole month no one noticed any change in his conduct, except that his heart was lighter than heretofore.

At last Jón made a settlement of all he possessed, giving by far the greater part of his property to Sigrídur, and his personal wealth to his wife and other children, who were well off with it. And every one thus saw that he was most fond of his daughter from the lower regions; and what, all things considered, was the wonder? When Jón died, many felt deeply his loss and wept bitterly for him; for he had been a good man and a warm friend.

Some years afterwards Sigrídur married a young and hopeful peasant, and their farm throve till none in the district could compare with it. They lived happily and everybody looked up to them with respect and fondness. Of their many children the descendants are scattered widely through the south country.

The Wizards in the Westmann Islands

DURING THE TIME when that dread pest, yclept the Black Death, raged through Iceland, eighteen sorcerers banded together, and went out to the Westmann Islands, in order to escape, as long as possible, the scourge. When, after a while, by means of their magic arts, they discovered that the plague was abating its fury, they were curious to know how many people were left alive in the country.

So they agreed to send one of their company to land, that he might find how matters stood, and make his report to the others. They chose for this errand a man who was neither first nor last in the knowledge of their arts;

and when they put him ashore they told him that if he did not return to them by Christmas Day next, they would despatch a Sending to him who should kill him.

Far and wide wandered the man, north, south, and east, without finding a single living soul. All the dwellings stood wide open, and from floor to roof, even on threshold and on hill, lay the dead. At last, he came to a house which was shut up, and through his wonder at this half hoped to find there still some signs of human life. He knocked loudly at the door, which was instantly opened, and there came out a young and beautiful damsel, who, half-wild with joy to see again a living man, answered his salutation by falling on his neck, and embracing him; telling him at the same time with many tears that she had thought herself the only living creature in the whole land.

She begged him to stay with her some time, which he consented to do, and they went into the house and held a vast deal of talk together. She asked him whence he came, and what was the object of his journey; and he told her all about the company of wizards, their desire to know how many people were left alive in the land, and their strict command to him to be back in the Westmann Islands before next Christmas Day. But she begged for his company as long as he could possibly afford it her; and he, pitying her loneliness, agreed to stay with her some time. The girl told him, that within many and many a mile not one soul was left alive; for she had made a week's journey from home in all directions, hoping to find someone still living, but quite in vain.

So the man abode there, and Christmas Day drew nearer and nearer, until, at last, he felt bound to tell the girl that he must leave her now, or suffer the punishment of death for his disobedience to the commands of the other sorcerers. But the girl would not hear of his going so soon, and coaxed him to stay yet a little longer, saying, that surely his companions were not such unmerciful and heartless folks as to kill him for so slight a fault as staying with a poor lonely woman. By these words she quite overcame his determination to leave her till Christmas Eve came round. Then, said he, he truly must leave her as he valued his life. At first she tried to persuade him to stay with her by caresses and prayers; but finding him deaf to them, she changed her tone, and said, "Well, my good man, since you will go, go! And reach the Westmann Islands by Christmas Day if you can. I wish you luck in your journey, and somewhat more than common speed!" Then the man suddenly bethought himself that more than common speed must indeed be his, if he would make the journey in time; and so, knowing that it was totally useless for him to start now for the Westmann Islands, resolved to stay and await his death where he was. He passed the night in a sad state of mind; but the maiden, on the contrary, was as lively as lively could be, and asked him if he could now see what was going on among his companions. He said they had just rowed the Sending ashore from the islands. So she sat on the foot of the bed, which was near the door, and he lay behind her. After a while, he told her that he felt a strange heaviness come over him, which he knew to be owing to the magic arts of the wizards. Having told her this, he fell into a deep sleep.

By and by, the girl, who still sat at the bed's foot, woke him, and asked him if he knew now where the Sending was, or his way.

He said, "Within the bounds of the farm," and fell back again into a sleep so deep, that, shake him as she would, she could not rouse him from it.

When she had sat there a little while longer, she saw a brownish vapour enter the house through the open door. It glided softly towards her, and standing still before her, took the figure of a man. "Well," said the girl, "what do you want here?"

The Sending said to her, "I am sent hither by the wizards of the Westmann Islands to slay this man, who has broken his word to them as one who knows not what truth is. Move, therefore, from the bed, for while you sit there I cannot reach him."

"All in good time," replied she. "But, first of all, you must do me some service."

The Sending asked what service she would of him. "Make yourself, for instance," she answered, "as large as you can."

This, he said, he would assuredly do, willingly enough. Accordingly he made himself so large that he quite filled the house.

"That will do," said the girl. "Now, for instance, make yourself as small as you can."

So the Sending shrunk down and down and down, till from a monstrous giant he became the smallest fly you ever saw.

"Aha," said she, and stuck him forthwith into an empty marrow-bone, which she had in her pocket, and corked him in.

Then putting the bone back in her pocket, she woke the man. He started up, wondering that he was yet alive, and she asked him where was now the Sending.

"I know not," said he; and she answered, "I thought your companions were no such great wizards as you made them out to be. Trouble yourself no more about them; they will not slay you just yet; but let us spend Christmas Day in mirth and joy." So they spent Christmas Day in such revel as befitted the time and a late escape from death, and laughed and sang, till the rafters had not heard the like of it for many a long year.

Now, as New Year's day drew nigh, the man fell again into his old sadness, and became so gloomy that the girl noticed his strange manner, and asked him what ailed him.

He answered, "The wizards on the Westmann Islands are now preparing another Sending, and when that shall come here, it will be no easy task for me to escape from it."

"Oh," said the girl, "just wait till I have tried its strength, and then it will be time enough to be afraid of it. Meanwhile don't trouble your head about either your friends on the island or their threats."

And since the maiden was so light-hearted, he thought that surely he would be but a coward to be dull and sad, and accordingly put the brightest face he could upon the matter.

On New Year's eve he spoke to the girl, and said, "Now the Sending has been put ashore; and, gifted as it is with all the wrath of the wizards, it comes apace."

She begged him to come with her, and led him across the country till they came to a place where the grass was high and the shrubs were thick. In the midst of this, the girl stooped down, and removing a low mound of earth and grass which stood at her feet, came to a large slab of stone, which she lifted, and, by so doing, disclosed a passage, leading far below ground. They entered the passage, and after walking for a long time in darkness, greater than that of the blackest night, they came to a cavern, which was dimly lighted with some fat, burning in a human skull. Near this light, in a mean and wretched bed, lay an old man of the most horrible aspect. His eyes were as red as blood, and his mouth reached from ear to ear; and as for his nose, no words can tell its length and colour. So frightful was he, that the wizard quaked at the very idea of going near him.

"Oho!" said this old fellow, "strange news you have to tell me, no doubt, foster-daughter. It is long enough since I saw you last. What can I do for you?"

The girl told him all about the wizard, and his friends in the Westmann Islands, and how they had despatched a Sending to slay him, and in what way she had treated the same. Upon which the old man waxed quite lively, and asked to see the marrow-bone. So she immediately took it out of her pocket and gave it him.

As soon as he saw it, he waxed even livelier than before, and became at last so very brisk, that he was really quite another man. Taking the bone in his hand, with every appearance of pleasure, he turned it about and patted it, and rubbed it all over.

While he was mumbling over the bone, the girl noticed the islander growing sleepier and sleepier, and, at length, said to the old man, "If you will aid me at all, aid me now, for I know full well that the Sending is near at hand."

Without more ado, therefore, the old fellow took the cork out of the bone, and out crept the fly, whom he patted and stroked, and to whom he said, "Go now. Receive all the Sendings from the wizards on the Westmann Islands, and swallow them."

Immediately, with a loud roar like thunder, the fly flew from the cavern; and when it came to the upper world, behold! It became so large, that one jaw reached up to the heavens, and the other touched the earth; and when not only one Sending, but two or three came, it swallowed them all down; and so the islander was saved from the malice of his companions.

After thanking the old man for his timely help, the girl and the Westmann islander returned to the farm, where, as the story goes, they became man and wife; lived to a good old age, and increased and multiplied. Thus was the land repeopled. As for the other wizards, mighty little more was ever heard about them; just enough, indeed, to amount to nothing.

The Story of Grímur, Who Killed Skeljúngur

A CERTAIN MAN was named Kári, the son of Össur. He was the nephew of Hjálmúlfr, who had made himself possessor of Blönduhlíd, extending from the river Djúpadalsá to the river Nordurá, and who dwelt at Hjálmúlfsstadir, and is buried in the barrow called Ulfshaugur, south of the farm.

Kári came from Norway, in company with Hjálmúlfr, made himself possessor of the land between Nordurá and Merkigil, and dwelt at the farm called Flatatúga; whereupon he was named Túngukári.

He had a son, Thorgrímur, a strong and wise man, who married Ashildur, daughter of Thorbrandur, of Thorbrandsstadir, in Nordurárdalur, and with her he received the property belonging to the farm Silfrastadir, where he began his life as a farmer, and became very wealthy in flocks and herds.

Thorbrandur lived at Thorbrandsstadir, to a high age, and possessed, besides this farm, one called Haukagil. At the former of these he built the famous hall, so much spoken of in the Sagas, through which the highway ran, where there were tables of provisions always ready for every passer-by. Thorbrandur was buried on the other side of the river Nordurá, where a large mound was raised above him, in a place he had himself chosen, whence he could see over both Thorbrandsstadir and Haukagil.

Thorgrímur of Silfrastadir had a son by his wife, named Grímur, who was one of the handsomest and best-grown men in Skagafjördur. He had also a daughter, named Ingibjörg, who was both winsome and wise, and was looked upon as one of the chief ladies in all that neighbourhood.

Thorgrímur had large flocks, as his pasture-grounds were good, and was therefore in need of an active herdsman, if he wished all to go well with his sheep. Once it happened that a vessel from Norway came into the harbour of Kolbeinsá late in the summer. Thorgrímur, with many other farmers, rode down to the ship, the merchants of which had on board, besides other wares, a certain bondman named Skeljúngur. He was tall, strong, and of an indomitable temper.

Thorgrímur, being apprised by the merchants that this man was for sale, went to him and asked him for what work he was fit.

Skeljúngur answered, "Thralls are not fit for much. But in good weather I have not refused ere now to watch sheep, and if you will, I can do so still."

Thorgrímur said, "I will risk buying you if you will guard my sheep, which are numerous, and their pastures dangerous."

"Do as you like," answered Skeljúngur.

So the farmer purchased this bondman, and took him home to Silfrastadir, where he commenced his duties as herdsman towards the beginning of the winter, and Thorgrímur soon perceived that the man had the strength and courage of two, in everything he undertook.

Skeljúngur was very obedient to his master, but could not agree with the other men of the farm, and least of all with Grímur.

Amongst the servants at the farm was a bond-maid named Bóla, who was fiendishly evil-minded and malicious, insomuch that nobody could come to any understanding with her. Many fancied that her nature partook of that of the trolls; and her quarrels with Skeljúngur were so fierce and frequent, that the farmer had repeatedly to interfere between them.

At last, Bóla ran away from Silfrastadir in a fit of rage, and every one was convinced that she had taken up her abode in a deep rocky gulf, near the farm. In this gulf there were three high waterfalls, as a little river ran through it. The approach to the two lower ones was difficult; to the uppermost one, under which Bóla was supposed to have taken up her abode in a cave, nearly impossible. From this place she infested the neighbourhood, part of which, with the gulf itself, was subsequently called by her name.

Once, early in the winter, Thorgrímur lost five of his best wethers from Skeljúngur's keeping, and it was suspected that Bóla had taken them. Skeljúngur became very cross at this, and wanted to find out whether she had taken them or not. But the farmer entreated him to run no such risk, assuring him that it would be far better to remain quiet. The man obeyed him, and, for the present, desisted from any search into the matter.

Next autumn eight wethers were lost from Skeljúngur's charge, who still did not endeavour to find them, as the farmer had begged him not to do so.

The third autumn ten more were lost, and then Skeljúngur became so enraged that he would not listen in the least to what the farmer said. So he ran off in a state of blind and mad rage, like that in which the warriors of old could fight their best, and hastened to the gulf, and over the waterfall into the cave; which leap has been since called "Skeljúngur's leap."

Now, after this, nothing distinct is known concerning his struggle with Bóla; but the story runs, that, after a fierce and long fight with her, he contrived to suffocate her in the deep pool beneath the fall. This done, Skeljúngur returned to the farm, and said that he fancied the stealing of his sheep would not be continued now; but Thorgrímur, far from pleased, held his peace.

People soon found that Skeljúngur's temper had become more diabolical than ever, since his struggle with Bóla, so that it became almost impossible to treat with him; but he still continued faithful and attached to his master, and so time passed quietly on.

Now we must return to Grímur, the son of Thorgrímur, who had lived with his father to manhood, and was now the most active of all his fellows.

One day Grímur came to his father, and said, "Advance me some money from my inheritance. I wish to travel hence and become acquainted with the customs of other countries; for to sit here at home like a girl will prove but a scanty advantage to me."

The farmer replied, "You shall not need to ask twice. I will give you money enough; but I have a foreboding that at some future time we shall need you here; and then you had better be at home than away; and I fear that you will have some great dangers to overcome."

Grímur answered, "I will run the risk;" and after this went on board a vessel belonging to some Norway merchants, with plenty of money for his travels. He took an affectionate leave of his father, and sailed away. But the ship had started very late, having been prevented from sailing by the Greenland ice, and when once at sea, was so hard tossed by storms, as to lose her way and be driven hither and thither all the rest of the summer. At the approach of the winter, they were, in a heavy snow-storm, carried near the shores of an unknown country, where there was no harbour, and where the coast was surrounded by cliffs. Here they were wrecked, and every life was lost, and all the merchandise swallowed by the waves; Grímur alone being able to swim to shore, where he wandered about forlorn and tired, not knowing whither to go, till he heard the sound of some one cutting wood near him. He went in that direction, and found a young and strongly-built man, hewing wood with a large axe.

Grímur saluted this youth, who courteously received him, and asked him about his journey, and how he had come there.

Grímur answered, "I am an Icelander, by name Grímur. My ship, with all its merchandise and all my companions, has been wrecked, and all lost but myself. Tell me now, to what land I have been driven; who is its ruler? and whom do I now address?"

The other replied. "I am your namesake, for my name is also Grímur. You have come to the wildernesses of Greenland, a long way from the thickly-inhabited districts; but my father's hut is not far hence. His name also is Grímur, and my mother's Thórhildur, and I have a sister, two years older than myself, named Ingibjörg. No one else lives in the house, nor have we many neighbours.

Now, as matters stand, I think you can do no better than accompany me home to my father, appeal to his good feeling, and see what comes of it. And I suppose he will do better who aids you than he who is against you."

To this the Icelandic Grímur agreed, and the young men went towards the hut together.

The cottage was neat and strongly built, and the Greenland Grímur brought his namesake into the room where his father was sitting; an old man of noble aspect, hale for his age, and active in all his movements. His wife, an aged woman, was very neat in her dress, and imposing in her demeanour.

The old man saluted his son kindly, and said, "Who is the young fellow with you?"

His son replied, "He is an Icelander who has been wrecked on the shore, and has lost all his possessions. I beg you, my father, to help him, for he is an honourable and well-born youth."

His father said, "I was not curious concerning him, but as he has been driven to shore, to the compassion of his fellow creatures, take him with you, my son, we bid him welcome for the winter."

The young men thanked the farmer for his kindness, and from that time became, as it were, brothers. Ingibjörg was a noble and lovely maiden, and she and the Icelander became much attached to one another, at which no one wondered, as all were fond of him.

So the winter passed, until shortly before Christmas-time, when it happened one day, that the brothers, while gathering drift-wood on the shore, saw a monster in woman's form, with large and repulsive countenance, approaching them.

She addressed them with these words: "I must tell you, young men, that my mother Skráma, who lives in the mountains, invites you to her Christmas festivities, and is very anxious that you should accept her invitation."

The youths answered her only with curses, and spurned her invitation; whereupon she at once disappeared.

When they came home late in the evening, the old man asked them whether they had any news for him, but they said they had nothing new to relate to him. He continued, however. "I am sure that you have seen something unusual, and that you will not refuse to tell me the truth about it."

So they told him that they had seen the monster, and laughed to scorn her invitation; "for," they said, "what cared we for her?"

The old man answered, "It will not do for you to reject her invitation. And now, I will give you some useful information. In the mountains some way from here, is a valley with a cave in it, in which lives a trollwoman, Járngerdur by name, who is an awful and malignant creature. Her two daughters live with her, Skinnbrók and Skinnhetta, who are very dangerous to have to do with.

"Now, because I and Járngerdur have for long been opposed to one another, and I have always had the advantage, she will seek to take vengeance upon you, by her troll's arts. But it will not do for you two to go by yourselves to her, therefore I and my dog Grámúll will join your company. This Járngerdur is the worst troll of all the infernal tribe, and upon whomsoever her dying eyes shall fall, he will rot alive beneath their glare, in that very hour. Therefore we must make all possible preparations, and take every precaution, if we wish to escape from her alive."

The young men begged the old farmer to make for them every needful preparation, declaring that they trusted implicitly in his great experience.

On the morning of Christmas Eve they left the hut; had to reach the valley through heavy snow drifts, and would have lost their way to it, had not the dog Grámúll found the path for them. In the evening they saw before them a large cave in some rocks, and following the narrow passage, came into it. There was a blazing fire in the cave, by which two young, monstrous, and hideous trollwomen were sitting.

The one, Skinnbrók, said to the other, Skinnhetta, "See! we shall not lie alone tonight, and tomorrow we will cut those young men up for our Christmas feast. But if this old Grímur can carry out his intentions, we shall all perish. I would that the old man could have some punishment for his curiosity in coming here against our will."

Then Grímur the Icelander went close to the fire and said: "Is the Christmas meal ready? and the table dressed?"

The sisters started at this, and sprang to their feet; and Skinnbrók ran towards Grímur the Icelander, to struggle with him, saying, "I suppose you will not consider yourself the worse treated if you embrace such a fine lady as myself, before the Christmas feast?"

Then they fought together with brute fury, and dashed one another from corner to corner of the cave. After a while the Icelander found that, troll as she was, she began to flag and lose her breath; then he tried to trip her up, and at last flung her down so that her neck was broken, and he left her dead, he himself being tired and bruised after the struggle.

Now Skinnhetta, in her turn, attacked Grímur the Greenlander, and they had a long and fierce fight, each trying to throw the other into the fire; but at last Grímur succeeded in lifting her up from the ground and hurling her, head foremost, into the boiling kettle, where he kept her till she died. After that he rested himself.

Meanwhile, the old troll-mother had attacked Grímur the father, and their struggle was a deadly one. When the brothers saw that their father began to lose strength, they set the dog Grámúll upon the troll. The hound flew savagely at her, and tore her side so that her entrails were seen, and the dog rent them out. At this the troll fell down, and in dying fixed a horrible and ghastly glare upon Grámúll, till the dog rotted beneath her eyes, and crumbled to dust at her feet; and thus died Járngerdur and the dog that had slain her.

Then the men lighted a great fire outside the cave, and burned the bodies of the three trolls. They found over the bed of the old troll a spear, which was a great rarity; glittering as glass, and adorned with gold. After this they searched all through the cave, and found many good things and valuable; all of which they bound into bundles and took away with them, the old Grímur carrying the spear, and returned home.

Here Grímur the Icelander dwelt for a long time, beloved by them all, but by none more than by the daughter, Ingibjörg.

The story now returns to Iceland. It happened that the winter after Grímur's departure, a meeting was appointed at Hofmannaflöt. To this many of the strongest men in the country, and even the giants and the mountaineers, came to make trials of their strength in wrestling. There came also Lágálfur, the son of Litildrós. When he came from this meeting in the south, down the mountains to the Skagafjördur, he had to cross the River Nordurá, opposite to Silfrastadir. It was late in the day, and the snow drifted heavily, and just now Lágálfur saw a man of huge stature striding towards him along the bank of the river. The giant saluted Lágálfur, and asked him what news he had to tell. Lágálfur told him all the most important news, and asked with whom he was speaking.

The other answered: "I am Skeljúngur, and I come from my flocks. I dare say you are a great and strong man, but I am cold with standing over my sheep all day, and it would be good sport for us to wrestle a little, to warm ourselves."

Lágálfur replied: "I have for some time had good sport in wrestling with gallant men, but although you look like a rascal and a troll, I will not refuse to wrestle with you. Let each man look to himself."

Skeljúngur consented to this, and having thrown off their outer clothes, they began to wrestle. Lágálfur soon felt that Skeljúngur had the strength of two strong men, and that he must not spare his own strength against him. Now they wrestled with such fury that frozen stones started from the ground beneath their feet. When Lágálfur was tired of this undecided struggle, he tried to trip up his adversary, and a fit of blind madness and heroic fury seized them. At last Lágálfur lifted Skeljúngur by his hip and threw him so high, that when he fell both his thighs were broken upon the frozen ground, and both his shoulders dislocated. Then his enemy set upon him with such rage that he left him at the point of death.

After this, Lágálfur went to the farm Silfrastadir, where all the people were already assembled in the family-room, and sang outside the window a verse, telling how he had fought with and subdued Skeljúngur.

"Quickly over the earth I ran,
And dealt with that rascally shepherd-man;
The strength-failing thrall himself brought it to be
That he should be dealt with so hardly by me.
The hair-brained fellow was beaten, and found
A good drubbing on the stony ground.
Skeljúngur scarcely will find him again
To watch his sheep and to guard the pen."

From this farm he went to another house, named Frostastödum, and stopped at that end of the house at which the farmer slept, where was a window through which he could see into the house. He saw the farmer sitting there, a grey-headed man, and heard him scolding his wife for having taken a handful of meal from the leather sack hanging in the roof over the farmer's head, and at last he struck her with his hand upon the cheek, so that she wept. Then Lágálfur thrust through the window the spear which he held in his hand, so as to cut the cords of the leather meal-bag, which fell down suddenly on the farmer's head, and sent him fainting to the ground. As soon as he saw that the farmer had recovered his senses, he retired from the window and sang:

"The meal-sack fell from the roof above
Upon the old man's pate,
And the beaten wife sat bewailing her fate
Till Lágálfur's spear avenged the sweet love."

Then Lágálfur went home, and henceforth is no more seen in our story, which returns now to Silfrastadir.

The farmer began to suspect something about Skeljúngur, when he heard Lágálfur sing at the window, and he supposed that the latter had left the herdsman unable to help himself. He therefore ordered his servants to search for Skeljúngur, but they could not find him, as the night was very dark. Early in the morning, the farmer started off with his men to search again for him. They discovered the place where Lágálfur and Skeljúngur had fought, by the trodden ground, and the stones which had been kicked up by their feet, but of the man himself they could find nothing.

After a little time people began to be aware that Skeljúngur did not lie quiet in death, and that he was a goblin, and now lived in the mountain close to Silfrastadir. And it became dangerous to pass through the valley, for he used to kill the horses of travellers, and their dogs, and mislead themselves. But Thorgrímur received the worst harm of all from him; for his herdsman was killed the following Christmas, and the same fatal thing took place till the third Christmas.

Now the story returns to Greenland again. Grímur the Icelander had lived there in all happiness with the good farmer and his family all this time. He had learnt many things, and excelled everybody in bravery and skill.

Once in the last spring the old farmer came to him and said to him, "This night I have seen many visions, and I suppose that your father is in hard need of you, for his herdsman has become a dangerous goblin, destroying his property and killing his servants, and I tell you that you are the only man capable of killing this monster. Now you shall make ready to return to Iceland, and I will give you a little ship for the voyage, in which Grímur, my son and Ingibjörg, my daughter, shall accompany you. I see that your lines of fate lie together, and on your arrival in Iceland, you will marry your sister Ingibjörg to my son Grímur. He will bring her hither, but will return again to Iceland, where they will rear their family. Your fortune, however, will lead you away from your native land; but in whatever company you move, you will always be the foremost and best. And now I will equip you for your journey as well as I can."

Grímur the Icelander thanked the old man for his kind gifts, and promised to follow his advice.

When the ice had disappeared, the young men prepared their vessel for their voyage, and the farmer gave them everything they required, of the best quality. To the Icelander he gave many rarities, and, among others, the troll's spear which they had found in the cave, and, as he delivered it into his hand, said, "I think this will wear through many a rough combat."

After this the old Grímur bade farewell to his children and to his future son-in-law, and wished them God-speed. So they weighed anchor and sailed away into the Greenland sea, and a long and rough passage they had, between – the stormy weather and the ice, but at last they came safely into harbour in the mouth of the River Blanda, two days before Christmas.

The Icelander said, "I will ride as speedily as possible northwards to Silfrastadir, and I shall be none too early; but do you wait by the ship till my return."

So he procured two of the best riding-horses in the neighbourhood, and rode, dressed in glittering armour and carrying the troll's spear, along Blanda up through Vatnsskard. The snow had drifted, and the roads were heavy, but he rode so fast that, as the tale goes, one of his horses died in the middle of the journey, and the other by the wall of the grass-field of Silfrúnarstadir.

When he arrived there it was Christmas Eve, and the day far spent, and he went in to his father, who received him with great joy. Then he went to the family-room and threw off his riding-dress. He saw that all the people of the household looked sorrowful, and as he knew what was the cause of their sadness, he questioned them about Skeljúngur's habits. They told him that all night this goblin used to sit outside of the sleeping-room roof, kicking his heels into it, and that he was so dangerous, that no one dared go out after nightfall.

Grímur saw lying on the floor the fresh skin of the ox which had been killed for the Christmas feast, so he took it and cut out of it three strong ropes, and after that went out of the house, and directed his steps southward, carrying the spear in one hand, the ropes in the other, till he came to a mound called, after him, Grímshóll, where he found a stone standing on the south side, broad at the bottom and narrow at the top. Grímur went to it, and pierced three holes through it with his spear. Into these holes he put the three ropes, and made, by means of loops, three nooses, which could be drawn tight against the stone. This accomplished, he returned home, where a merry Christmas feast awaited him, for every one was glad of his return, and none more so than his father. As the night advanced, Grímur begged all the people to go to bed.

The servant men of the farm slept in a dormitory near the entrance, where there were many beds. Grímur lay down on the bed nearest the door, wrapped up in the fresh ox-skin from which he had cut the cords, and through the head of which he could see the door. One lamp was burning in the room, and Grímur told all the others to be neither afraid nor troubled if anyone should come unceremoniously into the house. Every one, with silent dread, expected Skeljúngur, and thus, in perfect quiet, some part of the night was spent.

After midnight some one was heard to mount on to the house and ride astride of the dormitory roof, kicking his heels with such fury that every rafter cracked again.

Then this house-rider jumped down, and, coming to the door, kicked it open.

Skeljúngur (for it was he) rolled his horrible eyes round the room, till none of the men could move for fear. When he saw that there was a new sleeper in the room, he went up to the bed nearest the door and caught hold of the ox-skin, but Grímur held it so tight that the other could not move it. Finding this, the other pulled with all his strength; but Grímur put his foot against the wainscot, and pushed against him till he broke the wainscot down. Then in their struggle they arrived at the door; and Grímur, seeing that he could not resist Skeljúngur except by stratagem, lay on the skin and let the other drag him out, planting his feet, however, against everything that came in his way, and thus they came to the outer door. Skeljúngur dragged the skin from the door across the field, in a southerly direction, but Grímur made the dragging as difficult for him as he could by planting his feet against every hillock and every stone that they passed. Active as the goblin was, he now began to be tired, and at last they came to Grímshóll.

By this time the night was far advanced towards dawn, and Grímur fought then and there more fiercely than ever, contriving finally to bind him to the stone by means of the nooses which he had prepared. Having securely fastened Skeljúngur to the rock, he went home in order to procure fire and fuel for burning him.

But when he came back he found that both Skeljungur and the stone had disappeared. He judged that the direction the goblin would have most probably taken with his load was a southerly one, down the slope of the mountain, so he followed that way. After a while he saw before him Skeljúngur dragging the great stone behind him with great difficulty. Then Grímur ran up to him and cut off his head, and, fetching the fire and fuel, burnt him there. After that he took his ashes to a well close by and threw them in, and, according to the current story, two fishes, covered with blue hair, sprung from them, and lived there until the Nordurá changed its course and swept over the well, when the fishes disappeared.

The stone, bound to which Skeljúngur lost his second life, is yet to be seen standing by the highway, sunk deep into the ground, and there is still one hole visible, which was pierced by the iron spear.

The poet Hjálmar Jónsson, who has written this story, asserts that he has seen, in his youth, two holes in the stone, the lower one of which was close to the surface of the earth. But this was forty years ago, and nobody can tell how large the stone may be.

On the spot where the goblin was burnt, was afterwards built a farm called Skeljúngsstadir, which is mentioned in Sturlúnga, for Eyólfur the Vehement rested there with his men when he attacked the Earl Gissur at Flugumýri.

Skeljúngshellir, or the cave of Skeljúngur, is also to be found in the adjacent mountain.

Now we will return to Grímur, who went home after this struggle very weary. Everybody in the farm thanked him with fair words for the riddance he had made, and everybody agreed that no one was his equal in all Skagafjördur. Now he told his father about his journey to Greenland, and mentioned all the conditions he had made with his Greenland friends, asking him frankly to consent to them, for that he had to thank those men for his preservation; nor, declared he, would his sister be better off with any husband than with Grímur the Greenlander.

Thorgrímur said that all their agreements should stand unbroken, "And my daughter," he continued, "shall go with your friend to Greenland, for I know that they will return and settle in Iceland to rear their family around them."

Grímur thanked his father for his kind answer, and his sister's departure from home was prepared for with all possible liberality, and both her father and brother accompanied her to the vessel lying in the mouth of the Blanda. Thorgrímur gave her a large number of gold and silver ornaments, and to Grímur the Greenlander a new body of sailors, sending also with him gifts for the old man in Greenland. Then they parted in affection, and when Thorgrímur kissed his daughter at farewell, he wept tears of fatherly love.

With a fair wind, Grímur the Greenlander and his bride sailed away.

Thorgrímur and his son rode northwards to Silfrastadir, taking with them Ingibjörg of Greenland, who was looked upon as very beautiful, and who made a right good wife; for, a short time after this, Grímur married her, and their marriage was a happy one. It was soon found that Grímur, after his struggle with the goblin, had become very irritable, and it was impossible for his neighbours to agree with him; so they induced him to go south, to Borgar-fjördur, but having dwelt a short time there, he sailed from Iceland with his wife Ingibjörg, and settled in Sweden, where he raised up a family, and none of his descendants are known to have come to Iceland.

And where he dwelt he became celebrated for his bravery.

People say that Grímur the Greenlander returned to Iceland with his wife Ingibjörg, and settled at Skaga, between Skagafjörður and Húnaflóa.

His son was Thorgrímur, the Weatherwise, who lived at Keta.

His son was Grímur, who lived at Hafnir.

His son again was Grímur, who lived there after his father's death, at the time when Thorgerdur Kolka came from Hornstrandir and built the farm called Kolkunes, trusting herself to Grímur's honour.

The priest Eyólfur of Vellir mentions her in his "Antiquarian Transactions" as a benevolent woman, and one of great account, and says that at her death a miraculous earthquake took place, doing much damage, both at Skaga and at other places, and swallowing up Gullbrekka, with all its inhabitants and cattle.

And there is now a great slough where the farm formerly stood.

And thus ends the story of Grímur, who killed Skeljúngur.

The Story of Gunnlaug the Worm-Tongue and Raven the Skald

Chapter I – Of Thorstein Egilson and his Kin

THERE WAS A MAN called Thorstein, the son of Egil, the son of Skallagrim, the son of Kveldulf the Hersir of Norway. Asgerd was the mother of Thorstein; she was the daughter of Biorn Hold. Thorstein dwelt at Burg in Burg-firth; he was rich of fee, and a great chief, a wise man, meek and of measure in all wise. He was nought of such wondrous growth and strength as his father Egil had been; yet was he a right mighty man, and much beloved of all folk.

Thorstein was goodly to look on, flaxen-haired, and the best-eyed of men; and so say men of lore that many of the kin of the Mere-men, who are come of Egil, have been the goodliest folk; yet, for all that, this kindred have differed much herein, for it is said that some of them have been accounted the most ill-favoured of men: but in that kin have been also many men of great prowess in many wise, such as Kiartan, the son of Olaf Peacock, and Slaying-Bardi, and Skuli, the son of Thorstein. Some have been great bards, too, in that kin, as Biorn, the champion of Hit-dale, priest Einar Skulison, Snorri Sturluson, and many others.

Now, Thorstein had to wife Jofrid, the daughter of Gunnar, the son of Hlifar. This Gunnar was the best skilled in weapons, and the lithest of limb of all bonderfolk who have been in Iceland; the second was Gunnar of Lithend; but Steinthor of Ere was the third. Jofrid was eighteen winters old when Thorstein wedded her; she was a widow, for Thorodd, son of Odd of Tongue, had had her to wife aforetime. Their daughter was Hungerd, who was brought up at Thorstein's at Burg. Jofrid was a very stirring woman; she and Thorstein had many children betwixt them, but few of them come into this tale. Skuli was the eldest of their sons, Kollsvein the second, Egil the third.

Chapter II – Of Thorstein's Dream

One summer, it is said, a ship came from over the main into Gufaros. Bergfinn was he hight who was the master thereof, a Northman of kin, rich in goods, and somewhat stricken in years, and a wise man he was withal.

Now, goodman Thorstein rode to the ship, as it was his wont mostly to rule the market, and this he did now. The Eastmen got housed, but Thorstein took the master to himself, for thither he prayed to go. Bergfinn was of few words throughout the winter, but Thorstein treated him well. The Eastman had great joy of dreams.

One day in spring-tide Thorstein asked Bergfinn if he would ride with him up to Hawkfell, where at that time was the Thing-stead of the Burg-firthers; for Thorstein had been told that the walls of his booth had fallen in. The Eastman said he had good will to go, so that day they rode, some three together, from home, and the house-carles of Thorstein withal, till they came up under Hawkfell to a farmstead called Foxholes. There dwelt a man of small wealth called Atli, who was Thorstein's tenant. Thorstein bade him come and work with them, and bring with him hoe and spade. This he did, and when they came to the tofts of the booth, they set to work all of them, and did out the walls.

The weather was hot with sunshine that day, and Thorstein and the Eastman grew heavy; and when they had moved out the walls, those two sat down within the tofts, and Thorstein slept, and fared ill in his sleep. The Eastman sat beside him, and let him have his dream fully out, and when he awoke he was much wearied. Then the Eastman asked him what he had dreamt, as he had had such an ill time of it in his sleep.

Thorstein said, "Nay, dreams betoken nought."

But as they rode homeward in the evening, the Eastman asked him again what he had dreamt.

Thorstein said, "If I tell thee the dream, then shalt thou unriddle it to me, as it verily is."

The Eastman said he would risk it.

Then Thorstein said: "This was my dream; for methought I was at home at Burg, standing outside the men's-door, and I looked up at the house-roof, and on the ridge I saw a swan, goodly and fair, and I thought it was mine own, and deemed it good beyond all things. Then I saw a great eagle sweep down from the mountains, and fly thitherward and alight beside the swan, and chuckle over her lovingly; and methought the swan seemed well content thereat; but I noted that the eagle was black-eyed, and that on him were iron claws: valiant he seemed to me.

"After this I thought I saw another fowl come flying from the south quarter, and he, too, came hither to Burg, and sat down on the house beside the swan, and would fain be fond with her. This also was a mighty eagle.

"But soon I thought that the eagle first-come ruffled up at the coming of the other. Then they fought fiercely and long, and this I saw that both bled, and such was the end of their play, that each tumbled either way down from the house-roof, and there they lay both dead.

"But the swan sat left alone, drooping much, and sad of semblance.

"Then I saw a fowl fly from the west; that was a falcon, and he sat beside the swan and made fondly towards her, and they flew away both together into one and the same quarter, and therewith I awoke.

"But a dream of no mark this is," he says, "and will in all likelihood betoken gales, that they shall meet in the air from those quarters whence I deemed the fowl flew."

The Eastman spake: "I deem it nowise such," saith he.

Thorstein said, "Make of the dream, then, what seemeth likest to thee, and let me hear."

Then said the Eastman: "These birds are like to be fetches of men: but thy wife sickens now, and she will give birth to a woman-child fair and lovely; and dearly thou wilt love her; but high-born men shall woo thy daughter, coming from such quarters as the eagles seemed to fly from, and shall love her with overweening love, and shall fight about her, and both lose their lives thereby. And thereafter a third man, from the quarter whence came the falcon, shall woo her, and to that man shall she be wedded. Now, I have unravelled thy dream, and I think things will befall as I have said."

Thorstein answered: "In evil and unfriendly wise is the dream interpreted, nor do I deem thee fit for the work of unriddling dreams."

Then Eastman said, "Thou shalt find how it will come to pass."

But Thorstein estranged himself from the Eastman thenceforward, and he left that summer, and now he is out of the tale.

Chapter III – Of the Birth and Fostering of Helga the Fair

This summer Thorstein got ready to ride to the Thing, and spake to Jofrid his wife before he went from home. "So is it," he says, "that thou art with child now, but thy child shall be cast forth if thou bear a woman; but nourished if it be a man."

Now, at this time when all the land was heathen, it was somewhat the wont of such men as had little wealth, and were like to have many young children on their hands, to have them cast forth, but an evil deed it was always deemed to be.

And now, when Thorstein had said this, Jofrid answers, "This is a word all unlike thee, such a man as thou art, and surely to a wealthy man like thee it will not seem good that this should be done."

Thorstein answered: "Thou knowest my mind, and that no good will hap if my will be thwarted."

So he rode to the Thing; but while he was gone Jofrid gave birth to a woman-child wondrous fair. The women would fain show her to the mother; she said there was little need thereof, but had her shepherd Thorvard called to her, and spake to him:

"Thou shalt take my horse and saddle it, and bring this child west to Herdholt, to Thorgerd, Egil's daughter, and pray her to nourish it secretly, so that Thorstein may not know thereof. For with such looks of love do I behold this child, that surely I cannot bear to have it cast forth. Here are three marks of silver, have them in reward of thy work; but west there Thorgerd will get thee fare and food over the sea."

Then Thorvard did her bidding; he rode with the child to Herdholt, and gave it into Thorgerd's hands, and she had it nourished at a tenant's of hers who dwelt at Freedmans-stead up in Hvamfirth; but she got fare for Thorvard north in Steingrims-firth, in Shell-creek, and gave him meet outfit for his sea-faring: he went thence abroad, and is now out of the story.

Now when Thorstein came home from the Thing, Jofrid told him that the child had been cast forth according to his word, but that the herdsman had fled away and stolen her horse. Thorstein said she had done well, and got himself another herdsman. So six winters passed, and this matter was nowise wotted of.

Now in those days Thorstein rode to Herdholt, being bidden there as guest of his brother-in-law, Olaf Peacock, the son of Hoskuld, who was then deemed to be the chief highest of worth among all men west there. Good cheer was made Thorstein, as was like to be; and one day at the feast it is said that Thorgerd sat in the high seat talking with her brother Thorstein, while Olaf was talking to other men; but on the bench right over against them sat three little maidens. Then said Thorgerd,—

"How dost thou, brother, like the look of these three little maidens sitting straight before us?"

"Right well," he answers, "but one is by far the fairest; she has all the goodliness of Olaf, but the whiteness and the countenance of us, the Mere-men."

Thorgerd answered: "Surely this is true, brother, wherein thou sayest that she has the fairness and countenance of us Mere-folk, but the goodliness of Olaf Peacock she has not got, for she is not his daughter."

"How can that be," says Thorstein, "being thy daughter none the less?"

She answered: "To say sooth, kinsman," quoth she, "this fair maiden is not my daughter, but thine."

And therewith she told him all as it had befallen, and prayed him to forgive her and his own wife that trespass.

Thorstein said: "I cannot blame you two for having done this; most things will fall as they are fated, and well have ye covered over my folly: so look I on this maiden that I deem it great good luck to have so fair a child. But now, what is her name?"

"Helga she is called," says Thorgerd.

"Helga the Fair," says Thorstein. "But now shalt thou make her ready to come home with me."

She did so, and Thorstein was led out with good gifts, and Helga rode with him to his home, and was brought up there with much honour and great love from father and mother and all her kin.

Chapter IV – Of Gunnlaug Worm-Tongue and his Kin

Now at this time there dwelt at Gilsbank, up in White-water-side, Illugi the Black, son of Hallkel, the son of Hrosskel. The mother of Illugi was Thurid Dandle, daughter of Gunnlaug Worm-Tongue.

Illugi was the next greatest chief in Burg-firth after Thorstein Egilson. He was a man of broad lands and hardy of mood, and wont to do well to his friends; he had to wife Ingibiorg, the daughter of Asbiorn Hordson, from Ornolfsdale; the mother of Ingibiorg was Thorgerd, the daughter of Midfirth-Skeggi. The children of Illugi and Ingibiorg were many, but few of them have to do with this story. Hermund was one of their sons, and Gunnlaug another; both were hopeful men, and at this time of ripe growth.

It is told of Gunnlaug that he was quick of growth in his early youth, big, and strong; his hair was light red, and very goodly of fashion; he was dark-eyed, somewhat ugly-nosed, yet of lovesome countenance; thin of flank he was, and broad of shoulder, and the best-wrought of men; his whole mind was very masterful; eager was he from his youth up, and in all wise unsparing and hardy; he was a great skald, but somewhat bitter in his rhyming, and therefore was he called Gunnlaug Worm-Tongue.

Hermund was the best beloved of the two brothers, and had the mien of a great man.

When Gunnlaug was fifteen winters old he prayed his father for goods to fare abroad withal, and said he had will to travel and see the manners of other folk. Master Illugi was slow to take the matter up, and said he was unlike to be deemed good in the out-lands "when I can scarcely shape thee to my own liking at home."

On a morning but a very little afterwards it happened that Illugi came out early, and saw that his storehouse was opened, and that some sacks of wares, six of them, had been brought out into the road, and therewithal too some pack-gear. Now, as he wondered at this, there came up a man leading four horses, and who should it be but his son Gunnlaug. Then said he:

"I it was who brought out the sacks."

Illugi asked him why he had done so. He said that they should make his faring goods.

Illugi said: "In nowise shalt thou thwart my will, nor fare anywhere sooner than I like!" and in again he swung the ware-sacks therewith.

Then Gunnlaug rode thence and came in the evening down to Burg, and goodman Thorstein asked him to bide there, and Gunnlaug was fain of that proffer. He told Thorstein how things had gone betwixt him and his father, and Thorstein offered to let him bide there as long as he liked, and for some seasons Gunnlaug abode there, and learned law-craft of Thorstein, and all men accounted well of him.

Now Gunnlaug and Helga would be always at the chess-playing together, and very soon each found favour with the other, as came to be proven well enough afterwards: they were very nigh of an age.

Helga was so fair, that men of lore say that she was the fairest woman of Iceland, then or since; her hair was so plenteous and long that it could cover her all over, and it was as fair as a band of gold; nor was there any so good to choose as Helga the Fair in all Burgfirth, and far and wide elsewhere.

Now one day, as men sat in the hall at Burg, Gunnlaug spake to Thorstein: "One thing in law there is which thou hast not taught me, and that is how to woo me a wife."

Thorstein said, "That is but a small matter," and therewith taught him how to go about it.

Then said Gunnlaug, "Now shalt thou try if I have understood all: I shall take thee by the hand and make as if I were wooing thy daughter Helga."

"I see no need of that," says Thorstein. Gunnlaug, however, groped then and there after his hand, and seizing it said, "Nay, grant me this though."

"Do as thou wilt, then," said Thorstein; "but be it known to all who are hereby that this shall be as if it had been unspoken, nor shall any guile follow herein."

Then Gunnlaug named for himself witnesses, and betrothed Helga to him, and asked thereafter if it would stand good thus. Thorstein said that it was well; and those who were present were mightily pleased at all this.

Chapter V – Of Raven and his Kin

There was a man called Onund, who dwelt in the south at Mossfell: he was the wealthiest of men, and had a priesthood south there about the nesses. He was married, and his wife was called Geirny. She was the daughter of Gnup, son of Mold-Gnup, who settled at Grindwick, in the south country. Their sons were Raven, and Thorarin, and Eindridi; they were all hopeful men, but Raven was in all wise the first of them. He was a big man and a strong, the sightliest of men and a good skald; and when he was fully grown he fared between sundry lands, and was well accounted of wherever he came.

Thorod the Sage, the son of Eyvind, then dwelt at Hjalli, south in Olfus, with Skapti his son, who was then the spokesman-at-law in Iceland. The mother of Skapti was Ranveig, daughter of Gnup, the son of Mold-Gnup; and Skapti and the sons of Onund were sisters' sons. Between these kinsmen was much friendship as well as kinship.

At this time Thorfin, the son of Selthorir, dwelt at Red-Mel, and had seven sons, who were all the hopefullest of men; and of them were these – Thorgils, Eyjolf, and Thorir; and they were all the greatest men out there. But these men who have now been named lived all at one and the same time.

Next to this befell those tidings, the best that ever have befallen here in Iceland, that the whole land became Christian, and that all folk cast off the old faith.

Chapter VI – How Helga was Vowed to Gunnlaug, and of Gunnlaug's Faring Abroad

Gunnlaug Worm-Tongue was, as is aforesaid, whiles at Burg with Thorstein, whiles with his father Illugi at Gilsbank, three winters together, and was by now eighteen winters old; and father and son were now much more of a mind.

There was a man called Thorkel the Black; he was a house-carle of Illugi, and near akin to him, and had been brought up in his house. To him fell an heritage north at As, in Water-dale, and he prayed Gunnlaug to go with him thither. This he did, and so they rode, the two together, to As. There they got the fee; it was given up to them by those who had the keeping of it, mostly because of Gunnlaug's furtherance.

But as they rode from the north they guested at Grimstongue, at a rich bonder's who dwelt there; but in the morning a herdsman took Gunnlaug's horse, and it had sweated much by then he got it back. Then Gunnlaug smote the herdsman, and stunned him; but the bonder would in nowise bear this, and claimed boot therefor. Gunnlaug offered to pay him one mark. The bonder thought it too little.

Then Gunnlaug sang,

"Bade I the middling mighty
To have a mark of waves' flame;
Giver of grey seas glitter,
This gift shalt thou make shift with.
If the elf sun of the waters
From out of purse thou lettest,
O waster of the worm's bedy
Awaits thee sorrow later."

So the peace was made as Gunnlaug bade, and in such wise the two rode south.

Now, a little while after, Gunnlaug asked his father a second time for goods for going abroad.

Illugi says, "Now shalt thou have thy will, for thou hast wrought thyself into something better than thou wert." So Illugi rode hastily from home, and bought for Gunnlaug half a ship which lay in Gufaros, from Audun Festargram – this Audun was he who would not flit abroad the sons of Oswif the Wise, after the slaying of Kiartan Olafson, as is told in the story of the Laxdalemen, which thing though betid later than this. And when Illugi came home, Gunnlaug thanked him well.

Thorkel the Black betook himself to seafaring with Gunnlaug, and their wares were brought to the ship; but Gunnlaug was at Burg while they made her ready, and found more cheer in talk with Helga than in toiling with chapmen.

Now one day Thorstein asked Gunnlaug if he would ride to his horses with him up to Long-water-dale. Gunnlaug said he would. So they ride both together till they come to the mountain-dairies of Thorstein, called Thorgils-stead. There were stud-horses of Thorstein, four of them together, all red of hue. There was one horse very goodly, but little tried: this horse Thorstein offered to give to Gunnlaug. He said he was in no need of horses, as he was going away from the country; and so they ride to other stud-horses. There was a grey horse with four mares, and he was the best of horses in Burgfirth. This one, too, Thorstein offered to give Gunnlaug, but he said, "I desire these in no wise more than the others; but why dost thou not bid me what I will take?"

"What is that?" said Thorstein.

"Helga the Fair, thy daughter," says Gunnlaug.

"That rede is not to be settled so hastily," said Thorstein; and therewithal got on other talk. And now they ride homewards down along Long-water.

Then said Gunnlaug, "I must needs know what thou wilt answer me about the wooing."

Thorstein answers: "I heed not thy vain talk," says he.

Gunnlaug says, "This is my whole mind, and no vain words."

Thorstein says, "Thou shouldst first know thine own will. Art thou not bound to fare abroad? And yet thou makest as if thou wouldst go marry. Neither art thou an even match for Helga while thou art so unsettled, and therefore this cannot so much as be looked at."

Gunnlaug says, "Where lookest thou for a match for thy daughter, if thou wilt not give her to the son of Illugi the Black; or who are they throughout Burg-firth who are of more note than he?"

Thorstein answered: "I will not play at men-mating," says he, "but if thou wert such a man as he is, thou wouldst not be turned away."

Gunnlaug said, "To whom wilt thou give thy daughter rather than to me?"

Said Thorstein, "Hereabout are many good men to choose from. Thorfin of Red-Mel hath seven sons, and all of them men of good manners."

Gunnlaug answers, "Neither Onund nor Thorfin are men as good as my father. Nay, thou thyself clearly fallest short of him – or what hast thou to set against his strife with Thorgrim the Priest, the son of Kiallak, and his sons, at Thorsness Thing, where he carried all that was in debate?"

Thorstein answers, "I drave away Steinar, the son of Onund Sioni, which was deemed somewhat of a deed."

Gunnlaug says, "Therein thou wast holpen by thy father Egil; and, to end all, it is for few bonders to cast away my alliance."

Said Thorstein, "Carry thy cowing away to the fellows up yonder at the mountains; for down here, on the Meres, it shall avail thee nought."

Now in the evening they come home; but next morning Gunnlaug rode up to Gilsbank, and prayed his father to ride with him a-wooing out to Burg.

Illugi answered, "Thou art an unsettled man, being bound for faring abroad, but makest now as if thou wouldst busy thyself with wife-wooing; and so much do I know, that this is not to Thorstein's mind."

Gunnlaug answers, "I shall go abroad all the same, nor shall I be well pleased but if thou further this."

So after this Illugi rode with eleven men from home down to Burg, and Thorstein greeted him well. Early in the morning Illugi said to Thorstein, "I would speak to thee."

"Let us go, then, to the top of the Burg, and talk together there," says Thorstein; and so they did, and Gunnlaug went with them.

Then said Illugi, "My kinsman Gunnlaug tells me that he has begun a talk with thee on his own behalf, praying that he might woo thy daughter Helga; but now I would fain know what is like to come of this matter.

His kin is known to thee, and our possessions; from my hand shall be spared neither land nor rule over men, if such things might perchance further matters."

Thorstein said, "Herein alone Gunnlaug pleases me not, that I find him an unsettled man; but if he were of a mind like thine, little would I hang back."

Illugi said, "It will cut our friendship across if thou gainsayest me and my son an equal match."

Thorstein answers, "For thy words and our friendship then, Helga shall be vowed, but not betrothed, to Gunnlaug, and shall bide for him three winters: but Gunnlaug shall go abroad and shape himself to the ways of good men; but I shall be free from all these matters if he does not then come back, or if his ways are not to my liking."

Thereat they parted; Illugi rode home, but Gunnlaug rode to his ship. But when they had wind at will they sailed for the main, and made the northern part of Norway, and sailed landward along Thrandheim to Nidaros; there they rode in the harbour, and unshipped their goods.

Chapter VII – Of Gunnlaug in the East and the West

In those days Earl Eric, the son of Hakon, and his brother Svein, ruled in Norway. Earl Eric abode as then at Hladir, which was left to him by his father, and a mighty lord he was. Skuli, the son of Thorstein, was with the earl at that time, and was one of his court, and well esteemed.

Now they say that Gunnlaug and Audun Festargram, and seven of them together, went up to Hladir to the earl. Gunnlaug was so clad that he had on a grey kirtle and white long-hose; he had a boil on his foot by the instep, and from this oozed blood and matter as he strode on. In this guise he went before the earl with Audun and the rest of them, and greeted him well. The earl knew Audun, and asked him tidings from Iceland. Audun told him what there was toward. Then the earl asked Gunnlaug who he was, and Gunnlaug told him his name and kin. Then the earl said: "Skuli Thorstein's son, what manner of man is this in Iceland?"

"Lord," says he, "give him good welcome, for he is the son of the best man in Iceland, Illugi the Black of Gilsbank, and my foster-brother withal."

The earl asked, "What ails thy foot, Icelander?"

"A boil, lord," said he.

"And yet thou wentest not halt?"

Gunnlaug answers, "Why go halt while both legs are long alike?"

Then said one of the earl's men, called Thorir: "He swaggereth hugely, this Icelander! It would not be amiss to try him a little."

Gunnlaug looked at him and sang:

"A courtman there is
Full evil I wis,
A bad man and black,
Belief let him lack."

Then would Thorir seize an axe. The earl spake: "Let it be," says he; "to such things men should pay no heed. But now, Icelander, how old a man art thou?"

Gunnlaug answers: "I am eighteen winters old as now," says he.

Then says Earl Eric, "My spell is that thou shalt not live eighteen winters more."

Gunnlaug said, somewhat under his breath: "Pray not against me, but for thyself rather."

The earl asked thereat, "What didst thou say, Icelander?"

Gunnlaug answers, "What I thought well befitting, that thou shouldst bid no prayers against me, but pray well for thyself rather."

"What prayers, then?" says the earl.

"That thou mightest not meet thy death after the manner of Earl Hakon, thy father."

The earl turned red as blood, and bade them take the rascal in haste; but Skuli stepped up to the earl, and said: "Do this for my words, lord, and give this man peace, so that he depart at his swiftest."

The earl answered, "At his swiftest let him be off then, if he will have peace, and never let him come again within my realm."

Then Skuli went out with Gunnlaug down to the bridges, where there was an England-bound ship ready to put out; therein Skuli got for Gunnlaug a berth, as well as for Thorkel, his kinsman; but Gunnlaug gave his ship into Audun's ward, and so much of his goods as he did not take with him.

Now sail Gunnlaug and his fellows into the English main, and come at autumntide south to London Bridge, where they hauled ashore their ship.

Now at that time King Ethelred, the son of Edgar, ruled over England, and was a good lord; this winter he sat in London. But in those days there was the same tongue in England as in Norway and Denmark; but the tongues changed when William the Bastard won England, for thenceforward French went current there, for he was of French kin.

Gunnlaug went presently to the king, and greeted him well and worthily. The king asked him from what land he came, and Gunnlaug told him all as it was. "But," said he, "I have come to meet thee, lord, for that I have made a song on thee, and I would that it might please thee to hearken to that song." The king said it should be so, and Gunnlaug gave forth the song well and proudly; and this is the burden thereof:

"As God are all folk fearing
The free lord King of England,
Kin of all kings and all folk,
To Ethelred the head tow."

The king thanked him for the song, and gave him as song-reward a scarlet cloak lined with the costliest of furs, and golden-broidered down to the hem; and made him his man; and Gunnlaug was with him all the winter, and was well accounted of.

One day, in the morning early, Gunnlaug met three men in a certain street, and Thororm was the name of their leader; he was big and strong, and right evil to deal with. He said, "Northman, lend me some money."

Gunnlaug answered, "That were ill counselled to lend one's money to unknown men."

He said, "I will pay it thee back on a named day."

"Then shall it be risked," says Gunnlaug; and he lent him the fee withal.

But some time afterwards Gunnlaug met the king, and told him of the money-lending. The king answered, "Now hast thou thriven little, for this is the greatest robber and riever; deal with him in no wise, but I will give thee money as much as thine was."

Gunnlaug said, "Then do we, your men, do after a sorry sort, if, treading sackless folk under foot, we let such fellows as this deal us out our lot. Nay, that shall never be."

Soon after he met Thororm and claimed the fee of him. He said he was not going to pay it.

Then sang Gunnlaug:

"Evil counselled art thou,
Gold from us withholding;
The reddener of the edges,
Pricking on with tricking.
Wot ye what? They called me,
Worm-Tongue, yet a youngling;
Nor for nought so hight I;
Now is time to show it!"

"Now I will make an offer good in law," says Gunnlaug; "that thou either pay me my money, or else that thou go on holm with me in three nights' space."

Then laughed the Viking, and said, "Before thee none have come to that, to call me to holm, despite of all the ruin that many a man has had to take at my hands. Well, I am ready to go."

Thereon they parted for that time.

Gunnlaug told the king what had befallen; and he said, "Now, indeed, have things taken a right hopeless turn; for this man's eyes can dull any weapon. But thou shalt follow my rede; here is a sword I will give thee – with that thou shalt fight, but before the battle show him another."

Gunnlaug thanked the king well therefor.

Now when they were ready for the holm, Thororm asked what sort of a sword it was that he had. Gunnlaug unsheathed it and showed him, but had a loop round the handle of the king's sword, and slipped it over his hand; the bearserk looked on the sword, and said, "I fear not that sword."

But now he dealt a blow on Gunnlaug with his sword, and cut off from him nigh all his shield; Gunnlaug smote in turn with the king's gift; the bearserk stood shieldless before him, thinking he had the same weapon he had shown him, but Gunnlaug smote him his deathblow then and there.

The king thanked him for this work, and he got much fame therefor, both in England and far and wide elsewhere.

In the spring, when ships sailed from land to land, Gunnlaug prayed King Ethelred for leave to sail somewhither; the king asks what he was about then. Gunnlaug said, "I would fulfil what I have given my word to do," and sang this stave withal:

"My ways must I be wending
Three kings' walls to see yet,
And earls twain, as I promised
Erewhile to land-sharers.
Neither will I wend me
Back, the worms'-bed lacking,
By war-lord's son, the wealth-free,
For work done gift well given."

"So be it, then, skald," said the king, and withal he gave him a ring that weighed six ounces; "but," said he, "thou shalt give me thy word to come back next autumn, for I will not let thee go altogether, because of thy great prowess."

Chapter VIII – Of Gunnlaug in Ireland

Thereafter Gunnlaug sailed from England with chapmen north to Dublin. In those days King Sigtrygg Silky-Beard, son of King Olaf Kvaran and Queen Kormlada, ruled over Ireland; and he had then borne sway but a little while. Gunnlaug went before the king, and greeted him well and worthily. The king received him as was meet. Then Gunnlaug said, "I have made a song on thee, and I would fain have silence therefor."

The king answered, "No men have before now come forward with songs for me, and surely will I hearken to thine." Then Gunnlaug brought the song, whereof this is the burden—

"Swaru's steed
Doth Sigtrygg feed."

And this is therein also:

"Praise-worth I can
Well measure in man,
And kings, one by one—
Lo here, Kvararis son!
Gruageth the king
Gift of gold ring?
I, singer, know
His wont to bestow.
Let the high king say,
Heard he or this day,
Song drapu-measure
Dearer a treasure?"

The king thanked him for the song, and called his treasurer to him, and said, "How shall the song be rewarded?"

"What hast thou will to give, lord?" says he.

"How will it be rewarded if I give him two ships for it?" said the king.

Then said the treasurer, "This is too much, lord; other kings give in regard of songs good keepsakes, fair swords, or golden rings."

So the king gave him his own raiment of new scarlet, a gold-embroidered kirtle, and a cloak lined with choice furs, and a gold ring which weighed a mark. Gunnlaug thanked him well.

He dwelt a short time here, and then went thence to the Orkneys.

Then was lord in Orkney, Earl Sigurd, the son of Hlodver; he was friendly to Icelanders. Now Gunnlaug greeted the earl well, and said he had a song to bring him. The earl said he would listen thereto, since he was of such great kin in Iceland.

Then Gunnlaug brought the song; it was a shorter lay, and well done. The earl gave him for lay-reward a broad axe, all inlaid with silver, and bade him abide with him.

Gunnlaug thanked him both for his gift and his offer, but said he was bound east for Sweden; and thereafter he went on board ship with chapmen who sailed to Norway.

In the autumn they came east to King's Cliff, Thorkel, his kinsman, being with him all the time. From King's Cliff they got a guide up to West Gothland, and came upon a cheaping-stead, called Skarir: there ruled an earl called Sigurd, a man stricken in years. Gunnlaug went before him, and told him he had made a song on him; the earl gave a willing ear hereto, and Gunnlaug brought the song, which was a shorter lay.

The earl thanked him, and rewarded the song well, and bade him abide there that winter. Earl Sigurd had a great Yule-feast in the winter, and on Yule-eve came thither men sent from Earl Eric of Norway, twelve of them together, and brought gifts to Earl Sigurd. The earl made them good cheer, and bade them sit by Gunnlaug through the Yule-tide; and there was great mirth at drinks.

Now the Gothlanders said that no earl was greater or of more fame than Earl Sigurd; but the Norwegians thought that Earl Eric was by far the foremost of the two. Hereon would they bandy words, till they both took Gunnlaug to be umpire in the matter. Then he sang this stave:

"Tell ye, staves of spear-din,
How on sleek-side sea-horse
Oft this earl hath proven
Over-toppling billows;
But Eric, victory's ash-tree,
Oft hath seen in east-seas
More of high blue billows
Before the bows a-roaring."

Both sides were content with his finding, but the Norwegians the best. But after Yule-tide those messengers left with gifts of goodly things, which Earl Sigurd sent to Earl Eric.

Now they told Earl Eric of Gunnlaug's finding: the earl thought that he had shown upright dealing and friendship to him herein, and let out some words, saying that Gunnlaug should have good peace throughout his land. What the earl had said came thereafter to the ears of Gunnlaug.

But now Earl Sigurd gave Gunnlaug a guide east to Tenthland, in Sweden, as he had asked.

Chapter IX – Of the Quarrel between Gunnlaug and Raven before the Swedish King

In those days King Olaf the Swede, son of King Eric the Victorious, and Sigrid the High-Counselled, daughter of Skogul Tosti, ruled over Sweden. He was a mighty king and renowned, and full fain of fame.

Gunnlaug came to Upsala towards the time of the Thing of the Swedes in spring-tide; and when he got to see the king, he greeted him. The king took his greeting well, and asked who he was. He said he was an Iceland-man.

Then the king called out: "Raven," says he, "what man is he in Iceland?"

Then one stood up from the lower bench, a big man and a stalwart, and stepped up before the king, and spake: "Lord," says he, "he is of good kin, and himself the most stalwart of men."

"Let him go, then, and sit beside thee," said the king.

Then Gunnlaug said, "I have a song to set forth before thee, king, and I would fain have peace while thou hearkenest thereto."

"Go ye first, and sit ye down," says the king, "for there is no leisure now to sit listening to songs."

So they did as he bade them.

Now Gunnlaug and Raven fell a-talking together, and each told each of his travels. Raven said that he had gone the summer before from Iceland to Norway, and had come east to Sweden in the forepart of winter. They soon got friendly together.

But one day, when the Thing was over, they were both before the king, Gunnlaug and Raven.

Then spake Gunnlaug, "Now, lord, I would that thou shouldst hear the song."

"That I may do now," said the king.

"My song too will I set forth now," says Raven.

"Thou mayst do so," said the king.

Then Gunnlaug said, "I will set forth mine first if thou wilt have it so, king."

"Nay," said Raven, "it behoveth me to be first, lord, for I myself came first to thee."

"Whereto came our fathers forth, so that my father was the little boat towed behind? Whereto, but nowhere?" says Gunnlaug. "And in likewise shall it be with us."

Raven answered, "Let us be courteous enough not to make this a matter of bandying of words. Let the king rule here."

The king said, "Let Gunnlaug set forth his song first, for he will not be at peace till he has his will."

Then Gunnlaug set forth the song which he had made to King Olaf, and when it was at an end the king spake. "Raven," says he, "how is the song done?"

"Right well," he answered; "it is a song full of big words and little beauty; a somewhat rugged song, as is Gunnlaug's own mood."

"Well, Raven, thy song," said the king.

Raven gave it forth, and when it was done the king said, "How is this song made, Gunnlaug?"

"Well it is, lord," he said; "this is a pretty song, as is Raven himself to behold, and delicate of countenance. But why didst thou make a short song on the king, Raven? Didst thou perchance deem him unworthy of a long one?"

Raven answered, "Let us not talk longer on this; matters will be taken up again, though it be later."

And thereat, they parted.

Soon after Raven became a man of King Olaf's, and asked him leave to go away. This the king granted him. And when Raven was ready to go, he spake to Gunnlaug, and said, "Now shall our friendship be ended, for that thou must needs shame me here before great men; but in time to come I shall cast on thee no less shame than thou hadst will to cast on me here."

Gunnlaug answers: "Thy threats grieve me nought. Nowhere are we likely to come where I shall be thought less worthy than thou."

King Olaf gave to Raven good gifts at parting, and thereafter.

Chapter X – How Raven Came Home to Iceland, and asked for Helga to Wife

Now this spring Raven came from the east to Thrandheim, and fitted out his ship, and sailed in the summer to Iceland. He brought his ship to Leiruvag, below the Heath, and his friends and kinsmen were right fain of him. That winter he was at home with his father, but the summer after he met at the Althing his kinsman, Skapti the law-man.

Then said Raven to him, "Thine aid would I have to go a-wooing to Thorstein Egilson, to bid Helga his daughter."

Skapti answered, "But is she not already vowed to Gunnlaug Worm-Tongue?"

Said Raven, "Is not the appointed time of waiting between them passed by? And far too wanton is he withal, that he should hold or heed it aught."

"Let us then do as thou wouldst," said Skapti.

Thereafter they went with many men to the booth of Thorstein Egilson, and he greeted them well.

Then Skapti spoke: "Raven, my kinsman, is minded to woo thy daughter Helga. Thou knowest well his blood, his wealth, and his good manners, his many mighty kinsmen and friends."

Thorstein said, "She is already the vowed maiden of Gunnlaug, and with him shall I hold all words spoken."

Skapti said, "Are not the three winters worn now that were named between you?"

"Yes," said Thorstein; "but the summer is not yet worn, and he may still come out this summer."

Then Skapti said, "But if he cometh not this summer, what hope may we have of the matter then?"

Thorstein answered, "We are like to come here next summer, and then may we see what may wisely be done, but it will not do to speak hereof longer as at this time."

Thereon they parted. And men rode home from the Althing. But this talk of Raven's wooing of Helga was nought hidden.

That summer Gunnlaug came not out.

The next summer, at the Althing, Skapti and his folk pushed the wooing eagerly, and said that Thorstein was free as to all matters with Gunnlaug.

Thorstein answered, "I have few daughters to see to, and fain am I that they should not be the cause of strife to any man. Now I will first see Illugi the Black." And so he did.

And when they met, he said to Illugi, "Dost thou not think that I am free from all troth with thy son Gunnlaug?"

Illugi said, "Surely, if thou williest it. Little can I say herein, as I do not know clearly what Gunnlaug is about."

Then Thorstein went to Skapti, and a bargain was struck that the wedding should be at Burg, about winter-nights, if Gunnlaug did not come out that summer; but that Thorstein should be free from all troth with Raven if Gunnlaug should come and fetch his bride.

After this men ride home from the Thing, and Gunnlaug's coming was long drawn out. But Helga thought evilly of all these redes.

Chapter XI – Of How Gunnlaug Must Needs Abide away from Iceland

Now it is to be told of Gunnlaug that he went from Sweden the same summer that Raven went to Iceland, and good gifts he had from King Olaf at parting.

King Ethelred welcomed Gunnlaug worthily, and that winter he was with the king, and was held in great honour.

In those days Knut the Great, son of Svein, ruled Denmark, and had new-taken his father's heritage, and he vowed ever to wage war on England, for that his father had won a great realm there before he died west in that same land.

And at that time there was a great army of Danish men west there, whose chief was Heming, the son of Earl Strut-Harald, and brother to Earl Sigvaldi, and he held for King Knut that land that Svein had won.

Now in the spring Gunnlaug asked the king for leave to go away, but he said, "It ill beseems that thou, my man, shouldst go away now, when all bodes such mighty war in the land."

Gunnlaug said, "Thou shalt rule, lord; but give me leave next summer to depart, if the Danes come not."

The king answered, "Then we shall see."

Now this summer went by, and the next winter, but no Danes came; and after midsummer Gunnlaug got his leave to depart from the king, and went thence east to Norway, and found Earl Eric in Thrandheim, at Hladir, and the earl greeted him well, and bade him abide with him. Gunnlaug thanked him for his offer, but said he would first go out to Iceland, to look to his promised maiden.

The earl said, "Now all ships bound for Iceland have sailed."

Then said one of the court, "Here lay, yesterday, Hallfred Troublous-Skald, out tinder Agdaness."

The earl answered, "That may well be; he sailed hence five nights ago."

Then Earl Eric had Gunnlaug rowed put to Hallfred, who greeted him with joy; and forthwith a fair wind bore them from land, and they were right merry.

This was late in the summer: but now Hallfred said to Gunnlaug, "Hast thou heard of how Raven, the son of Onund, is wooing Helga the Fair?"

Gunnlaug said he had heard thereof but dimly. Hallfred tells him all he knew of it, and therewith, too, that it was the talk of many men that Raven was in nowise less brave a man than Gunnlaug. Then Gunnlaug sang this stave:

"Light the weather wafteth;
But if this east wind drifted
Week-long, wild upon us
Little were I recking;
More this word I mind of
Me with Raven mated,
Than gain for me the gold-foe
Of days to make me grey-haired."

Then Hallfred said, "Well, fellow, may'st thou fare better in thy strife with Raven than I did in mine. I brought my ship some winters ago into Leiruvag, and had to pay a half-mark in silver to a house-carle of Raven's, but I held it back from him. So Raven rode at us with sixty men, and cut the moorings of the ship, and she was driven up on the shallows, and we were bound for a wreck. Then I had to give selfdoom to Raven, and a whole mark I had to pay; and that is the tale of my dealings with him."

Then they two talked together alone of Helga the Fair, and Gunnlaug praised her much for her goodliness; and Gunnlaug sang:

"He who brand of battle
Beareth over-wary,
Never love shall let him
Hold the linen-folded;
For we when we were younger
In many a way were playing
On the outward nesses
From golden land outstanding."

"Well sung!" said Hallfred.

Chapter XII – Of Gunnlaug's Landing, and How He Found Helga Wedded to Raven

They made land north by Fox-Plain, in Hraunhaven, half a month before winter, and there unshipped their goods. Now there was a man called Thord, a bonder's son of the Plain, there. He fell to wrestling with the chapmen, and they mostly got worsted at his hands.

Then a wrestling was settled between him and Gunnlaug. The night before Thord made vows to Thor for the victory; but the next day, when they met, they fellto wrestling. Then Gunnlaug tripped both feet from under Thord, and gave him a great fall; but the foot that Gunnlaug stood on was put out of joint, and Gunnlaug fell together with Thord.

Then said Thord, "Maybe that other things go no better for thee."

"What then?" says Gunnlaug.

"Thy dealings with Raven, if he wed Helga the Fair at winter-nights. I was anigh at the Thing when that was settled last summer."

Gunnlaug answered naught thereto.

Now the foot was swathed, and put into joint again, and it swelled mightily; but he and Hallfred ride twelve in company till they come to Gilsbank, in Burg-firth, the very Saturday night when folk sat at the wedding at Burg. Illugi was fain of his son Gunnlaug and his fellows; but Gunnlaug said he would ride then and there down to Burg. Illugi said it was not wise to do so, and to all but Gunnlaug that seemed good. But Gunnlaug was then unfit to walk, because of his foot, though he would not let that be seen. Therefore there was no faring to Burg.

On the morrow Hallfred rode to Hreda-water, in North-water dale, where Galti, his brother and a brisk man, managed their matters.

Chapter XIII – Of the Winter-Wedding at Skaney, and How Gunnlaug gave the King's Cloak to Helga

Tells the tale of Raven, that he sat at his wedding-feast at Burg, and it was the talk of most men that the bride was but drooping; for true is the saw that saith, "Long we remember what youth gained us," and even so it was with her now.

But this new thing befell at the feast, that Hungerd, the daughter of Thorod and Jofrid, was wooed by a man named Sverting, the son of Hafr-Biorn, the son of Mold-Gnup, and the wedding was to come off that winter after Yule, at Skaney, where dwelt Thorkel, a kinsman of Hungerd, and son of Torn Valbrandsson; and the mother of Torn was Thorodda, the sister of Odd of the Tongue.

Now Raven went home to Mossfell with Helga his wife. When they had been there a little while, one morning early before they rose up, Helga was awake, but Raven slept, and fared ill in his sleep. And when he woke Helga asked him what he had dreamt. Then Raven sang:

"In thine arms, so dreamed I,
Hewn was I, gold island!
Bride, in blood I bled there,

Bed of thine was reddened.
Never more then mightst thou,
Mead-bowl's pourer speedy,
Bind my gashes bloody—
Lind-leek-bough thou likst it."

Helga spake: "Never shall I weep therefor," quoth she; "ye have evilly beguiled me, and Gunnlaug has surely come out." And therewith she wept much.

But, a little after, Gunnlaug's coming was bruited about, and Helga became so hard with Raven, that he could not keep her at home at Mossfell; so that back they had to go to Burg, and Raven got small share of her company.

Now men get ready for the winter-wedding. Thorkel of Skaney bade Illugi the Black and his sons. But when master Illugi got ready, Gunnlaug sat in the hall, and stirred not to go. Illugi went up to him and said, "Why dost thou not get ready, kinsman?"

Gunnlaug answered, "I have no mind to go."

Says Illugi, "Nay, but certes thou shalt go, kinsman," says he; "and cast thou not grief over thee by yearning for one woman. Make as if thou knewest nought of it, for women thou wilt never lack."

Now Gunnlaug did as his father bade him; so they came to the wedding, and Illugi and his sons were set down in the high seat; but Thorstein Egilson, and Raven his son-in-law, and the bridegroom's following, were set in the other high seat, over against Illugi.

The women sat on the dais, and Helga the Fair sat next to the bride. Oft she turned her eyes on Gunnlaug, thereby proving the saw, "Eyes will bewray if maid love man."

Gunnlaug was well arrayed, and had on him that goodly raiment that King Sigtrygg had given him; and now he was thought far above all other men, because of many things, both strength, and goodliness, and growth.

There was little mirth among folk at this wedding. But on the day when all men were making ready to go away the women stood up and got ready to go home. Then went Gunnlaug to talk to Helga, and long they talked together: but Gunnlaug sang:

"Light-heart lived the Worm-Tongue
All day long no longer
In mountain-home, since Helga
Had name of wife of Raven;
Nought foresaw thy father,
Hardener white of fight-thaw,
What my words should come to.
—The maid to gold was wedded."

And again he sang:

"Worst reward I owe them,
Father thine, O wine-may,
And mother, that they made thee
So fair beneath thy maid-gear;
For thou, sweet field of sea-flame,
All joy hast slain within me.—
Lo, here, take it, loveliest
E'er made of lord and lady!"

And therewith Gunnlaug gave Helga the cloak, Ethelred's gift, which was the fairest of things, and she thanked him well for the gift.

Then Gunnlaug went out, and by that time riding-horses had been brought home and saddled, and among them were many very good ones; and they were all tied up in the road. Gunnlaug leaps on to a horse, and rides a hand-gallop along the homefield up to a place where Raven happened to stand just before him; and Raven had to draw out of his way. Then Gunnlaug said,—

"No need to slink aback, Raven, for I threaten thee nought as at this time; but thou knowest forsooth, what thou hast earned."

Raven answered and sang,

"God of wound-flamed glitter,
Glorier of fight-goddess,
Must we fall a-fighting

For fairest kirtle-bearer?
Death-staffs many such-like
Fair as she is are there
In south-lands o'er the sea floods.
Sooth saith he who knoweth."

"Maybe there are many such, but they do not seem so to me," said Gunnlaug.

Therewith Illugi and Thorstein ran up to them, and would not have them fight.

Then Gunnlaug sang,

"The fair-hued golden goddess
For gold to Raven sold they,
(Raven my match as men say)
While the mighty isle-king,
Ethelred, in England
From eastward way delayed me,
Wherefore to gold-waster
Waneth tongue's speech-hunger."

Hereafter both rode home, and all was quiet and tidingless that winter through; but Raven had nought of Helga's fellowship after her meeting with Gunnlaug.

Chapter XIV – Of the Holmgang at the Althing

Now in summer men ride a very many to the Althing: Illugi the Black and his sons with him, Gunnlaug and Hermund; Thorstein Egilson and Kolsvein his son; Onund, of Mossfell, and his sons all, and Sverting, Hafr-Biorn's son. Skapti yet held the spokesmanship-at-law.

One day at the Thing, as men went thronging to the Hill of Laws, and when the matters of the law were done there, then Gunnlaug craved silence, and said:

"Is Raven, the son of Onund, here?"

He said he was.

Then spake Gunnlaug, "Thou well knowest that thou hast got to wife my avowed bride, and thus hast thou made thyself my foe. Now for this I bid thee to holm here at the Thing, in the holm of the Axe-water, when three nights are gone by."

Raven answers, "This is well bidden, as was to be looked for of thee, and for this I am ready, whenever thou williest it."

Now the kin of each deemed this a very ill thing. But, at that time it was lawful for him who thought himself wronged by another to call him to fight on the holm.

So when three nights had gone by they got ready for the holmgang, and Illugi the Black followed his son thither with a great following. But Skapti, the lawman, followed Raven, and his father and other kinsmen of his.

Now before Gunnlaug went upon the holm he sang,

"Out to isle ofeel-field
Dight am I to hie me:
Give, O God, thy singer
With glaive to end the striving.
Here shall I the head cleave
Of Helga's love's devourer,
At last my bright sword bringeth
Sundering of head and body."

Then Raven answered and sang,

"Thou, singer, knowest not surely
Which of us twain shall gain it;
With edge for leg-swathe eager,
Here are the wound-scythes bare now.
In whatso-wise we wound us,
The tidings from the Thing here,
And fame of thanes' fair doings,
The fair young maid shall hear it."

Hermund held shield for his brother, Gunnlaug; but Sverting, Hafr-Biorn's son, was Raven's shield-bearer. Whoso should be wounded was to ransom himself from the holm with three marks of silver.

Now, Raven's part it was to deal the first blow, as he was the challenged man. He hewed at the upper part of Gunnlaug's shield, and the sword brake asunder just beneath the hilt, with so great might he smote; but the point of the sword flew up from the shield and struck Gunnlaug's cheek, whereby he got just grazed; with that their fathers ran in between them, and many other men.

"Now," said Gunnlaug, "I call Raven overcome, as he is weaponless."

"But I say that thou art vanquished, since thou art wounded," said Raven.

Now, Gunnlaug was nigh mad, and very wrathful, and said it was not tried out yet.

Illugi, his father, said they should try no more for that time.

Gunnlaug said, "Beyond all things I desire that I might in such wise meet Raven again, that thou, father, wert not anigh to part us."

And thereat they parted for that time, and all men went back to their booths.

But on the second day after this it was made law in the law-court that, henceforth, all holmgangs should be forbidden; and this was done by the counsel of all the wisest men that were at the Thing; and there, indeed, were all the men of most counsel in all the land. And this was the last holmgang fought in Iceland, this, wherein Gunnlaug and Raven fought.

But this Thing was the third most thronged Thing that has been held in Iceland; the first was after Njal's burning, the second after the Heath-slaughters.

Now, one morning, as the brothers Hermund and Gunnlaug went to Axe-water to wash, on the other side went many women towards the river, and in that company was Helga the Fair. Then said Hermund,—

"Dost thou see thy friend Helga there on the other side of the river?"

"Surely, I see her," says Gunnlaug, and withal he sang:

"Born was she for men's bickering:
Sore bale hath wrought the war-stemy

And I yearned ever madly
To hold that oak-tree golden.
To me then, me destroyer
Of swan-mead's flame, unneedful
This looking on the dark-eyed,
This golden land's beholding."

Therewith they crossed the river, and Helga and Gunnlaug spake awhile together, and as the brothers crossed the river eastward back again, Helga stood and gazed long after Gunnlaug.

Then Gunnlaug looked back and sang:

"Moon of linen-lapped one,
Leek-sea-bearing goddess,
Hawk-keen out of heaven
Shone all bright upon me;
But that eyelid's moonbeam
Of gold-necklaced goddess
Her hath all undoing
Wrought, and me made nought of."

Chapter XV – How Gunnlaug and Raven Agreed to go East to Norway, to Try the Matter Again

Now after these things were gone by men rode home from the Thing, and Gunnlaug dwelt at home at Gilsbank.

On a morning when he awoke all men had risen up, but he alone still lay abed; he lay in a shut-bed behind the seats. Now into the hall came twelve men, all full armed, and who should be there but Raven, Onund's son; Gunnlaug sprang up forthwith, and got to his weapons.

But Raven spake, "Thou art in risk of no hurt this time," quoth he, "but my errand hither is what thou shalt now hear: Thou didst call me to a holmgang last summer at the Althing, and thou didst not deem matters to be fairly tried therein; now I will offer thee this, that we both fare away from Iceland, and go abroad next summer, and go on holm in Norway, for there our kinsmen are not like to stand in our way."

Gunnlaug answered, "Hail to thy words, stoutest of men! This thine offer I take gladly; and here, Raven, mayest thou have cheer as good as thou mayest desire."

"It is well offered," said Raven, "but this time we shall first have to ride away." Thereon they parted.

Now the kinsmen of both sore misliked them of this, but could in no wise undo it, because of the wrath of Gunnlaug and Raven; and, after all, that must betide that drew towards.

Now it is to be said of Raven that he fitted out his ship in Leiruvag; two men are named that went with him, sisters' sons of his father Onund, one hight Grim, the other Olaf, doughty men both. All the kinsmen of Raven thought it great scathe when he went away, but he said he had challenged Gunnlaug to the holmgang because he could have no joy soever of Helga; and he said, withal, that one must fall before the other.

So Raven put to sea, when he had wind at will, and brought his ship to Thrandheim, and was there that winter and heard nought of Gunnlaug that winter through; there lie abode him the summer following: and still another winter was he in Thrandheim, at a place called Lifangr.

Gunnlaug Worm-Tongue took ship with Hallfred Troublous-Skald, in the north at The Plain; they were very late ready for sea.

They sailed into the main when they had a fair wind, and made Orkney a little before the winter. Earl Sigurd Lodverson was still lord over the isles, and Gunnlaug went to him and abode there that winter, and the earl held him of much account.

In the spring the earl would go on warfare, and Gunnlaug made ready to go with him; and that summer they harried wide about the South-isles and Scotland's firths, and had many fights, and Gunnlaug always showed himself the bravest and doughtiest of fellows, and the hardiest of men wherever they came.

Earl Sigurd went back home early in the summer, but Gunnlaug took ship with chapmen, sailing for Norway, and he and Earl Sigurd parted in great friendship.

Gunnlaug fared north to Thrandheim, to Hladir, to see Earl Eric, and dwelt there through the early winter; the earl welcomed him gladly, and made offer to Gunnlaug to stay with him, and Gunnlaug agreed thereto.

The earl had heard already how all had befallen between Gunnlaug and Raven, and he told Gunnlaug that he laid ban on their fighting within his realm; Gunnlaug said the earl should be free to have his will herein.

So Gunnlaug abode there the winter through, ever heavy of mood.

Chapter XVI – How the Two Foes Met and Fought at Dingness

But on a day in spring Gunnlaug was walking abroad, and his kinsman Thorkel with him; they walked away from the town, till on the meads. before them they saw a ring of men, and in that ring were two men with weapons fencing; but one was named Raven, the other Gunnlaug, while they who stood by said that Icelanders smote light, and were slow to remember their words.

Gunnlaug saw the great mocking hereunder, and much jeering was brought into the play; and withal he went away silent.

So a little while after he said to the earl that he had no mind to bear any longer the jeers and mocks of his courtiers about his dealings with Raven, and therewith he prayed the earl to give him a guide to Lifangr: now before this the earl had been told that Raven had left Lifangr and gone east to Sweden; therefore, he granted Gunnlaug leave to go, and gave him two guides for the journey.

Now Gunnlaug went from Hladir with six men to Lifangr; and, on the morning of the very day whereas Gunnlaug came in in the evening, Raven had left Lifangr with four men. Thence Gunnlaug went to Vera-dale, and came always in the evening to where Raven had been the night before.

So Gunnlaug went on till he came to the uppermost farm in the valley, called Sula, wherefrom had Raven fared in the morning; there he stayed not his journey, but kept on his way through the night.

Then in the morning at sun-rise they saw one another. Raven had got to a place where were two waters, and between them flat meads, and they are called Gleipni's meads: but into one water stretched a little ness called Dingness. There on the ness Raven and his fellows, five together, took their stand. With Raven were his kinsmen, Grim and Olaf.

Now when they met, Gunnlaug said, "It is well that we have found one another."

Raven said that he had nought to quarrel with therein.

"But now," says he, "thou mayest choose as thou wilt, either that we fight alone together, or that we fight all of us man to man."

Gunnlaug said that either way seemed good to him.

Then spake Raven's kinsmen, Grim and Olaf, and said that they would little like to stand by and look on the fight, and in like wise spake Thorkel the Black, the kinsman of Gunnlaug.

Then said Gunnlaug to the earl's guides, "Ye shall sit by and aid neither side, and be here to tell of our meeting;" and so they did.

So they set on, and fought dauntlessly, all of them. Grim and Olaf went both against Gunnlaug alone, and so closed their dealings with him that Gunnlaug slew them both and got no wound. This proves Thord Kolbeinson in a song that he made on Gunnlaug the Worm-Tongue:

"Grim and Olaf great-hearts
In Gondul's din, with thin sword
First did Gunnlaug fell there
Ere at Raven fared he;
Bold, with blood be-drifted
Bane of three the thane was;
War-lord of the wave-horse
Wrought for men folks' slaughter."

Meanwhile Raven and Thorkel the Black, Gunnlaug's kinsman, fought until Thorkel fell before Raven and lost his life; and so at last all their fellowship fell. Then they two alone fought together with fierce onsets and mighty strokes, which they dealt each the other, falling on furiously without stop or stay.

Gunnlaug had the sword Ethelred's gift, and that was the best of weapons. At last Gunnlaug dealt a mighty blow at Raven, and cut his leg from under him; but none the more did Raven fall, but swung round up to a tree-stem, whereat he steadied the stump.

Then said Gunnlaug, "Now thou art no more meet for battle, nor will I fight with thee any longer, a maimed man."

Raven answered: "So it is," said he, "that my lot is now all the worser lot, but it were well with me yet, might I but drink somewhat."

Gunnlaug said, "Bewray me not if I bring thee water in my helm."

"I will not bewray thee," said Raven. Then went Gunnlaug to a brook and fetched water in his helm, and brought it to Raven; but Raven stretched forth his left hand to take it, but with his right hand drave his sword into Gunnlaug's head, and that was a mighty great wound.

Then Gunnlaug said, "Evilly hast thou beguiled me, and done traitorously wherein I trusted thee."

Raven answers, "Thou sayest sooth, but this brought me to it, that I begrudged thee to lie in the bosom of Helga the Fair."

Thereat they fought on, recking of nought; but the end of it was that Gunnlaug overcame Raven, and there Raven lost his life.

Then the earl's guides came forward and bound the head-wound of Gunnlaug, and in meanwhile, he sat and sang:

"O thou sword-storm stirrer,
Raven, stem of battle
Famous, fared against me
Fiercely in the spear din.
Many a flight of metal
Was borne on me this morning,
By the spear-walls' builder,
Ring-bearer, on hard Dingness."

After that they buried the dead, and got Gunnlaug on to his horse thereafter, and brought him right down to Lifangr. There he lay three nights, and got all his rights of a priest, and died thereafter, and was buried at the church there.

All men thought it great scathe of both of these men, Gunnlaug and Raven, amid such deeds as they died.

Chapter XVII – The News of the Fight Brought to Iceland

Now this summer, before these tidings were brought out hither to Iceland, Illugi the Black, being at home at Gilsbank, dreamed a dream: he thought that Gunnlaug came to him in his sleep, all bloody, and he sang in the dream this stave before him; and Illugi remembered the song when he woke, and sang it before others:

"Knew I of the hewing
Of Raven's hilt-finned steel-fish
Byrny-shearing – sword-edge
Sharp clave leg of Raven.
Of warm wounds drank the eagle,
When the war-rod slender,
Cleaver of the corpses,
Clave the head of Gunnlaug."

This portent befel south at Mossfell, the self-same night, that Onund dreamed how Raven came to him, covered all over with blood, and sang:

"Red is the sword, but I now
Am undone by Sword-Odin.
'Gainst shields beyond the sea-flood
The ruin of shields was wielded.
Methinks the blood-fowl blood-stained
In blood o'er men's heads stood there,
The wound-erne yet wound-eager
Trod over wounded bodies?"

Now the second summer after this, Illugi the Black spoke at the Althing from the Hill of Laws, and said:

"Wherewith wilt thou make atonement to me for my son, whom Raven, thy son, beguiled in his troth?"

Onund answers, "Be it far from me to atone for him, so sorely as their meeting hath wounded me. Yet will I not ask atonement of thee for my son."

"Then shall my wrath come home to some of thy kin," says Illugi. And withal after the Thing was Illugi at most times very sad.

Tells the tale how this autumn Illugi rode from Gilsbank with thirty men, and came to Mossfell early in the morning. Then Onund got into the church with his sons, and took sanctuary; but Illugi caught two of his kin, one called Biorn and the other Thorgrim, and had Biorn slain, but the feet smitten from Thorgrim. And thereafter Illugi rode home, and there was no righting of this for Onund.

Hermund, Illugi's son, had little joy after the death of Gunnlaug his brother, and deemed he was none the more avenged even though this had been wrought.

Now there was a man called Raven, brother's son to Onund of Mossfell; he was a great sea-farer, and had a ship that lay up in Ramfirth: and in the spring Hermund Illugison rode from home alone north over Holt-beacon Heath, even to Ramfirth, and out as far as Board-ere to the ship of the chapmen. The chapmen were then nearly ready for sea; Raven, the ship-master, was on shore, and many men with him; Hermund rode up to him, and thrust him through with his spear, and rode away forthwith: but all Raven's men were bewildered at seeing Hermund.

No atonement came for this slaying, and therewith ended the dealings of Illugi the Black and Onund of Mossfell.

Chapter XVIII – The Death of Helga the Fair

As time went on, Thorstein Egilson married his daughter Helga to a man called Thorkel, son of Hallkel, who lived west in Hraundale. Helga went to his house with him, but loved him little, for she cannot cease to think of Gunnlaug, though he be dead. Yet was Thorkel a doughty man, and wealthy of goods, and a good skald.

They had children together not a few, one of them was called Thorarin, another Thorstein, and yet more they had.

But Helga's chief joy was to pluck at the threads of that cloak, Gunnlaug's gift, and she would be ever gazing at it.

But on a time there came a great sickness to the house of Thorkel and Helga, and many were bed-ridden for a long time. Helga also fell sick, and yet she could not keep abed.

So one Saturday evening Helga sat in the fire-hall, and leaned her head upon her husband's knees, and had the cloak Gunnlaug's gift sent for; and when the cloak came to her she sat up and plucked at it, and gazed thereon awhile, and then sank back upon her husband's bosom, and was dead. Then Thorkel sang this:

"Dead in mine arms she droopeth,
My dear one, gold-rings bearer,
For God hath changed the life-days
Of this Lady of the linen.
Weary pain hath pined her,
But unto me, the seeker
Of hoard of fishes highway,
Abiding here is wearier."

Helga was buried in the church there, but Thorkel dwelt yet at Hraundale: but a great matter seemed the death of Helga to all, as was to be looked for.

And here endeth the story.

The Elves, Giants & Beasts

IN THE REMOTEST TIMES the Icelandic superstition was strongly imbued with the then-prevailing warlike spirit, and wore a harsher and more demoniacal character than later on. Stories of elves were but scarce in those days, whereas those of goblins, beasts, giants and ghosts were abundant.

Yet it cannot be doubted that elves formed, at any rate, some part of the superstition. It is evident that they belonged to the race of the Land-voettir, and as such, were peaceful, faint-hearted, defenceless and inoffensive beings who could, nevertheless, do harm if ill-treated.

In this chapter stories of the creatures are combined, to give an overall feel for the brilliant Icelandic supernatural folktales.

The Giantess and the Granite Boat

ONCE UPON A TIME there lived a king and queen who were greatly beloved by all their people. They had only one son, named Sigurd, who, even as a boy, was distinguished for his marvellous skill and dexterity in all manly sports and pastimes, whilst his strength was only equalled by his wisdom and his handsome person.

Years passed on. Sigurd had become a man, when one day the king called him to him.

"My son," he said, "it is now time for you to choose a fitting bride. I am getting old, and cannot expect to live much longer. You must take my place in a few years, and must try to gain men's respect and esteem by showing yourself capable of winning a princess worthy to share your throne. Visit first the country of Hardrada, my friend. His daughter is indeed, I hear, a marvel of beauty and goodness."

Sigurd at once prepared to start on his journey. With a few chosen companions, he set sail in his noble galley, the high prow breasting the waves, and the stern, all gorgeous with carving and gilding, glittering in the sun. After sailing for some days over the tossing waters, the vessel at length reached Hardrada's country. It was night, one of those glorious summer nights of the north, when the moon is almost as brilliant as the sun. The bold shore, with its strange, grotesque crags and peaks, seemed utterly unapproachable, till suddenly a large creek or fiord was seen, at the head of which rose the king's palace. The windows were all ablaze with light, and the sounds of music and revelry told the travellers that some banquet was in progress.

Leaving their ship, Sigurd and his companions proceeded towards the palace, where they received the warmest of welcomes from the king and his daughter Helga. The princess was indeed all she had been pictured, tall and beautiful, and so gentle and charming that Sigurd made up his mind to win her. Next morning he acquainted the king with the object of his journey, and gained his consent. Hardrada was indeed anxious to have a son-in-law to share the cares of his kingdom, which, now that he was an old man, weighed heavily upon him. As a condition of his remaining with Hardrada, Sigurd only stipulated that he should return to his own country directly his father sent for him.

So the marriage of Sigurd the brave with Helga the Fair took place with great pomp and rejoicing, thanes and nobles coming from all parts to bring presents to the young people.

Sigurd and his wife loved each other very dearly, and their happiness was completed when, after the lapse of a year, a son was born to them, inheriting the beauty of the mother, and the strength and handsome form of the father. Three happy years thus passed away, little Kurt being two years old, when Sigurd received the news of his father's death and a recall to his native land.

It was a sad parting between Helga and her father; but Sigurd dared not linger, and once more the beautiful Viking ship started on its voyage through the sun-tipped waves, bearing the young king and his wife and child.

For several days the wind was favourable; but when within a day's sail of Sigurd's country the vessel ran into an extraordinary calm. Day after day the sun blazed down fierce and strong; not a breath of air was to be felt. In the forepart of the vessel, the men had all gone below. Sigurd's companions were also asleep, while he and his wife remained on deck, beneath the awning, talking quietly, with little Kurt playing at their feet. After a little, a strange drowsiness seemed to overpower Sigurd himself, and, declaring he could no longer keep awake, he too went below, and fell asleep like the others.

Helga was now quite alone on deck with her boy. Suddenly, as she was playing with him, she saw a strange object moving slowly along the smooth surface of the water. Shading her eyes with her hands, she watched it, and as it came nearer she made out that it was a boat, with a curious, ungainly form seated in it rowing.

Nearer and nearer it came, with silent, swift strokes, and as it touched the vessel with a hard sound the queen saw that it was very large and cut out of granite. With one spring the terrible giantess who had been rowing it was on deck. Like one in a dream, the queen could neither move nor utter a sound to arouse the king or the ship's crew. She seemed held by an invisible power. The giantess came up to her, and, snatching away the child, placed him behind her; then she proceeded to take off all the young queen's beautiful embroidered robes, leaving her only a single linen garment, and as she herself put on Helga's clothes, she gradually also assumed her shape and likeness. Lastly, she seized the queen and placed her in the granite boat, saying as she did so, in a terrible voice—

"Obey my words and my magic spell. Thou must neither rest nor pause on the way, till thou reachest my brother in the lower regions."

The poor queen, half fainting and utterly powerless, sat still and silent in the boat like a statue. With a strong push the giantess sent the boat from the vessel's side, and it was speedily lost to sight. Then little Kurt began to cry. In vain the giantess tried to soothe him; the more she attempted it the worse he became, till at length, losing all patience, she snatched him up and carried him down to the king.

Waking him roughly, she upbraided him loudly for leaving her alone on deck with the child.

"It was most careless and negligent of you," she went on. "Some one ought to have been left on guard while you were asleep. No one can tell what may happen when one is thus left alone. As it is, I found it impossible to quiet the child; I have therefore brought him down here, which is the proper place for him. It is high time you roused your lazy crew. A favourable wind has at last sprung up, and we can have a chance of getting off this wretched ship."

Sigurd was astonished at being addressed by his queen in such terms. In all their married life he had never heard her speak like that. He, however, decided to take no notice of it; she must be overtired with the heat, he thought, and, answering her very gently, he endeavoured to quiet the child. The little fellow, however, sobbed and cried as much as ever.

By this time the crew were aroused, the sails hoisted, and, the wind freshening splendidly, they reached land the following day. Here the whole country was still in mourning for the late king. But the people rejoiced greatly when it became known that Sigurd had returned in safety.

He was crowned amid universal acclamations, and at once took the reins of government into his hands.

But ever since the strange calm at sea the king's little son had never ceased crying and sobbing, especially in the presence of his supposed mother, while before that time he had been a remarkably happy, affectionate child. The king, therefore, chose a nurse for him from among the people at his court, and when he was with her the little fellow seemed to be once more the bright, happy child he had been.

The king could not, however, understand the change that had come over the queen ever since their journey. She who formerly had always been so good and gentle, was now obstinate, cross, and untruthful. And ere long others began to notice the disagreeable, quarrelsome nature of the king's wife.

Now, there were at the court two young men who were so devoted to playing chess that they would sit for hours over their game, instead of joining in the outdoor sports of the other young courtiers. As they were the king's cousins, their room was in the palace, and it happened to be next to that of the queen. She had been particularly rude and disagreeable to them ever since she came, and they would have been glad to revenge themselves upon her in any way.

One day, hearing her moving about and talking angrily, they looked through a slit in the door, and distinctly heard her say—

"When I yawn slightly, I grow small and dainty, like a young maiden; when I give a bigger yawn, I grow into half a giantess; but when I stretch out my arms and yawn with all my might, I return to my original size, and become a mighty giantess."

And as she said these words, she stretched herself, yawned frightfully, as if her jaws would break, and suddenly grew into a monstrous and terrible giantess. Then, stamping her foot, the floor opened, and up came a three-headed giant, bearing a huge trough of raw meat. Greeting the queen as his sister, he placed the trough before her, and she devoured the contents, never resting till she had emptied it.

The two young courtiers watched this strange scene, though they could not hear all that the giantess and her brother said to one another. They were horrified to see how greedily she devoured the raw meat, and amazed at the quantity she ate, for at the king's table she only picked daintily at the dishes. As soon as she had emptied the trough, the three-headed giant disappeared in the same manner as he had come, and the queen, giving a slight yawn, at once assumed her human figure again. The young princes then returned to their game, discussing the mystery in undertones.

And what of the king's little son all this time? One evening, when the nurse had lighted her lamp, and was playing with the child in her arms, some of the boards in the centre of the floor opened, and a most lovely lady, wearing only a single white linen garment, stepped forth. Her waist was encircled by a heavy iron ring, to which was attached a chain, which descended right down through the hole in the floor.

With a soft little cry, she ran up to the nurse, took the little boy in her arms, kissed him and fondled him, and, after lavishing no end of caresses on him, gently placed him back in his nurse's arms and disappeared in the same way as she had come, the floor closing over her again. All this time she never spoke a single word.

The nurse was greatly amazed at the incident, but, startled though she was, she did not say a word to any one. The next evening the same thing occurred. The white-robed lady came up through the floor, took the child, kissed and caressed him lovingly, and then replaced him in his nurse's arms. But this time, when she prepared to descend, she murmured, in sorrowful tones, "Twice this happiness has been permitted. Once more, and then all will be over."

Then she disappeared, and the floor closed over her as before.

The nurse became greatly alarmed when she heard the white lady say those words. She feared that some danger must threaten the child, and yet she had been much taken with the stranger, who had caressed the boy as if he were her own. She therefore thought it best to speak to the king, tell him what had happened, and beg him to be present at the time when the white-robed lady was wont to appear. The king listened attentively to the woman's story, and, suspecting foul play, promised he would be there.

The following evening, therefore, found him betimes in the nursery, seated in a chair, with his sword drawn, close to the spot where the stranger had always appeared. He had not long to wait. With a faint grating noise the boards opened, and forth stepped the beautiful white-robed figure, with the iron ring round her waist, and the long trailing chain.

In an instant Sigurd recognized in her his own beloved wife, Helga, and quick as lightning he seized her in his arms, and with one stroke of his sword cut the chain that fastened her. Immediately the most terrible groans and rumblings issued from the earth, the whole castle rocked and trembled, and every one thought that an earthquake was taking place. But in a short time the unearthly sounds ceased without any damage having been done.

Then Helga related to her dear lord all that had befallen her – how the wicked giantess had come to the ship in her granite boat when they were all asleep, and with her magic power had taken away all her clothes and put them on herself.

"When she had placed me in the granite boat, it floated on by itself, until the ship was quite out of sight," she continued, "and then I perceived we were going towards a large dark object, which, as we came near to land, I saw was a huge three-headed giant. He wanted me to marry him, but I steadfastly refused to be his wife, whereupon he chained me up in a big lonely cave, telling me I should never be free unless I consented. Every second day he came, repeating the same request and the same threats. Then, as time went on and I saw no hope of help, I began to think how I could escape his hands. At last I told him that I would be his wife if he would allow me to visit my son on the earth for three days running. At first he would not consent, but when I persisted he gave in; but I had to promise that I would not say who I was. He then placed this iron ring round my waist, to which he attached a chain, the other end being fastened to himself. I hoped that perhaps one evening you might be there when I came to see our little Kurt. How sadly my heart failed me when the second evening passed without my seeing you! But my prayers never ceased, and now my reward has come. The terrible groans when you cut the chain must have been the giant. He would fall when the strain was suddenly taken off the chain, for he lives right under the castle. He probably broke his neck when he fell, and the terrible shock must have been his death throes."

Now the king saw clearly why he could not reconcile the behaviour of the giantess with that of the gentle Helga, his own dear queen. The hideous impostor, who had now reverted to her original form, was summoned before the State Council, and, as additional evidence against her, the two young princes related what they had heard and seen. She was condemned to be stoned to death, and her body was put into a sack and torn to pieces by wild horses.

Then the real queen was invested with all her rightful honours, and soon won the hearts of her people. And little Kurt's nurse was not forgotten. She was married to a great nobleman, the king and queen giving her a rich dowry. She and her husband remained to the end of their days the friends of Sigurd and Helga.

The Five Brothers

ONCE UPON A TIME long years ago, when giants still lived upon the earth, there dwelt an old man and his wife in a small wooden hut, sheltered from the rough winter winds by the tall mountains and rocks that surrounded it. The world would have said they were very poor; but they thought themselves rich, for they had five handsome, healthy boys, who were the delight of their eyes. There was only a year's difference in age between the lads, and they were always together.

One day, the old couple went to cut grass on a slope some distance off, leaving the boys alone at home. It was a bright, warm morning, and, tired of playing indoors, the children went out into the little garden, and soon their merry shouts were heard echoing from the hills. Presently, up the path towards them came an old woman, feeble and lame.

"May an old woman beg for a draught of water?" she said, in a weak voice.

Stopping their games at once, the eldest boy ran to the well, while the others made her sit down by the door and rest. In a moment he was back with a pitcher of cool, sparkling water.

"There, grannie," he said, "that will refresh you. I let the bucket run down ever so far, to make the water nice and cold."

The old dame thanked him heartily, and, having quenched her thirst, asked what their names were. The boys laughed merrily.

"We have no names," they said. "We are all so near in age that we do everything together; and when father or mother want anything they just call out 'Boys!' and there we are, always at hand."

"You have kind hearts," the old woman said; "you are good to the aged and feeble. I was nearly dying of thirst, and could not have gone further without your help. Would that I could reward you as I should like! Alas! I have not the power. But one thing I can do for you. You shall no longer be nameless. I am going to bestow a name on each. You, my young cup-bearer," turning to the eldest boy, "shall be called 'Watchwell;' your brothers, 'Holdwell,' 'Hitwell,' 'Spywell,' and 'Climbwell.' May these names in the future bring you good fortune, as a reward for your kindness to a poor old woman."

Then she bade them good-bye, reminded them once more of their names, told them to act up to them, and turned away down the path.

In the evening, when their parents returned, the boys related what had occurred, and repeated the strange names they had been given. The old people were much astonished, and asked where the stranger had come from, and all particulars about her. But the boys could only tell what had happened, and the whole thing would soon have been forgotten, had it not been for the names. These they did not forget, and, strange to say, the more they were used the more the owner of each name seemed to develop the special quality that his name denoted, Watchwell, in addition, constituting himself the general guardian of the five. Was there a burden to carry, Holdwell's strong arms were ready. Did the parents require faggots for the winter, Hitwell would cut a pile, up in the dark pine woods on the mountains, that gladdened their hearts. Not a rabbit or bird could escape the keen eyes of Spywell, and by constant practice little Climbwell could scale the steepest cliffs along the fiord.

Years rolled on; the bright boys had grown up into tall, handsome young men, and all this time they had never crossed the high rocky hills that walled in their valley, never seen the great world that lay outside.

But, now that they were men, a great wish was rising in their hearts to go forth from the old home and play their part among other men. The old people gave them their blessing, and bade them continue to stand by one another as they had ever done, for, if they only did that, there was nothing they could not achieve.

And so the young men departed, following the steep track over the high mountains at first, and then gradually leaving the hill country behind them as they went ever onwards. Sometimes they rested at a farmhouse, sometimes in a village, but nowhere did they find any permanent work. Many a farmer would gladly have engaged Watchwell and Spywell to guard his flocks, but he had no employment for Holdwell and Climbwell, and when the two last could have joined the village lads in fishing or seabird hunting, there was, again, no post for the other three. Still, they would not be discouraged. They had stout hearts and strong limbs, and the good fortune they sought must be found elsewhere. So on they went, climbing high mountains and fording swift rivers, till at last they entered an interminable dark pine wood with a tangled undergrowth of brambles and tall ferns. Hitwell cleared a path before them, and at length they emerged on a vast plain.

The sun was setting, and pouring a flood of crimson, gold, and purple over the scene before them. The rays lit up the tall spires and high grey walls of a large city, and turned the broad, flowing river that encircled it into molten gold.

The brothers stood still entranced.

"It must be the city of the king," cried Watchwell, at length.

"Yes," said Spywell; "look, there is the royal flag flying on the tower of the palace."

They soon traversed the plain, and as darkness began to fall, they arrived at the great drawbridge over the river, and were directed to the palace by the warder. The king received them, and listened to their request for employment in his service. The brothers were such fine, handsome fellows that he was much taken with them as they stood before him. They were very tall, and had bright blue eyes, and fair curling hair. He told them that he could give employment to all five, if they would remain throughout the winter at his court, and watch and guard his daughters at the coming Christmas Eve.

"Do not, however, pledge yourselves to stay, until you learn the nature of the task that lies before you," he said. "For I have made a vow that the life of the next man who fails in this duty shall be forfeited. Perhaps you five brothers acting together can be more careful than strangers. Now listen. Two years ago," he went on, "I had five fair daughters, but, alas! the Christmas before last my golden-haired Elma disappeared mysteriously in the dead of night. Search was made in all directions; no trace of her could be found. Last Christmas Eve the princesses' apartments were carefully watched and guarded; no strangers were admitted, only old and faithful servants were near them. But when morning came, Irene, my second daughter, was nowhere to be found, nor was there any sign of her captors' footsteps near the window of the room where she slept. I have now made a vow, and I shall keep it; but I also offer a reward. He who defends them faithfully this year shall wed the next eldest princess who would without his care have disappeared, and he shall be to me as a son. It will be death or honour. Choose, young men, now, while you are still quite free."

"We will stay and guard the princesses," they cried with one voice. "It is a task that will call all our qualities into full play. No robber can escape the eyes of Spywell, Holdwell will act up to his name, till Climbwell and Hitwell reach him, and I," and Watchwell drew himself up proudly, "I will be the one to forfeit my life if we fail."

So they remained at the court, and became great favourites with the king, who began to feel almost sorry that he had imposed sentence of death on the man who should fail to defend his daughters. He, therefore, determined to do what he could to make them safe, and caused a great tower to be built on to the palace with thick walls and windows very high up, and here the princesses were to sleep on Christmas Eve.

And now the time drew near. As usual great festivities were held for several days. On the last night, when the dancing and merry-making were all over, the three princesses – Frida, Ida, and Meya – were led to the tower by the king, attended by their ladies. As they lay down on the big couch, covered with silken embroideries, he bade them a last goodnight, and charged the five brothers to guard them with their lives. Then he left the tower, double-locking the great iron door that led into the rest of the castle. All was still. The brothers lay down on a rough bench in the ante-chamber, but the door of the princesses' room was wide open, and a lamp was kept burning there.

It had been a long and tiring day, and the younger brothers were soon fast asleep. But Watchwell never closed an eye. Wrapped in his long cloak, he leant against the wall and watched.

The night drew on. But what was that? He thought he saw a dark shadow slowly approach the window of the princesses' room. As he looked, a monstrous hand opened the lattice, and stretched out gropingly towards the couch on which the king's daughters lay asleep.

Watchwell touched his brothers. In an instant Holdwell had grasped the mysterious hand so tightly that the owner could not move it; and Hitwell, with one blow of his sword, severed it from the wrist. A terrible wild cry of pain and baffled anger filled the air, and, looking forth, the brothers saw a fearful giant striding rapidly away from the palace, and shaking his remaining hand threateningly towards the tower. The noise had aroused the king, who was quickly on the spot, while Watchwell and his brothers hurried after the monster. Faster and faster he went, seeing he was pursued, but, though he was speedily out of sight, Spywell's keen eye traced his footsteps all the way.

On, on, on, they went, till at last they came to the foot of a high mountain. Steep and precipitous before them the sides rose up – no foothold to be seen anywhere. Climbwell, however, never hesitated. He showed his brothers a strong silken cord that he always carried with him, then, making a bold spring to a tiny ledge he had noticed, he commenced to climb, never taking a false step, till he reached the summit in safety. Then, lowering the silken rope, he drew up his brothers one after the other.

When they reached the top they found an enormous cavern, and just inside the entrance sat a huge giantess, on a low stool, crying bitterly. The brothers asked what ailed her.

"What matters it to you?" she said, and cried more than ever. But at last she told them that the previous night her husband had lost one of his hands, and she feared he would die, he was in such terrible pain. Then they told her that they could heal her husband if she would let them in, but "no one," they said, "must be there but ourselves; we must bind all others lest they should find out the secret of our healing power."

The giantess, who was quite as wicked as her husband, and had hoped to entice these young men, by her pretended grief, into the cavern, so as to provide a dinner for herself and her husband, did not at all like the suggestion of being bound. But she thought, perhaps, they might be able to heal her husband first, so she submitted for the moment, comforting herself with the hope that she could easily break the rope and set herself free when the young men had cured her husband.

Holdwell bound her with Climbwell's strong silken rope, and then they passed into the inner cavern. The giant was lying on his couch, and gave a howl of rage when he saw them. But, crippled by the loss of his hand, he was no match for the young men, who speedily put an end to him. Then they also killed the wicked giantess, who had quite a heap of human bones beside her, and proceeded to explore the inner cavern. They thought it might, perhaps, contain some hidden treasure. But nothing was to be found, and they were on the point of leaving, when Spywell descried a small door cunningly let into the rock. Speedily breaking it open, a subterranean passage was seen, leading to another cavern, and there they discovered the two lost princesses – Elma, very pale and emaciated; whilst Irene, who had not been imprisoned so long, was more rosy and not so thin. The giant had evidently intended securing all five princesses before eating them.

The king's daughters were greatly overjoyed when they saw their noble deliverers, and heard that they were prisoners no longer. They quickly departed, Spywell and Climbwell having discovered an easier road for them to return by.

They arrived at the palace as night was falling, and the joy of the king at having his five daughters united once more can well be imagined.

A great banquet was hastily prepared, and before the assembled nobles and guests he related the brave deeds of Watchwell and his brothers, and announced that he had decided to wed his five daughters to the five heroes. "It is but right and fitting that men such as these, brave, noble and true, should reign over this land when I am gone," he said, "and to whom could I more worthily entrust my dear daughters than to those who have saved their lives?"

Never was there so magnificent a wedding-feast. It lasted a whole month, and the dresses of the five princesses were perfect marvels of gold and silver embroidery and precious stones. Then to each brother was appointed a position in the State which would call his special quality into play. They lived long and happily with their respective wives, greatly beloved and honoured by all, and when at length the old king died, Watchwell succeeded to the throne, and his wise and good reign, together with his beautiful and beloved Queen Elma, is still spoken of to this day.

The Story of Audunn and the Bear

Chapter I

THERE WAS A MAN called Audunn; he came of a family of the Western Firths, and was not well off. Audunn left Iceland from the Western Firths with the assistance of Thorsteinn, a substantial farmer, and of Thorir, a ship's captain, who had stayed with Thorsteinn during the winter. Audunn had been on the same farm, working for Thorir, and as his reward he got his passage to Norway under Thorir's care.

Audunn had set aside the greater part of his property, such as it was, for his mother, before he took ship, and it was determined that this should support her for three years.

Now they sailed to Norway and had a prosperous voyage, and Audunn spent the following winter with the skipper Thorir, who had a farm in Moérr. The summer after that, they sailed out to Greenland, where they stayed for the winter.

It is told that in Greenland, Audunn bought a white bear, a magnificent beast, and paid for him all he had. Next summer they returned to Norway, and their voyage was without mishap. Audunn brought his bear with him, intending to go south to Denmark to visit King Sveinn, and to present the beast to him. When he reached due south of Norway and came to the place where the King was in residence, Audunn went ashore, leading his bear, and hired lodgings.

King Haraldr was soon told that a bear had been brought to the place, a magnificent creature, belonging to an Icelander. The King immediately sent men to fetch Audunn, and when he entered the King's presence, Audunn saluted him as was proper. The King acknowledged the salute suitably and then asked:

Is it true that you have a great treasure, a white bear?

Audunn answered and said that he had got a bear of some sort.

The King said: Will you sell him to us for the price you paid for him?

Audunn answered: I would not care to do that, my Lord.

Will you then, said the King, have me pay twice the price? That would be fairer if you gave all you had for him.

I would not care to do that, my Lord, answered Audunn, but the King said:

Will you give him to me then?

No, my Lord, answered Audunn.

The King asked: What do you mean to do with him then? – and Audunn answered: I mean to go south to Denmark and give him to King Sveinn.

Can it be that you are such a fool, said King Haraldr, that you have not heard about the war between these two countries? Or do you think your luck so good that you will be able to bring valuable possessions to Denmark, while others cannot get there unmolested, even though they have pressing business?

Audunn answered: My Lord, that is for you to decide, but I shall agree to nothing other than that which I had already planned.

Then the King said: Why should we not have it like this, that you go your own way, just as you choose, and then visit me on your way back, and tell me how King Sveinn rewards you for the bear? It may be that luck will go with you.

I will promise you to do that, said Audunn.

Audunn now followed the coast southward and eastward into the Vik, and from there to Denmark, and by that time every penny of his money had been spent, and he had to beg food for himself as well as for the bear. He called on one of King Sveinn's stewards, a man named Aki, and asked him for some provisions, both for himself and for his bear. – I intend, said he, to give the bear to King Sveinn.

Aki said that he would sell him some provisions if he liked, but Audunn answered that he had nothing to pay for them, – but yet, said he, I would like to carry out my plan, and to take the beast to the King.

Aki answered: I will supply such provisions as the two of you need until you go before the King, but in exchange I will have half the bear. You can look at it in this way: the beast will die on your hands, since you need a lot of provisions and your money is spent, and it will come to this, that you will have nothing out of the bear.

When Audunn considered this, it seemed to him that there was some truth in what the steward had said, and they agreed on these terms: he gave Aki half the bear, and the King was then to set a value on the whole.

Now they were both to visit the King, and so they did. They went into his presence and stood before his table. The King wondered who this man could be, whom he did not recognize, and then said to Audunn: Who are you?

Audunn answered: I am an Icelander, my Lord, and I came lately from Greenland, and now from Norway, intending to bring you this white bear. I gave all I had for him, but I have had a serious setback, so now I only own half of the beast. – Then Audunn told the King what had happened between him and the steward, Aki.

The King asked: Is that true, what he says, Aki?

True it is, said Aki.

The King said: And did you think it proper, seeing that I had placed you in a high position, to let and hinder a man who had taken it on himself to bring me a precious gift, for which he had given all he had? King Haraldr saw fit to let him go his way in peace, and he is no friend of ours. Think, then, how far this was honest on your part. It would be just to have you put to death, but I will not do that now; you must rather leave this land at once, and never come into my sight again. But to you, Audunn, I owe the same gratitude as if you were giving me the whole of the bear, so now stay here with me.

Audunn accepted the invitation and stayed with King Sveinn for a while.

Chapter II

After some time had passed Audunn said to the King: I desire to go away now, my Lord.

The King answered rather coldly: What do you want to do then, since you do not wish to stay with us?

Audunn answered: I wish to go south on a pilgrimage.

If you had not such a good end before you, said the King, I should be vexed at your desire to go away.

Now the King gave Audunn a large sum of silver, and he travelled south with pilgrims bound for Rome. The King arranged for his journey, asking him to visit him when he came.

Audunn went on his way until he reached the city of Rome in the south. When he had stayed there as long as he wished, he turned back, and a severe illness attacked him, and he grew terribly emaciated. All the money which the King had given him for his pilgrimage was now spent, and so he took up his staff and begged his food. By now his hair had fallen out and he looked in a bad way. He got back to Denmark at Easter, and went to the place where the King was stationed. He dared not let the King see him, but stayed in a side-aisle of the church, intending to approach the King when he went to church for Nones. But when Audunn beheld the King and his courtiers splendidly arrayed, he did not dare to show himself.

When the King went to drink in his hall, Audunn ate his meal out of doors, as is the custom of Rome pilgrims, so long as they have not laid aside their staff and scrip. In the evening, when the King went to Vespers, Audunn intended to meet him, but shy as he was before, he was much more so now that the courtiers were merry with drink. As they were going back, the King noticed a man, and thought he could see that he had not the confidence to come forward and meet him. But as the courtiers walked in, the King turned back and said:

Let the man who wants to meet me come forward; I think there must be someone who does.

Then Audunn came forward and fell at the feet of the King, but the King hardly recognized him. As soon as he knew who he was, he took Audunn by the hand and welcomed him: – You have changed a lot since we met last, – he said, and then he led Audunn into the hall after him. When the courtiers saw Audunn they laughed at him, but the King said:

There is no need for you to laugh at this man, for he has provided better for his soul than you have.

The King had a bath prepared for Audunn and then gave him clothes, and now he stayed with the King.

Chapter III

It is told that one day in the spring the King invited Audunn to stay with him for good, and said he would make him his cup-bearer, and do him great honour.

Audunn answered: May God reward you, my Lord, for all the favours you would show me, but my heart is set on sailing out to Iceland.

The King said: This seems a strange choice to me, – but Audunn answered: My Lord, I cannot bear to think that I should be enjoying high honour here with you, while my mother is living the life of a beggar out in Iceland. For by now, all that I contributed for her subsistence before I left Iceland, has been used up.

The King answered: That is well spoken and like a man, and good fortune will go with you. This was the one reason for your departure which would not have offended me. So stay with me until the ships are made ready for sea. – And this Audunn did.

One day towards the end of spring King Sveinn walked down to the quay, where men were getting ships ready to sail to various lands, to the Baltic lands and Germany, to Sweden and Norway. The King and Audunn came to a fine vessel, and there were some men busy fitting her out. The King asked:

How do you like this ship, Audunn?

Audunn answered: I like her well, my Lord.

The King said: I will give you this ship and reward you for the white bear.

Audunn thanked the King for his gift as well as he knew how.

After a time, when the ship was quite ready to sail, King Sveinn said to Audunn:

If you wish to go now, I shall not hinder you, but I have heard that you are badly off for harbours in your country, and that there are many shelterless coasts, dangerous to shipping. Now, supposing you are wrecked, and lose your ship and your goods, there will be little to show that you have visited King Sveinn and brought him a precious gift.

Then the King handed him a leather purse full of silver: You will not be altogether penniless, said he, even if you wreck your ship, so long as you can hold on to this. But yet it may be, said the King, that you will lose this money, and then it will be of little use to you that you have been to see King Sveinn and given him a precious gift.

Then the King drew a ring from his arm and gave it to Audunn, saying: Even if it turns out so badly that you wreck your ship and lose your money, you will still not be a pauper if you reach land, for many men have gold about them in a shipwreck, and if you keep this ring there will be something to show that you have been to see King Sveinn. But I will give you this advice, said the King, do not give this ring away, unless you should feel yourself so much indebted to some distinguished man – then give the ring to him, for it is a fitting gift for a man of rank. And now farewell.

Chapter IV

After this Audunn put to sea and made Norway, and had his merchandise brought ashore, and that was a more laborious task than it had been last time he was in Norway. Then he went into the presence of King Haraldr, wishing to fulfil the promise he had given him before he went to Denmark. Audunn gave the King a friendly greeting, which he accepted warmly.

Sit down, said the King, and drink with us, and so Audunn did. Then King Haraldr asked: What reward did King Sveinn give you for the bear?

Audunn answered: This, my Lord, that he accepted him from me.

I would have given you that, said the King, but what else did he give you?

Audunn said: He gave me silver to make a pilgrimage to Rome, but

King Haraldr said:

King Sveinn gives many people silver for pilgrimages and for other things, even if they do not bring him valuable gifts. What more did he do for you?

He offered to make me his cup-bearer and to give me great honours.

That was a good offer, said the King, but he must have given you still more.

Audunn said: He gave me a merchantman with a cargo of wares most profitable for the Norway trade.

That was generous, said the King, but I would have rewarded you as well as that. Did he give you anything else?

Audunn said: He gave me a leather purse full of silver, and said that I would still not be penniless if I kept it, even if my ship were wrecked off Iceland.

The King said: That was magnificent, and more than I should have done. I would have thought my debt discharged if I had given you the ship. Did he give you anything else?

Certainly he gave me something else, my Lord, said Audunn; he gave me this ring which I am wearing on my arm, and said that I might chance to lose all my property, and yet not be destitute if I had this ring. But he advised me not to part with it unless I were under such an obligation to some noble man that I wished to give it to him. And now I have come to the right man, for it was in your power to take from me both my bear and my life, but you allowed me to go to Denmark in peace when others could not go there.

The King received the gift graciously and gave Audunn fine presents in exchange before they parted. Audunn laid out his merchandise on his voyage to Iceland, and sailed out that same summer, and people thought him the luckiest of men.

From this man Audunn was descended Thorsteinn Gyduson.

Helga

AN OLD MAN and his wife once lived in a cottage beside the sea, far away from any other habitations. They had three daughters; the eldest was called Fredegond, the second Olga, and the youngest Helga.

Now, although the parents were not rich, owning only a few acres of land, which they tilled themselves, Fredegond and Olga were treated as if they were princesses. They never did any work, but sat all day amusing themselves and decking themselves in any finery their father brought them home from the neighbouring town, whilst Helga, who was far more beautiful and clever than either of her sisters, was always kept in the background. She never shared in any pleasures that her elder sisters often enjoyed; no presents were ever brought home for her; but all day long, from early morning till late at night, poor Helga had to work and toil for the whole family, receiving nothing but sour looks, often accompanied by blows, from the elder sisters.

Now, it happened one day that the fire on their hearth had been allowed to go out. Helga was busy working in the fields, and as they had to send a long way to fetch fresh fire, the old man told Fredegond she must go for it

At first Fredegond grumbled, for she was trying to dress her hair in a new way; but then she thought a walk through the woods might be pleasant, so she started.

After she had gone some little distance, she came to a hillock, and heard a deep voice saying, "Would you rather have me with you or against you?"

Fredegond, thinking it was some labourer or woodcutter, said she did not care in the least, and that it was very impertinent of him to address her, and went on to the cave whence they fetched their fire.

When she got there, to her great surprise she saw a big cauldron, filled with meat, boiling on the fire, and beside it stood a pan, filled with dough, waiting to be made into cakes, but not a creature in sight.

Fredegond, being very hungry after her long walk, stirred up the fire beneath the cauldron, to make the meat boil quickly, and then began baking some cakes. But although she made one specially nice for herself, she let all the others burn, so that they were quite uneatable. Then as soon as the meat was cooked she took a bowl from a shelf, filled it with all the best bits, and sat down and made a good meal, finishing up with the cake.

Just as she had finished, a big black dog ran up to her, and began wagging his tail and begging for some food. But Fredegond angrily gave him a slap, and chased him away. Then the dog grew angry, and, jumping upon her, bit one of her hands.

Screaming with fright and pain, Fredegond jumped up, and, in her hurry to get away, forgot all about the fire she was to bring, and ran home to tell her parents what had happened.

They were very sorry, both for her sore hand, which they bathed and bandaged, and the lack of the fire. It was really very unfortunate, for that cave was the nearest place where they could procure some fire, as it was generally used by charcoal-burners. So, though very unwilling to send Olga, who was their pet and favourite, she had to go, for they all feared that if Helga were sent, she might run away and never come back again. And then there would be no one on whom to vent their bad tempers, or to do the work of the whole household – for did she not wait on father and mother and both her sisters? So it was decided that Olga should go.

But, alas! Olga fared even worse than her sister. She was so spoilt, that she thought she ought always to have the best of everything. So, when she reached the cave, she too helped herself to all the best bits of meat, and, making a nice cake for herself, threw the rest of the dough on the fire.

Then when the dog came up to her and wagged his tail and sat up and begged for some food, Olga took up some of the boiling broth and threw it on him. This made the dog so angry that he jumped up and bit off the point of her nose; and Olga ran home crying and screaming, with only half a nose and no fire.

This time the parents were quite beside themselves with anger, and decided that Helga must go and fetch the fire. If she succeeded, well and good; and if not, why, the dog might eat her, for all they cared. It would be a good riddance.

So, taking up the big fire-shovel, Helga went on her way to the cave. As she passed the hillock, she too heard a voice, saying, "Would you rather I was with you than against you?"

To this question she answered, "A well-known proverb says, 'There is nothing so bad that it is not better to have it on your side than against you;' so, as I do not know who you are who ask me this question, I would rather that you were with me than against me."

And hearing nothing further and seeing no one, Helga continued her way till she reached the cave. Here she found everything the same as her sisters had done. The cauldron was on the fire, and the dough was ready for baking, but, instead of thinking only of herself, Helga looked after the meat, and saw that it was nicely cooked; then, with great care, she made up the dough into cakes, and never thought of taking anything for herself, although she was very hungry, for she had had nothing for her breakfast but some hard, dry crusts, and a glass of cold water. Neither would she now help herself to any of the fire without asking leave from the owner of the cave.

Feeling very tired after her long walk, Helga sat down on a bench to rest. But she had hardly done so, when she heard a loud rumbling noise; the ground began to tremble; and Helga, fearful that the cave might fall in, rose hastily from her seat. But as she turned to run out, she saw a big, three-headed giant standing at the entrance of the cave, followed by a large black dog.

Helga was terribly frightened; but being fond of animals, she held out her hand and patted the dog, and she quite regained courage when the giant, in a kind voice, said, "You have done the work well, which you found waiting here. It is only right, therefore, that you should get your share. Sit down, therefore, on that bench, and share my dinner; afterwards you can take home some of the fire you have come for."

The giant then got a bowl from the shelf and helped Helga to some broth out of the big cauldron, carefully giving her the tenderest bits of meat. As he did so, the ground again began to shake and tremble, and fearful noises, like claps of thunder, frightened Helga greatly.

But the giant in a gentle voice bade her sit down beside him, and she finished her broth.

Then the giant got up and gave her one of the cakes she had baked; but no sooner had she finished it, than the ground again began to shake and tremble, the thunder pealed, and flash after flash of lightning lit up the inside of the cave. Helga got so terrified that she ran up to the giant for protection, and as she clung to his arm the noises ceased, and as the darkness passed away Helga saw that the giant had disappeared, and that she was holding on to the arm of a handsome young prince.

"Nay, do not be frightened," he said; "I can never thank you enough, dear Helga, for you have rescued me from the horrible enchantment the wicked fairy Gondomar pronounced on me at my birth. I am Torquil, the son of King Osbert, who reigns in the neighbouring island; but because my father refused to marry Gondomar, and chose my mother instead, the wicked fairy condemned me to go through life a three-headed monster, until some young girl should, despite my frightful appearance, place full trust and confidence in me."

As Prince Torquil said these words, he seated himself beside Helga on a stone, thickly covered with soft green moss. Then Helga told him her history, and why she came to the cave, and also the fate of her sisters who had gone to the cave on the same errand, adding that she must hasten back with the fire, else her father and mother would scold and beat her.

"You shall not be ill treated any more," replied Torquil; and he went to the back of the cave, and presently returned, carrying a casket and a small bundle in his hands.

"See, this casket contains gold, and pearls, and precious stones," he said. "You can give some of these to your sisters; but this," and he placed the bundle on a stool, "you must wear under your own dress, when you get home, and be very careful that no one sees it."

So saying, he undid the bundle, and unfolded a beautiful dress of cloth of gold, all worked with silver and precious stones.

Helga could not repress a cry of admiration when she saw the lovely gown, and warmly thanked the prince for all his beautiful gifts.

Torquil then filled her fire-shovel with burning coals, and carried it for her some part of the way home; but ere they came in sight of the cottage he stopped, and, taking her hand, placed a heavy gold ring on her finger.

"Keep this ring, dear Helga," he said, "and let no one take it from you. It will not be long ere I come to claim my bride, but I must first return to my parents and tell them the joyful news that the wicked charm is broken at last." With these words he took a loving farewell of Helga, and started her on her homeward journey.

When she reached the cottage, and her parents saw that she had succeeded in bringing back the fire, Helga, for once in her life, received a kind word of welcome; but when she showed them the casket and was about to give her sisters some of the jewels, they seized upon it, and dividing the contents among themselves, returned Helga the empty casket. They might also have taken away her beautiful dress, but, after Torquil left her, she had taken the precaution to slip it on under her old gown, so no one knew anything about it.

And thus some days passed on. Matters relapsed into their former way. Fredegond and Olga did nothing all day but deck themselves with the jewels out of the casket, quarrelling and fighting over them and Helga, as before, had to do the work for the whole family, when one day the mother, who had been to the higher meadow for some herbs she wanted, came back and said that she had seen a beautiful big ship lying at anchor on the shore below their cottage.

The old man hastened down to the strand to find out who the owner of the fine vessel might be, and seeing a boat pulling off from it, he waited till the stranger, who was a handsome young man, had landed, and then entered into conversation with him. But though he plied him with many questions, he could not find out his name.

Then the young man in his turn began to question him, and asked him how many children he had.

"Only two daughters," replied the old man, "and such good and beautiful girls they are too," he added.

"I should much like to see them," said the stranger.

The old man, greatly delighted, led the way back to his cottage, where his two eldest daughters had hurried on their best frocks and decked themselves with all the jewels out of Helga's casket.

The stranger expressed himself as being very pleased with the girls.

"But," he asked, "why has one of your daughters got her hand tied up with a cloth, and the other one a handkerchief fastened across her nose?"

At first the father said they had met with an accident, and slipped down the cliffs; but when the stranger pressed for further particulars, the story of the dogs and the cave had to be told.

"But surely you have another daughter?" said the stranger; "one who, I know, is always kind to all animals."

At first the old man and his wife both declared they only had those two daughters; but when the stranger kept on urging him, he at last admitted that he had another girl. "But she is so ugly, lazy, and wicked," he added, "that she is more like some wild animal than a human being."

But the stranger said he did not mind that at all, and that he must see her. So the old man was obliged at last to call Helga.

The poor girl came out from the kitchen dressed just as she was, in her shabby old dress, when the young man went up to her; and as he took her hand the ragged old gown slipped from her shoulders, and there, to the astonishment and rage of her sisters, stood Helga, arrayed in the beautiful garment the prince had given her.

Prince Torquil rated the old man and the two wicked sisters soundly for all their unkindness to Helga. He also made the sisters give up all the jewels they had taken from her. But Helga begged that they might be allowed to keep a few; and the prince consenting, she gave each of them two chains, two brooches, two bracelets, and two pairs of ear-rings. Then Torquil led Helga down to the shore and took her on board his beautiful ship, where his sister gave her a kindly welcome; and when they reached his own country, King Osbert and his queen prepared a great wedding-feast, and Torquil and Helga were married, and lived long and happily together.

The Genesis of the Hid-folk

ONCE UPON A TIME, God Almighty came to visit Adam and Eve. They received him with joy, and showed him everything they had in the house. They also brought their children to him, to show him, and these He found promising and full of hope. Then He asked Eve whether she had no other children than these whom she now showed him. She said, "None."

But it so happened that she had not finished washing them all, and, being ashamed to let God see them dirty, had hidden the unwashed ones. This God knew well, and said therefore to her, "What man hides from God, God will hide from man." These unwashed children became forthwith invisible, and took up then abode in mounds, and hills, and rocks. From these are the elves descended, but we men from those of Eve's children whom she had openly and frankly shown to God. And it is only by the will and desire of the elves themselves that men can ever see them.

A traveller once lost his way, and knew not whither to turn or what to do. At last, after wandering about for some time, he came to a hut, which he had never seen before; and on his knocking at the door, an old woman opened it, and invited him to come in, which he gladly did. Inside, the house seemed to be a clean and good one. The old woman led him to the warmest room, where were sitting two young and beautiful girls. Besides these there were none else in the house. He was well received and kindly treated, and having eaten a good supper was shown to bed.

He asked whether one of the girls might stay with him, as his companion for the night, and his request was granted.

And now wishing to kiss her, the traveller turned towards her, and placed his hand upon her; but his hand sank through her, as if she had been of mist, and though he could well see her lying beside him, he could grasp nothing but the air. So he asked what this all meant, and she said, "Be not astonished, for I am a spirit. When the devil, in times gone by, made war in heaven, he, with all his armies, was driven into outer darkness. Those who turned their eyes to look after him as he fell, were also driven out of heaven; but those who were neither for nor against him, were sent to the earth and commanded to dwell there in the rocks and mountains. These are called Elves and Hid-folk. They can live in company with none but their own race. They do either good or evil, which they will, but what they do they do thoroughly. They have no bodies as you other mortals, but can take a human form and be seen of men when they wish. I am one of these fallen spirits, and so you can never hope to embrace me."

To this fate the traveller yielded himself, and has handed down to us this story.

The Fisherman of Götur

IT IS TOLD that long ago, a peasant living at Götur in Mýrdalur, went out fishing round the island of Dyrhólar. In returning from the sea, he had to cross a morass. It happened once,

that, on his way home, after nightfall, he came to a place where a man had lost his horse in the bog, and was unable to recover it without help. The fisherman to whom this man was a stranger, aided him in freeing his horse from the peat.

When the animal stood again safe and sound upon the dry earth, the stranger said to the fisherman, "I am your neighbour, for I live in Hvammsgil, and am, as you, returning from the sea. But I am so poor, that I cannot pay you for this service, as you ought to be paid. I will promise you, however, this much – that you shall never go to sea without catching fish, nor ever, if you will take my advice, return with empty hands. But you must never put to sea without having first seen me pass your house as if going towards the shore. Obey me in this matter and I promise you that you shall launch, at no time, your boat in vain."

The fisherman thanked him for this advice, and sure enough it was, that, for three years afterwards, never putting to sea till he had first seen his neighbour pass his door, he always launched his boat safely, and always came home full-handed.

But at the end of the three years, it fell out that one day, in the early morning, the fisherman looking out from his house, saw the wind and weather favourable and all other fishers hurrying down to the sea, to make the best of so good a time. But though he waited hour after hour, in the hope of seeing his neighbour pass, the man of Hvammsgil never came. At last losing his patience, he started out without having seen him go by. When he came down to the shore, he found that all the boats were launched and far away.

Before night the wind rose and became a storm, and every boat that had that day put to sea was wrecked, and every fisher drowned, the peasant of Götur alone escaping, for he had been unable to go out fishing. The next night he had a strange dream, in which his neighbour from Hvammsgil came to him and said, "Although you did not yesterday follow my advice, I yet so far felt kindly towards you, that I hindered you from going out to sea, and saved you thus from drowning ; but look no more forth to see me pass, for we have met for the last time." And never again did the peasant see his neighbour pass his door.

The Grateful Elfwoman

A PEASANT'S WIFE once dreamed that a woman came to her bedside, whom she knew to be a Huldukona, and who begged her to give her milk for her child, two quarts a day, for the space of a month, placing it always in a part of the house which she pointed out.

The goodwife promised to do so, and remembered her promise when she awoke. So she put a milkbowl every morning in the place which the other had chosen, and left it there, always on her return finding it empty. This went on for a month; and at the end of the month she dreamed that the same woman came to her, thanked her for her kindness, and begged her to accept the belt which she should find in the bed when she awoke, and then vanished. In the morning the goodwife found beneath her pillow, a silver belt, beautifully and rarely wrought, the promised gift of the grateful elf-woman.

Thórdur of Thrastastadir

A CERTAIN MAN named Thórdur lived at Thrastastadir, in Skagafiördur.

One day, in the winter, he started from home, intending to go to the trading-town of Hofsós, but the snow had drifted so deeply that the way was thought unsafe. Not caring for this, he carried his merchandise in a bag and walked off across a bog, which he knew to be his shortest path to Hofsós. When he had gone a little way, he quite lost the track, but still walked straight on till nightfall, when he saw before him some warehouses, so lofty and so beautiful that they filled him with surprise. Going up to them he discovered a light in one of the windows, and at the same time heard some delightful music. So he looked in at the window and saw a number of people dancing. He then went to the door and knocked, and immediately it was opened by a well-dressed man, who asked him what he would? Thórdur told him how he had lost his way, and begged, if it were possible, for a night's shelter. "Come in and be welcome," said the man, "you shall have shelter here. Bring in your bag too, and tomorrow I will trade with you, and I promise you that you shall not find the bargains of Hofsós better than mine."

Thórdur could scarcely believe his ears, but thought he must be dreaming. So the man let him into the chief room, spite of Thórdur's plain and muddy dress. There were many assembled there; the lady of the house, her children, and her servants, all gaily and brightly drest, making merry.

The man who had opened the door to Thórdur, and who was no other than the master of the house, said to the lady, "Wife, here is a man who has lost his way and who needs both rest and food – treat him well."

"I grieve to hear of his distress," replied she, and rising, brought in a good and plentiful supper, which she set before Thórdur, while the master of the house fetched wine and glasses, and begged Thórdur to drink with him. Thórdur did so, and thought he had never tasted such wine in all his life, nor ever met such goodly company, though he could not, for all that, help wondering at the strangeness of the adventure. Glass after glass of wine he drank, and by-and-by, becoming tipsy, went to bed and fell into a deep sleep.

Next morning, at breakfast, he was offered wine even better than that of the night before, and having drunk it, was conducted by the master to the trading-room, which was well filled with every kind of merchandise. Then and there Thórdur showed the man his wares, and received from him in exchange more than half again what he would have got for them at Hofsós. With the money he bought corn and linen, and many other small things, at a much lower price than he was wont to pay elsewhere for the like, and filled with them his sack.

When the trading was finished the master offered him as a gift, a cloak for his wife and cakes for his children, saying to him, "These and many other good turns shall you have at my hands, as tokens of my gratitude to you for having saved my son from death." Thórdur wondered what the man could mean, but the other said, "Once, you were standing under the rock called Thordarhofdi, in company with other young men, waiting for a good wind to take your boat to Drángey. Your companions amused themselves by throwing stones against the rock, under which, as the sun was very hot, my son had laid himself down to sleep; for he was tired, having been up all the night. You bade them cease their sport, for it was a foolish one, you said, and a useless one. They laughed at you for this notion of yours, and called you strange and fanciful for your pains. But had you not prevented them from throwing stones, they would have killed my son."

After this Thórdur took leave of all in the house, for the sky was now clear and the path good, and started on his homeward way, the master walking some steps with him, to wish him "God-speed." Thórdur marched on steadily for a while; but chancing to look back for the house wherein he had passed the night, he saw nothing of it, but, in its place, the rocks of the Thórdarhöfdi. Then he understood that the kind merchant was an elf, and hastening home, told his wife all that had befallen him, and gave her the cloak. As for the wares he had got instead of his own, he showed them to all his neighbours, and never were the like of them, for goodness, seen in all that country, nor in any other country under the sun.

The Magic Scythe

A CERTAIN DAY-LABOURER once started from his home in the south, to earn wages for hay-cutting, in the north country. In the mountains, he was suddenly overtaken by a thick mist and sleet-storm, and lost his way. Fearing to go on further, he pitched his tent in a convenient spot, and taking out his provisions, began to eat.

While he was engaged upon his meal, a brown dog came into the tent, so ill-favoured, dirty, wet, and fierce-eyed, that the poor man felt quite afraid of it, and gave it as much bread and meat as it could devour. This the dog swallowed greedily, and ran off again into the mist. At first the man wondered much to see a dog in such a wild place, where he never expected to meet with a living creature, but after a while he thought no more about the matter, and having finished his supper, fell asleep, with his saddle for a pillow.

At midnight he dreamed that he saw a tall and aged woman enter his tent, who spoke thus to him, "I am beholden to you, good man, for your kindness to my daughter, but am unable to reward you as you deserve. Here is a scythe which I place beneath your pillow: it is the only gift I can make you, but despise it not. It will surely prove useful to you, as it can cut down all that lies before it. Only beware of putting it into the fire to temper it. Sharpen it, however, you will, but in that way never." So saying she was seen no more.

When the man awoke and looked forth, he found the mist all gone and the sun high in heaven; so getting all his things together and striking his tent, he laid them upon the pack-horses, saddling, last of all, his own horse. But on lifting his saddle from the ground, he found beneath it a small scythe-blade, which seemed well worn and was rusty. On seeing this he, at once, recalled to mind his dream, and taking the scythe with him, set out once more on his way. He soon found again the road which he had lost, and made all speed to reach the well-peopled district to which he was bound.

When he arrived at the north country, he went from house to house, but did not find any employment, for every farmer had labourers enough, and one week of hay-harvest was already past. He heard it said, however, that one old woman in the district, generally thought by her neighbours to be skilled in magic and very rich, always began her hay-cutting a week later than anybody else, and though she seldom employed a labourer, always contrived to finish it by the end of the season. When, by any chance – and it was a rare one – she did engage a workman, she was never known to pay him for his work.

Now the peasant from the south was advised to ask this old woman for employment, having been warned of her strange habits.

He accordingly went to her house, and offered himself to her as a day-labourer. She accepted his offer, and told him that he might, if he chose, work a week for her, but must expect no payment.

"Except," she said, "you can cut more grass in the whole week than I can rake in on the last day of it."

To these terms he gladly agreed, and began mowing. And a very good scythe he found that to be which the woman had given him in his dream; for it cut well, and never wanted sharpening, though he worked with it for five days unceasingly. He was well content, too, with his place, for the old woman was kind enough to him.

One day, entering the forge next to her house, he saw a vast number of scythe-handles and rakes, and a big heap of blades, and wondered beyond measure what the old lady could want with all these. It was the fifth day – the Friday – and when he was asleep that night, the same elf-woman whom he had seen upon the mountains, came again to him, and said:

"Large as are the meadows you have mown, your employer will easily be able to rake in all that hay tomorrow, and if she does so, will – as you know – drive you away without paying you. When, therefore, you see yourself worsted, go into the forge, take as many scythe-handles as you think proper, fit their blades to them and carry them out into that part of the land where the hay is yet uncut. There you must lay them on the ground, and you shall see how things go."

This said, she disappeared, and in the morning the labourer getting up, set to work, as usual, at his mowing.

At six o'clock the old witch came out, bringing five rakes with her, and said to the man:

"A goodly piece of ground you have mowed, indeed!"

And so saying she spread the rakes upon the hay. Then the man saw, to his astonishment, that though the one she held in her hand raked in great quantities of hay, the other four raked in no less, each, all of their own accord and with no hand to wield them.

At noon, seeing that the old woman would soon get the best of him, he went into the forge and took out several scythe-handles, to which he fixed their blades, and bringing them out into the field laid them down upon the grass which was yet standing. Then all the scythes set to work of their own accord, and cut down the grass so quickly that the rakes could not keep pace with them. And so they went on all the rest of the day, and the old woman was unable to rake in all the hay which lay in the fields. After dark, she told him to gather up his scythes and take them into the house again, while she collected her rakes, saying to him:

"You are wiser than I took you to be, and you know more than myself: so much the better for you, for you may stay as long with me as you like."

He spent the whole summer in her employment, and they agreed very well together, mowing with mighty little trouble a vast amount of hay. In the autumn she sent him away, well laden with money, to his own home in the south. Next summer, and more than one summer following he spent in her employ, always being paid as his heart could desire, at the end of the season.

After some years, he took a farm of his own in the south country, and was always looked upon by all his neighbours as an honest man, a good fisherman, and an able workman in whatever work he might put his hand to. He always cut his own hay, never using any scythe but that which the elf-woman had given him upon the mountains; nor did any of his neighbours ever finish their mowing before him.

One summer it chanced that, while he was out fishing, one of his neighbours came to his house and asked his wife to lend him her husband's scythe, as he had lost his own. The farmer's wife looked for one, but could only find the one upon which her husband set such store. This, however, a little loth, she lent to the man, begging him at the same time never to temper it in the fire, for that, she said, her good man never did. So the neighbour promised, and taking it with him, bound it to a handle and began to work with it. But, sweep as he would, and strain as he would (and sweep and strain he did right lustily), not a single blade of grass fell. Wroth at this, the man tried to sharpen it, but with no avail. Then he took it into his forge, intending to temper it, for, thought he, what harm could that possibly do; but as soon as the flames touched it, the steel melted like wax, and nothing of it was left but a little heap of ashes. Seeing this, he went in haste to the farmer's house, where he had borrowed it, and told the woman what had happened: she was at her wits' end with fright and shame when she heard it, for she knew well enough how her husband set store by this scythe, and how angry he would be at its loss.

And angry indeed he was, when he came home, and he beat his wife well for her folly in lending what was not hers to lend. But his wrath was soon over, and he never again, as he never had before, laid the stick about his wife's shoulders.

The Father of Eighteen Elves

AT A CERTAIN FARM, long ago, it happened that all the household were out one day, making hay, except the goodwoman and her only child, a boy of four years old. He was a strong, handsome, lusty little fellow, who could already speak almost as well as his elders, and was looked upon by his parents with great pride and hope. But as his mother had plenty of other work to do besides watching him, she was obliged to leave him alone for a short time, while she went down to the brook to wash the milk-pails. So she left him playing in the door of the cottage, and came back again as soon as she had placed the milk-pails to dry. Directly she spoke to the child, it began to cry in a strange and unnatural way, which amazed her not a little, as it had always been so quiet and sweet-tempered. When she tried to make the child speak to her, as it was wont to do, it only yelled the more, and so it went on for a long time, always crying and never would be soothed, till the mother was in despair at so wonderful a change in her boy, who now seemed to have lost his senses.

Filled with grief, she went to ask the advice of a learned and skilful woman in the neighbourhood, and confided to her all her trouble.

Her neighbour asked her all sorts of questions – How long ago this change in the child's manner had happened? What his mother thought to be the cause of it? and so forth. To all of which the wretched woman gave the best answers she could. At last the wise woman said:

"Do you not think, my friend, that the child you now have is a changeling? Without doubt it was put at your cottage door in the place of your son, while you were washing the milk-pails."

"I know not," replied the other, "but advise me how to find it out."

So the wise woman said, "I will tell you. Place the child where he may see something he has never seen before, and let him fancy himself alone.

As soon as he believes no one to be near him, he will speak. But you must listen attentively, and if the child says something that declares him to be a changeling, then beat him without mercy."

That was the wise woman's advice, and her neighbour, with many thanks for it, went home.

When she got to her house, she set a cauldron in the middle of the hearth, and taking a number of rods, bound them end to end, and at the bottom of them fastened a porridge-spoon. This she stuck into the cauldron in such a way that the new handle she had made for it reached right up the chimney: as soon as she had prepared everything, she fetched the child, and placing him on the floor of the kitchen left him and went out, taking care, however, to leave the door ajar, so that she could hear and see all that went on.

When she had left the room, the child began to walk round and round the cauldron, and eye it carefully, and after a while he said:

"Well! I am old enough, as anybody may guess from my beard, and the father of eighteen elves, but never, in all my life, have I seen so long a spoon to so small a pot."

On hearing this the goodwoman waited not a moment, but rushed into the room and snatching up a bundle of fire-wood flogged the changeling with it, till he kicked and screamed again. In the midst of all this, the door opened, and a strange woman, bearing in her arms a beautiful boy, entered and said, "See how we differ! I cherish and love your son, while you beat and ill-use my husband;" with these words, she gave back to the farmer's wife her own son, and taking the changeling by the hand, disappeared with him.

But the little boy grew up to manhood, and fulfilled all the hope and promise of his youth.

The Divine & the Devil

THIS CHAPTER includes stories which touch upon religious matters. God and the devil continually clash and it is often the devil who falls victim to his own maliciousness.

Many of the tales here show a profound horror of every kind of irreligion; in a few of the stories, primarily 'The Wonderful Quern', 'Late Will the Souls of Priests Be Filled' and 'The Soul of My Own John', the concept of the soul and the devil's relationship to it is explored; and exorcism is resorted to in 'The Exorcism' to destroy the influence of evil. An intriguing mix of stories awaits.

The Steward of Skálholt

THERE WAS ONCE a bishop at Skálholt who was extremely harsh and merciless to his stewards. Unwillingly, therefore, they lived with him, and left him dishonoured. Many wished evil to the bishop for his harshness, and prayed that the Devil himself might come to him in their stead; and at last it fell out that the bishop, being in want of a steward, was at a loss to get one.

Then came there a man to him, elderly, red-haired, and broad-shouldered, offering his services as a steward. This offer the bishop accepted, the more gladly as he was in so great a strait.

The man had nought to say concerning his wages, but that the matter would rest till he left. Nor did he tell the bishop anything of his family and descent, nor mentioned whence he came; saying that this was of no consequence, inasmuch as all the bishop wanted to know was how he performed his duties.

He now took charge of the household concerns, and for a while it was clear that the bishop was satisfied.

In the same parish there dwelt an old peasant, an acquaintance of the bishop, skilled in the ancient arts; and the relations between this farmer and the steward soon waxed unfriendly.

Once the farmer had an interview with the bishop, in order to inform him that he strongly feared his steward would prove no gain to him at last. He asked the bishop, furthermore, wherefore he never chid the man; for that he always entered the church after the Gospel was read, and left it before the blessing was pronounced upon the people.

The bishop answered that he had never taken heed of this. But when he found that the farmer's words were true, he chid his steward, who gave back a peevish and wrathful answer, and said that he had so many things to take care of, that it would ill suit him to lounge about in church a needlessly long while: said too, that he would have his own will as to the time he spent in church, or else would speedily take his leave.

Hereat the bishop's anger calmed down. And now for six years more did the steward continue to serve him.

Nothing of note meanwhile came to pass.

But at the end of this time the steward was hated by all men, save alone the bishop; although his patience was nearly worn out by the man's violent and headstrong temper and behaviour.

In the middle of the Easter-night the old farmer, who had formerly spoken to his Reverence about his steward, came to Skálholt, and stole on the sly up to the churchyard, where he watched three men moving round about the church, of whom the steward was one. He saw that they were casting ropes and cables over the church at the command of the steward; wherefrom the farmer judged that the others were his servants. Both were ugly and rascally looking fellows.

When they had corded the church as much as they thought fit, the farmer heard the steward say that tomorrow, when he came out of the church, they should stand one at each side of it, ready to pull the ropes, while he himself would stand at the door looking after his own rope; and by this plan they would be sure to sink the church, with all the people therein.

When the farmer saw their preparations, and knew what plot lurked in them against the bishop and his flock, he stole away alone from the churchyard, up to the house, and going into the bishop's bedroom, roused him, and told him what fate awaited him on the morrow.

This unlooked-for news put the bishop out of countenance, but the farmer deemed redelessness the worst policy in this strait. He told the bishop to watch all the rest of the night, and prepare himself for preaching the sermon the next day, minding that it were a hard one.

"But I," said the farmer, "will sit on the corner bench, and if it should happen that the steward meet with some hindrance from me as he goes out, then watch well, and pronounce at once your blessing from the pulpit, and this will, by God's grace, suffice."

Now the bishop did as the farmer bade him, and when the peal of bells told out the worship to the people the farmer went to the church, took forth his pocket-knife and cut cross-marks upon the church, in sundry places. None but himself knew wherefore he did this; but he hereby cut the ropes which the steward had girt about it in the night.

The bishop mounted the pulpit, and, after the Gospel was read, the steward entered the church. In a mighty bustle he came in, and fiendish he looked, and much struck he was that the bishop had mounted the pulpit already.

The bishop seeing him enter, preached with great force and inspiration. No man's child in the church listened to the preacher without tears; but the steward was now pale as death, and now black and gloomy as soot, and as the sermon approached its end, he jumped up, in order to go out. The farmer stood up from his corner and moved against the door, telling the steward that he had no need to hurry, and that it would be as well for him, by way of a change, to await the out-giving of the blessing. Thereat the steward became violent, and would thrust the farmer away from the door, but with no avail.

The bishop seeing what was going on, pronounced at once the blessing with uplifted hands; and, at the same moment, the steward began to sink into the earth.

Now the farmer had in his bosom the book of the Psalms of David; this he took forth, and dealt the steward a goodly blow therewith on the crown, and, at the last syllable of the benediction, the skull of the Devil-steward vanished into the ground, under the repeated psalm-thumps of the old farmer.

After this the bishop began a good sermon of thanksgiving for this manifest salvation of himself and of his flock, from the vile plot and plan of the devil; and became, thenceforth, the best of masters to his stewards.

Boat Language

SOMETIMES ONE MAY hear a certain kind of cracking in boats that are in the boat-stand in calm weather. This cracking is the language of the boats, which it is not for every one

to understand. But one man, on a time, understood the boat language. He came to the sea shore when two boats were standing close together, and was witness that they thus talked:

1st Boat: "Long have we been together, but tomorrow must we part company."

2nd Boat: "Nay! That shall never be; we must not part. Thirty years now have we been neighbours, and have grown old; and if one is wrecked, we shall both go under."

1st Boat: "Natheless, that will not be: Good weather tonight, but other weather tomorrow, and none will row out but thy master; but I shall be left behind, and also the other boats. But thou wilt go, never to return. Never more shall we stand here together."

2nd Boat: "That never shall be, nor will I let myself be launched."

lst Boat: "Bound thou wilt be to go down to the sea. This is the last of nights that we shall be together."

2nd Boat: "Never will I let myself be launched, without thou goest down with me into the sea."

1st Boat: "It is not to be avoided."

2nd Boat: "Nay! Without the devil himself come too."

After this the boats spoke in so low a voice, that the listener was unable to make out their secret mutterings.

Next morning the weather was very suspicious, and none deemed fit to row out, except one boat-master and his crew. Down to the sea they went, as did many who would not out-row.

"Now," said the boat-master, as wont he was, "your skin-clothes on, in Jesus' name." And the crew clothed them in their skin-clothes.

"Let us launch the boat, in Jesus' name," quoth the boat-master, as wont he was.

So they all fell to launching, but the boat was not to be moved.

The boat-master prayed the other boat-men, who stood by, to aid them; but neither was this of any avail. Now every one of the standers by had lent his aid to launch the boat, and the master said, as before, "Now, let us launch in Jesus' name," but, in spite of all the hands at work, not an inch moved the boat.

Then cried the master loud, and said: "Hallo, there! In the name of the devil, forth with it!"

No sooner had the words been spoken than forth shot the boat into the sea, and nigh had flung itself out of the grasp of the men who launched it.

Now out, and away, went this boat with its crew; but nought has ever been seen of the boat since, nor aught been heard of its crew.

The Wonderful Quern

THERE WAS ONCE a very rich man who owned a great manor. He was married, and had by his wife two sons, of whom both were also married when these things came to pass. One of these brothers was rich as his father had been, and had by his wife four children. But the other was poor, living only on what his father vouchsafed him. When the father died, the brothers began to divide their inheritance. But the end of this affair was that the rich brother got the manor, and nigh all the rest of the inheritance, saying, forsooth, that his brother had well got his due, heretofore, in scrap after scrap, and draught after draught.

Hereafter held the rich brother the manor, and the poor one paid often a visit to him from his cottage, to ask of him (as of his parents before him), for that which he was in need of at the time. His brother was wont to grant something to him; but grumbling and snarling for ever. And thus did he keep up the wretched life of his brother, and his brother's wife.

Once the rich brother slaughtered a goodly ox, and the poor one deemed it as well to take this chance of asking his brother for a piece. But his wife kept him back from going, for, said she, he would get nought but his brother's harsh growling.

He said that, for that he cared nothing, and went to his brother's, in spite of all she could say.

He arrived first when they had dismembered the beast, and all the limbs lay on the slaughter-field; and, when he arrived, his brother was walking to and fro about the goodly carcass of his ox.

The poor brother begged him to give him enough meat for one meal of soup; "for," said he, "it is easy enough for you, now that you have so much at your hand."

The rich brother answered him harshly, said it was useless for him to go on with his begging, his ox had never been meant for his jaws.

But the poor brother still went on with his begging, till the rich one, at last, in a fit of rage, took one of the thighs of the ox, and threw it into his face, saying:

"Go, with this thigh, to the devil!"

So the poor brother took the thigh, and went home with it.

When his wife saw him coming with his great burden she was glad, although she by no means could understand his brother's having been, this time, so kind; and forthwith she made ready to put it into the pot and boil it.

Her husband prayed her to wait for awhile, as his brother had not given him the thigh, but bidden him go to the devil himself therewith, and he was in no mind to steal this charge out of hand from the devil. He therefore bade her, moreover, give him journey-needs, and new shoes, for he would start forth with the thigh, not delaying, in order to render it to the devil.

The goodwife bade him not thus make a fool of himself, for his brother had given him the thigh, although he had expressed himself in an awkward way, being wearied by entreaties.

Her husband said that she might interpret the matter how she would, but that he was bent upon doing with the thigh as he had been bidden.

She therefore equipped her husband as best she could. The man started off with the thigh, and walked for a long time, not knowing whither to go, to be sure of finding the devil.

At last, he met on his way a man, who asked whither he was carrying his thigh on his back.

He answered that he was going with it to the devil.

Then the stranger asked if he knew where the haunts of the devil were.

The other answered No, and begged the stranger by all means to tell him the way, if he knew it.

He replied that, in truth, that way was utterly unknown to him; but he would, nevertheless, try to be of some help to the man by giving him a ball of thread, the end of which he should hold in his hand, letting the ball run before him till he came to a certain hillock. Thereupon, when the ball stopped, he should knock with the staff (which the stranger gave him likewise), and the hillock would open of itself at the knock, and he should cast the thigh into the gap, taking good heed not to be too near himself. He would then see two querns coming up into the hole, one black, and the other white; this one he should take, not heeding the other. After that he should take the ball, and let it run before him as before, and follow it with his quern.

The poor man thanked the stranger for his rede, took leave of him, and went afresh on his way. Now all fell out as the stranger had foretold. He found the hillock, opened it with the staff, and flung into the yawning rift the thigh, saying, "Take, Fiend! My brother sends you this thigh of his ox."

Then out rolled two querns, and when he had managed to catch hold of the white one, he went on his way after the ball, till he came to the spot where he had before met the stranger, who was still there. The poor man greeted him, asking him what he should do with the quern.

The other answered that he should make a strong and roomy case for it, and put it in a fit place, where it would, he said, grind of its own accord all it was bidden to grind, the only thing needed being to repeat this verse:

Grind neither malt nor salt;
Grind in the name of the Lord.

After this they parted, when the poor man had heartily thanked the stranger for his rede and his aid.

He now came home to his wife, and told her all about his travels. He next made a strong and solid case for the quern, a fine piece of furniture for the house, and put .the quern in thorough trim. Then it ground everything he bade it; food, and all needful things for the house and the husbandry, so that they lacked nothing.

Once it came into the farmer's mind that it would be a good thing to have some money to spend, although, in truth, they needed none, as they had plenty of everything.

So he bade the quern grind gold, and repeated the same verse as before. And the quern ground on, and ground pure gold. This was done time after time, so that he shortly became mighty rich in gold.

Then said he to his wife, that he fain would know how much gold they had. She answered that she deemed that not needful; she only knew that they had plenty of it, as of everything else. But the farmer had no peace till he had found out by what means to measure his gold.

As they themselves had no measure, he ran to his brother's house, and asked him for a measure.

The rich brother bade his wife to lend him the measure. She did so, but said to herself, "What, in the wide world, can they have to measure?" And so saying, she took resin and smeared the measure with it, where the sides and the bottom meet, and then gave it to her brother-in-law.

He went home, and having measured his gold dust, gave back the measure.

His sister-in-law took the measure, and when he was gone, looked at it within, and found that all round the bottom clave gold dust to it. She then took it to her husband, and said, "Your brother measures gold, while we measure rye;" and he noticed that his brother had not, for a long while, begged aught of him, not, indeed, since he had got the ox-thigh. There was no question that the cottage-folk had something, for they looked well, and everything plainly throve with them. Then the goodwife bade the husband ask how matters might be with the others, for that this, his brother's happiness and welfare, could not be in the common course of things.

Now the rich brother went off, as he yearned to know how his brother had come into his wealth. So, when they met, the manor-farmer asked his brother what he had been measuring, the other day.

The latter told him the truth about it all.

The rich farmer asked him how this came about.

He answered that the devil had given him a quern, which ground every possible thing, obeying the afore-said verse, which he also told the other quite truthfully. "This," he said, "the devil does because I gave him the thigh of the ox, which you bade me, the other day, take to him."

His brother did not at all understand this, nor could he confess that he had ever sent his poor brother, with an ox thigh on his shoulders, to the devil; he had, said he, given him the thigh.

"Nay, nay!" answered the other, "you bade me take it to the devil, and so I did. For this he gave me the quern, and since this goodness of his I have needed neither yours nor any one else's help."

After this they parted, and the rich man went home, pondering and wondering over what he had heard.

And the couple were filled with jealousy of the cottage-folk, and thought long how they could manage to get the quern for themselves. At last they agreed upon offering to the farmer all they had for it, and when they had got it, they should buy a vessel and leave the country, with their quern.

The husband, therefore, went to try the bargain with his brother, who, however, was very loth to listen to his offers. Then he offered him his manor, and all his goods and chattels. The other answered that the manor had no great charm for him, as he could buy an estate quite as good whenever he liked. But as his brother eagerly wished for the quern, and as he himself was already rich enough, he would yield to his wishes, and let him have the quern, for all that he had.

Now they made the bargain, and the cottage-farmer moved to the manor, and took to himself all his brother's possessions. But the other bought himself a vessel, and embarked in it, taking nothing with him but his wife, his children, and his quern, thinking that he had made a marvellous gain by his bargain.

When he was at a good distance from the coast, he set to work to put the quern in trim, in order that it might grind them all they needed, and he repeated this verse:

Grind neither malt nor salt;
Grind in the name of the Lord.

But do and say whatever he would, the quern stood still and immovable, till at last he grew angry, and cried out, in a wild rage:

"Grind, then, both malt and salt;
Grind in the name of the Devil."

Then the quern began grinding malt and salt, and in a short while overcharged the vessel, and, as there were no means, anyhow, of stopping the quern, the end of it was that the vessel sank with all on board it, and has never since been seen. And it is told that the devil said he did not regret the change of quern-owners, for thereby he had got six souls for one.

But of the first quern-owner, it is told, that he had always riches and wealth enough after the loss of his quern, and, at last, began to think of his future and the fare of his soul. So he took two orphan children, gave them teaching, and bequeathed them his fortune at his and his wife's death; and they were fortunate and happy all their lives.

The Devil's Marriage

ONCE, A MOTHER and her daughter lived together. They were both well off, and the latter was deemed a good match. Many courted her with no avail, and people thought that, as she was a pious woman, she would live single, in the service of the Lord.

When the Devil heard of this, he liked it not at all, and turned himself into the shape of a young man, and wooed the girl, in order, thereby, to get her slowly into his power. He managed to make himself look so good and so pious, that he quite deceived the maiden. She accepted his troth, and they got wedded.

But when the Devil would enter the bed with his wife, she was so chaste and pure, that he could by no means bear to approach her, so feigned to be ill, and ordered a bath to be got ready for him, as only in that could he rest with some ease. This was done as the bridegroom desired, and he sat all night in his bath; and all the next day he spent in walking about, thinking how he could get himself out of this scrape.

On his way, he met a man, with whom he struck a bargain, that the stranger should be this woman's husband instead of himself, and should give him his first-born child, when it was seven years old, leaving it for him on the same spot whereon they now stood.

This the man promised to do, and the Devil gave him the same shape that he himself had worn, when he was wedded to his bride. The traveller then went to the bride, and she took him to be the true bridegroom, and this marriage turned out a very happy one.

As for children, they had only one son, and most tenderly did they love him. But when the boy had entered his seventh year, his father began to be very silent.

His wife entreated him to tell her why he was so uneasy in his mind, and, at last, he told her all the story.

"This you have hidden too long from me," said she; "but I will give you such rede in the matter as shall make nought the Devil's plan."

On the day when the boy had fulfilled his seventh year, the father went with his son to the spot where he had left the Devil, and, according to his wife's advice, he made a circle round the place, and consecrated it with holy song. He tarried with his son there till nightfall, and told him that whatever he might see during the night, he should not stir outside the circle, save to him who should give him his hand in Jesus' name.

After his father had left him, the lad first saw divers of his friends coming to the spot to offer him various dainties and sweets. Then he saw his parents, who tried to persuade him to come to them, now by coaxing, and now by threats. Next he saw children who played with sundry toys, and who begged him to come to them and join in their play. But the lad stayed firmly in his place, as no one came to reach him his hand, in the name of Jesus. After this he saw flashes and flames of fire, and eerie monster-shapes, and wonderful things of all kinds, until the dawn of day. At all these sights the boy was much frightened, but nevertheless kept his place. At the very beginning of day-break, his own parents came to him and gave him their hands, inside the circle in Jesus' name: and so the Devil lost his bargain.

Late Will the Souls of Priests Be Filled

THERE WAS ONCE a young and hopeful fellow, who fell in love with a maiden and betrothed himself to her, but she was greatly against all wedlock with him. This gave him great grief, insomuch that he went about as one daft.

Once, during his lonely wanderings about the country, he was startled by a man coming up to him and greeting him. He received his greeting coldly, and said that he did not know him.

The stranger was very friendly and kind, and said, "I know full well that you are in sorry mood, and the cause thereof I know well too; and if you will promise to be my bondsman at the end of this year, I will, at once, contrive that the girl shall no less wish to be wed to you than you wish now, to wed her."

The young man accepted this offer thankfully, and they agreed to these terms.

After this, they parted, and the youth went home.

Soon after, he met the girl at church, and, strangely enough, she had now changed her mind altogether, and was as warmly in love with the young man as he had been with her.

But he, deeming this change not too truthful, received her tokens of love rather coolly. But he was convinced anon that it was all sincerely meant; and it came to pass, at last, that he married the girl, and their marriage turned out a most happy one.

Now the year advanced to its end, from the time when the stranger who helped him forward to his marriage had met him, and he became deeply concerned in his mind as to who that man could have been. A month before the removing day he went to the priest, told him all the story, and begged his advice.

The priest said: "Too late hast thou told me this, for that stranger was no other than the devil himself."

Now, this put the farmer mightily out of countenance, and he entreated the priest all the more, not to spare his aid. The priest gladly yielded to his request; gathered many people to him, and bade them scoop out a certain large mound, leaving the greensward untouched, and carrying out of the way all the mould. This done, he pierced a hole through the top of the mound, and when this was accomplished the moving day had arrived.

Now, the priest took a knapsack, (which in Iceland is made of leather in the form of a cylinder, with wooden bottoms, and called a "sál;" or "soul" in our tongue;) removed both bottoms therefrom, and, having put a wooden cross in one end, fastened the bag in the hole at the top of the mound, where it stood upright, like a chimney-pot, the wood cross being in the lower end.

After this, be said to the farmer, "Wait for thy customer, on the mound, and make it a condition for him – if he will that thou shouldst be his bondsman – that he fill the "soul" with money, without causing loss to anybody; if he be unable to do this, declare that he has lost his bargain."

Thereupon, the priest left the farmer alone, who now did as he had been told. After a short while, came his customer, looking rather rougher than when they first met.

Quoth the farmer, "O! I forgot, when I last saw you, to ask a favour of you, which is of little matter to you, but of so great matter to me, that if you cannot do as I wish, I cannot possibly go to you to be your bondsman."

The Devil would know what this favour was.

"It is," said the man, "to fill that 'soul' with money, without causing loss to anybody."

The Devil viewed the "soul" with a fiendishly scornful look, and said: "Ah! Nothing else! That is no great feat;" and off he ran, and, after a short while, came back, dragging an immense sack after him, full of money and dripping with sea-water; this he poured at once into the "soul," but it remained as empty as before.

He went off for a second time, and brought back another drag-sack far larger than the first one, emptied it into the "soul," but the "soul" was as empty as before.

Off he went for the third time, and dragged back after him to the mound a far larger sack than either of the first two; but when he had poured this into the "soul," the "soul" was as empty as before.

For the fourth time, he rushed in devilish wrath to get one more money-sack, and brought one back, by far larger than any of the others.

When he had emptied this into the "soul," and the "soul" remained empty as ever, the cunning devil was struck with wonder, and, as he left the man and all hope of his bargain, he said: "Late indeed will the souls of priests be filled!"

The man was mighty glad of his deliverance from the fiend; and seeing that he was indebted to the priest for it, he divided the money equally between them. After this the devil came neither near them nor their money. And both farmer and priest were rich all the rest of their lives.

Rosamunda

ONCE THERE LIVED a king and queen in their realm. They had one son, whose name has not been given in the story. He was brought up like other princes, and taught all arts, and a castle was built for him, and nothing spared to make it a princely dwelling, as he was far above all other men.

In this same country, there was a nobleman, who had a daughter by name Rosamunda, a wondrous beauty. But, albeit she was good, and quite well-bred, there was this fault to be found with her, that she could learn nothing, either with hands or head, being dull-minded and clumsy-handed. But, for her beauty, she was famous all over the kingdom.

The king's son once saw her, and forthwith fell in love with her, for her lovliness, and she fell in love with him for high learning and skill.

After this, the prince had an interview with his father, and said he would woo for himself a wife.

"Where dost thou look for a wife?" said the king.

Then the prince answered: "None shall ever be my wife but Rosamunda."

"Name not that match!" said the king. "She is stupid and ignorant beyond all measure, and known to be so all over the country. It will not be seemly for you to choose such an one for your wife; and, beside, she is of baser birth than you."

The prince would not quarrel with his father about this, but could never turn his mind from Rosamunda; and, after this, he became very melancholy, and wandered about alone, and paid little attention to the pleasures and gaieties of the court.

Once, in his lonely wanderings, through forests and heaths, while he was deeply concerned about his future, there came to him a red-bearded, low-built man, and asked him why he, a king's son, wandered about thus lonely in these places, which was unseemly in him, and not becoming his rank: "Or," said he, "does aught ail you?"

The prince replied, "Little likely are you to help me out of my strait, although I revealed my sorrow to you."

The stranger answered: "You cannot be sure that I am not able to help you out of your distress; and, in order to shew you that I am not quite unacquainted with your life, I will tell you, that you are filled with grief because your father has prevailed on you not to wed Rosamunda the Fair, for that she is ignorant in head and hand."

This, the king's son said, was true, and prayed the stranger by all means to help him, since he knew all these things already.

Then the stranger took forth a small, slight rod of iron, and told the prince to give it to Rosamunda, who, when she would learn aught, should put it on the top of her tongue, but when she would accomplish any handiwork, should keep it between her fingers. This, he said, would make her an equally sharp learner, both in handiwork and book-learning, and, moreover, cause her to remember all she learnt, ever afterwards.

The king's son asked the man how much he might offer him for this.

The stranger replied: "This is so small a service, that I will charge nothing for it." And he said that he would come, besides, to Rosamunda, three years thence, to fetch the iron rod, but she should tell him, at the same time, his right name. "If she can do that without a mistake, she will," said he, "remember all she has learnt, even should she have given the iron rod away. But, if she cannot tell my name, I will take her, after these three years, as well as the iron rod. And my name is Rigdin-Rigdon."

The prince thanked him much for his advice, and took leave of him, going now home light in mind, and fixing the name of the man in his memory.

After this, the prince managed to get leave of his parents to fetch Rosamunda, in order to have all lady's arts taught to her, but on condition that, if she could learn nothing, he should not think of marrying her. This being agreed upon, the king's son went off with a splendid band of followers, fetched Rosamunda home to the king's court, and gave her the rod, telling her how to use it. But, in his glee at having brought her home to the court, he quite forgot the name of the man he had met in the wood.

Now all kinds of teachers were given to Rosamunda, in order to teach her all that was needed for a lady of her rank, and it avails not to spend many words on this, – that Rosamunda learnt everything, as soon as ever she saw or heard it.

But now the third year was fast waning, and the king's son could not, by any means, recall the name of the stranger. This cast him into deep gloom, and he was more concerned than ever before, that he should perchance have to lose his Rosamunda, who was, by this tune, as accomplished a damsel as she was beautiful.

In this strait, he wandered about the country, wrapped in thought, till he came once to an open space in a wood. It was a lawn, and in the midst of the lawn there was a mound. He heard a great chattering and peals of laughter in the hillock, and on listening nearer, he understood that the inmates of the mound were telling in tale how many souls they had each beguiled. When the prince heard this he was quite at a loss, for all at once the thought struck him that the man he had formerly met in the wood might have been one of these fellows. He listened, however, awhile to their ravings, although he found himself in a perilous strait in this place; – as it were between heaven and hell.

At last he heard the following song sung in the mound:

"Men who give me a fox's name
Have many a cause to do that same.
No mercy to the souls I shew,

When I claim of them what they owe.
I walk, like a lion, round about,
And many men's sight have I put out.
Harm and hurt to folk have I done,
And my name is Rigdin-Rigdon."

When the prince heard the name in the last verse, he at once remembered that it was the very name he had lost, and been so long thoughtful and anxious about. He now wrote down the name and returned home, easy and glad in mind.

Then he had a glass box made, so large that Rosamunda could stand inside it, and he wrote on the sides of it the name, Rigdin-Rigdon, in so many places, that nowhere about it could the eye be cast without seeing that name.

When the day arrived on which he awaited the coming of the man to fetch the rod, the prince made Rosamunda step inside the glass case, keeping with her the rod, and told her to give it to him that should come for it, and say at the same time, – "Rigdin-Rigdon." But whatever might happen, he warned her strongly not to lose courage, and by all means to remember the name, which he had written on purpose all over the box.

After this, the king's son left the room and locked it.

When a short time had passed, Rosamunda saw, all of a sudden, a man coming into the room through the locked door. He went straight up to the case, challenging her to come out.

She answered the challenge, stepped forward, and gave the rod to the man, saying; "Take it, Rigdin-Rigdon."

On hearing his name the stranger sank through the floor, where he stood.

Then the king's son wedded Rosamunda, and they had a share in the government of the realm, with their parents.

Rosamunda remembered all she had learnt by the aid of the rod, although its owner had been none other than the Devil himself. She was, in every way, a most wonderful queen, beloved by all; and she ruled the country, together with her husband, after the death of his parents, in happiness and peace, up to a high old age.

The Exorcism

IN THOSE TIMES when it was the custom of the Church to drive the Bad Spirit out of newborn children by charms and prayers, it happened that a priest was called to baptize a child.

The Priest began the exorcism by saying:

"Abi, male Spirite!"

But the Devil, having hidden himself in a corner of the church, roared out loudly:

"Pessime Grammatice!"

Then the Priest said:

"Abi, male Spiritu!"

The Devil answered:

"Wrong first, now awkward too!"

Then the Priest said:

"Abi, male Spiritus!"

And the Devil, as he went out, said:

"Sic debuisti dicere prius!"

The Priest and the Angel

THE BEGINNING of this story is that in the west part of the country was once a priest, who was as greedy as he was unjust, haughty, and whimsical. Amongst other things, he adopted the custom of having worship in the church no less on week days than on the Sabbath, and even said that it was a breach of the Sabbath not to come to church on week days.

Once, in the winter-time, a child was brought to the priest to be baptized, but the weather was bad, and looked foul. The people who had brought the child told him their errand, but he gave them a downright good scolding, as was his wont, and said, amongst other things, that they ought to have let him know of this beforehand, denied baptism to the child, and drove the people away. But the folk who had brought the child, and the child itself also, died from cold and storm on their way back home. This in no way troubled the priest's conscience, and he went on quite as before.

Next summer the priest sent a notice to his parishioners that he had fixed the following Thursday for service. This was in the high hay harvest.

No man said he would come, and yet none dared say he would not. When Thursday arrived, the priest awaited the coming of the people, and the celebration of worship. But when he found that his flock were too late in coming, he rushed into the church, and began walking up and down the floor. After he had been there awhile, an unknown man came to him and greeted him. The latter, in his haughty way, did not answer his greeting, only asking him whether he had seen any of the folk coming.

"What folk?" asked the stranger.

"Why, the church-folk, to be sure," said the priest.

"Why should they come to-day, a week day?" said the other. "Such a thing is unknown here, and every-one is, of course, busy in hay-making, so that none will come, and naturally enough."

The priest answered, "What does that matter to you? The folk are bound to come, as I have called them."

Quoth the other. "This indeed I call odd behaviour, and doubtless you are strange in many things more, my good priest, and unlike other people; and, if I sought, I could, I dare say, find much more that was odd about you."

Hereat the priest waxed wroth, and said: "What is there so wonderful about me?"

The man replied: "That I will shew you, if you like, and we will go out both together."

They did so; and when they got outside the door of the church the priest saw a large, oblong cask, filled to the brim with milk on one side, and blood on the other, which did not mingle together. At this the priest wondered, and went to the cask, and put his hand in, to try to mix them by stirring them about, but all in vain.

"This is certainly strange," said the priest.

"Sure enough," answered the other; "but you shall see more things of this kind."

The priest asked what this signified.

"That you shall know later," quoth the other.

Now they went into the churchyard, and came to a lake, whereon two grown birds were swimming, and one young one. No sooner had they touched the shore of the lake, than the young bird flew up, perched himself in the hair of the priest, and rooted it up without mercy. The priest tried to get rid of the bird, but being by no means able to do so, begged his fellow walker to drive the bird off, but he answered that he might not yet do so.

After this, they came to a large waterfall in a river, beneath which a man was standing with his mouth wide open, swallowing the whole of the waterfall; but it ran out again through the back of his head, as it were through a sponge. This, too, the priest found a strange sight.

Next they came to another river, with a waterfall in it which fell over a mighty rock. Underneath was a man, who swallowed the whole of the waterfall, but no water could the priest see run from him again. Neither what this meant would the stranger tell the priest.

Now they came to a fine grassy pasture. Here the priest saw two sheep, both lean and ill-favoured, and they were so thin-woolled that one could count the hairs on them. They devoured the grass like wild beasts, and anon fought with one another as if one would drive the other out of the pasture. This, too, the priest found strange, and asked if the sheep had been long in the pasture.

The other answered him curtly: "I believe so."

Next they came on to a rough and barren heath, where scarce aught was to be seen but pebbles and gravel. There the priest saw other two sheep, fat and well-favoured, chewing merrily the cud, and resting one at the other's side like brothers. They bent, too, their heads one to the other, as if neither could bear to lose sight of the other.

Furthermore, they walked on, till they came to a palace so comely and glorious, that the priest thought he never had seen the like before. It was surrounded with green downs, and the scent of countless flowers filled the air. And, on all sides, the chirping of happy birds rang and rang back, and, inside the palace one could hear the sweetest strains of music and of song, and behold all possible manner of glee and merry-making. And all was so highly beauteous and charming, as to go far beyond fancy.

Then the priest said to his fellow traveller: "Nay! No farther will I go; let me rest here."

Quoth the other: "No! Here must you not rest: another place is meant for you."

So, on they went for yet awhile, till the priest saw a house, the utter contrast of the palace. A foul stink filled the air, and everything was disgusting and frightful. There were also winged beasts in the shape of birds, who moved about for ever and shrieked. When the priest saw and heard all this, he was much struck with fear, and loathed the place so much that he begged the man to retreat thence, the sooner the better.

Then the stranger said: "Nay! Here shall you dwell. This is a place for all folk like you."

"Oh!" said the priest, "let me get hence, and counsel me how I may avoid having this for my dwelling-place."

"That will I do," answered the stranger; "but you must know that this is the place of torment for all ungodly people, and but a faint shadow of hell, which you have deserved by a long spell of misdoings; but you may avoid it by repenting and henceforth mending your life."

This the priest promised to do.

And now, returning the same way they had come, they came to the palace.

"This," said the stranger, "is the place prepared for good and holy people; and the charms of this place are a faint foretaste of the eternal joys of God's children, which you have hitherto spurned with your sins and vices."

Now came they to the goodly and gentle sheep on the heath.

"These sheep," said the stranger, "mean poor people, who live content with what God gives them, and do not murmur, although they have not always at hand whatever they may wish for, but live together in lovely accord."

Then they came to the ugly and riotous sheep.

"These," said the stranger, "mean the rich, who never are satisfied, and never thrive, albeit they have abundance of all things, for they ever are striving for more; and the discord and quarrelsomeness of these sheep betoken the envious talk which the rich hold one of another."

Then they came to the river, whose fall the man swallowed up.

Quoth the stranger: "This river betokens the malice-sin, which the children of this world for ever drink and swallow, but part with never again; and they die in their wickedness, never quitting the sin till the sin quits them."

Then came they on to the waterfall, that fell into the mouth of the man beneath it, but ran through his back again.

"This," said the stranger, "shows you the sin of weakness, which ever takes hold of the best of the children of God, but they drive it at once from their hearts again."

Next they came to the lake whereon the storm-birds had been swimming.

Then said the stranger: "These two large upgrown birds betoken the two people whom you drove from your door in the winter-time, out into the frost and storm, with the unbaptized child."

Next they came to the cask at the door of the church, in which the fluids had not mingled together.

Then said the stranger: "Here you may behold the blood you have sucked from the poor, and likewise that which you have sucked from the rich. They can never be mingled together, and therefore must you give recompense to the poor, and be more just in proportioning that which you take from rich and poor."

Now had their journey drawn to an end. They went into the church, and the priest begged the stranger to take the little bird out of his hair.

"That will I do," said the other; "but you must know that it is the avenging spirit of the child whom you refused to baptize, and now you must baptize it." The stranger then took the bird out of the priest's hair, and the priest baptized it. This done, the little bird flew away and was no more seen, but the priest knelt down in prayer. After he had finished his prayer, his companion went with him out of the church, and vanished in the churchyard, from the priest's sight.

Then the priest went home to the farm, but met there another priest, who greeted him and asked who he was.

The old priest told him, and asked, in his turn, who the other was. The latter answered that he had had charge of the living since the former priest who was there, had vanished some seven years ago.

The old priest was greatly amazed at this, and saw now that the Angel of God had come to him in this trance, and that he had been in it for seven years.

Of all he had seen he made a good lesson for himself, mended his life, and entered a monastery, where he stayed for the rest of his days.

And herewith ends the tale.

The Soul of My Own John

THERE LIVED once an old man and an old woman together. The old man was a troublesome fellow, disliked by people, lazy and of no use at home. Hereat his old wife was much annoyed, and chid him often herefor with sharp chidings, saying that he was good for nought but to squander away all she could earn. For herself, she drudged all she could and spared no toil in getting what they needed, and was always safe to have her way with whomsoever she had to deal. But although they quarrelled in this respect, the dame loved well her old carl, and never let him want.

Once the old man fell sorely sick.

The old woman watched over him, and when the man's strength began slowly to fail him, it came into her thoughts that he might perchance not be so well prepared for death as to leave it unquestionable that he would be allowed to enter into the heavenly kingdom. She therefore thought it would not be amiss to try, herself, to bring his soul to its latter end.

In order to accomplish this, she took a leather bag, drew it tight over the old fellow's face, and when he died his soul went into the bag, whose mouth the old woman at once tied up.

After this, she went to heaven with the leather bag in her apron, and when she came to the heavenly gate, knocked at it, and out came St. Peter, asking her what was her business there.

"All hail!" said the old woman. "I bring here the soul of my own John; you have, no doubt, heard talk of him, and I would beg of you to get him in here, if you please."

"Ah! Well!" said St. Peter; "but I am sorry to say that I cannot do it for you. I certainly have heard talk of your John, but never heard good of him yet."

Quoth the other: "I never could think for a moment, St. Peter, that you were so hard-hearted; and now it is clear that you have quite forgotten how you acted in days of yore, when you forsook your own Master."

When this was said, St. Peter backed in and locked the door, but the old woman stood groaning and sighing outside.

Now after a while she knocked again, and out came St. Paul.

She greeted him, and asked him his name, which he truly told her. She then prayed him to interest himself a whit for the soul of her own John; but he said he would have nought to do with her, as this John deserved no mercy.

Then the woman waxed angry, and said: "Oh, this becomes you, undoubtedly, well; I deem you have better deserved this same mercy, when, of old, you persecuted both God and the good. I ask no more boons of you."

Paul slammed the door to, at once. But when the old woman knocked for the third time, the Virgin Mary came out.

"All hail! My Good Lady!" said the old hag; "I hope you will allow my own John to come in, although Peter and Paul have both hindered his entrance."

" Ah," quoth the Virgin Mary, "my good old dame, I am sorry to say that I dare not do it; for your own John was such a wretched old John."

"Oh! Why should I blame you for this!" said the old woman. "To tell you the truth, however, I thought you knew that others could be weak as well as yourself. You surely have not forgotten that the only child you ever had, you could not father."

Mary did not want to hear any more, after this, but shut to the door in a hurry.

A fourth time the old woman knocked, and out came Christ, who asked her what she was travelling up here for.

She said humbly: "I would only ask you, my good Saviour, to allow this poor soul to enter the door."

Christ answered: " Oh! It is your own John, is it?

"No, woman, he never believed in me."

Now, just as he was shutting the door, the old woman betook her to her quickness of hand, and threw the leather bag, with the soul in it, through the door, which was yet ajar. The bag was blown far into the heavenly palace, but the door slammed into the lock.

Now a stone was lifted from the heart of this old woman, since her own John was, in spite of all, in heaven, and she went home glad in mind.

Nothing more do we know of her, or of her own John, or how it fared, at last, with his soul.

The Sin Sacks

THERE WAS ONCE a very zealous priest, whose preaching was hard, for he reminded his flock of their sins, without disguising them. In his parish there lived an old woman who seldom or never came to church, and the priest often chid her for it, and said she would scarcely get entrance into the kingdom of heaven, since she neglected so much the church. But to this the old woman paid no heed, and thus some time passed away.

Once the old woman fell ill, and begged that the priest might be brought to her, as the sins of men had caused her much deep grief.

The priest went at once to see the sick woman; and as he was about to begin his warning and comfort, seeing that her grief was a deep one, the old woman said: "Let me tell you what is my greatest and heaviest grief."

This the priest was glad to do, and listened most eagerly to the sinner's tale.

The old woman said: "A short while ago, I had a dream, and I dreamt that I came to the kingdom of heaven. There, I knocked at the door, begging for shelter, as I was cold and the weather was rough. A man came to the door with a large bunch of keys in his hand. I asked him his name. 'My name is Peter,' said he. I then knew with whom I had to deal, and entreated him to let me in. Quoth Peter: 'Nay, your place is not here.' 'O! let me in,' said I, 'I am so frightfully cold ; allow me only to get inside the door.' 'Nay,' quoth Peter, 'by no means.' I now saw that a large storehouse stood opposite the door, and I asked Peter to allow me to enter it. That, he said he would grant me, and opened the storehouse. Then I was glad and hurried in, but Peter stood in the door. Now when I was well in I saw a mighty heap of sacks, large and small. They were all filled with something, and their mouths were tied to. There were also sea-mittens, of which some were quite full, others half full, and some with only the thumb full. I asked Peter what was in these sacks. He answered, 'The sins of men.' 'You will not, I hope, refuse to let me see the sack of our minister,' said I; 'I am sure it cannot be large.' 'Large!' said St. Peter; 'Ah! it is not so very small, though. Look, it is yonder,' – pointing towards a huge sack. Now I was quite astonished, for it was by far the largest sack of them all. 'Oh!' said I, 'What a mighty big sack! But, prithee, where is my sack now? it is, I am sure, of no little size. 'Oh, that is all right enough,' quoth Peter, and pointed to one of the sea-mittens in whose thumb there was a very little. Hereat I was yet more astonished, and out I slipped again. Then Peter slammed to the door of the storehouse, and at this I awoke. This is what grieves me," said the old woman, "and therefore I sent for you, in order to tell you it."

But the priest, finding that this came rather home to himself, broke off his sick-visit, in a hurry.